The very last piece of this cowgirl puzzle was running a brush through her hair.

The way the stylist cut it made the best of her baby-fine hair with subtle layers and precision-cut ends. Rayna stepped as far back in the narrow trailer as possible so she could get as close as she could to a head-to-toe reflection. Out of nowhere, an emotion hit her, and she felt tears welling up in her eyes. Three steps forward, she got her hands on two cotton swabs and pressed one each into her tear ducts. After a moment or two, her makeup was saved, and she had fought back tears.

"Huh. What do you know? It actually worked."

Another text from Dean came through; she pushed the microphone icon and said, "I'm coming! Hold your horses!"

Rayna wrapped herself up in her winter gear and headed out the door. The fact that Dean was anxious for her to arrive made her smile. It reminded her so much of their lives together before. She did tend to run late, and that really hadn't changed. Dean was always waiting for her to arrive. The thought did cross her mind...

Maybe all of this time, Dean had been waiting patiently for her to finally come home.

Dear Reader!

Thank you for choosing *Big Sky Christmas*, the eighteenth Harlequin Special Edition book featuring the Brand family.

Stay-at-home mom Rayna "Ray" Brand believed she had it all until her husband filed for divorce just as their twin boys went off to college. After they sell the family home, and without any obvious marketable skills, Rayna returns to the one place that she can call home: Hideaway Ranch in Big Sky, Montana. While helping her sister turn Hideaway into a corporate destination, Rayna discovers she has more skills than she had originally thought: she can cook for the guests, and she's considering starting a goat-yoga class. Rayna is proud of her work at the family ranch, but that doesn't mean she's going to make Big Sky her last stop. She left after graduation and never looked back. But after her high school sweetheart, Dean Legend, comes back into the picture, Rayna has to make a touch choice— stay in Big Sky or lose her first love a second time around.

Cattleman and horse farrier Dean wears a lot of hats in his life: he's a caretaker for his ailing father, a single dad to his two school-age daughters, and running the family business, Legend Quality Cattle. His divorce took a toll and he's wary of any sign that someone from the opposite sex may be interested in him. As far as he's concerned, he's officially *off* the market!

Until Rayna Brand comes barreling into his life without any warning! He's always loved Rayna—she had been his first everything. First love, first kiss, first lover and first person he had proposed marriage to. She was also the first woman who had broken his heart. Will he put a padlock around his heart and shut the door on a second chance at romance with the woman of his dreams?

Happy Reading!

JoAnna

PS: My website (www.joannasimsromance.com) is under construction! Watch this space!

BIG SKY CHRISTMAS

JoAnna Sims

SPECIAL EDITION

Harlequin®
SPECIAL EDITION™

Recycling programs for this product may not exist in your area.

ISBN-13: 978-1-335-40203-5

Big Sky Christmas

Copyright © 2024 by JoAnna Sims

For questions and comments about the quality of this book, please contact us at CustomerService@Harlequin.com.

TM and ® are trademarks of Harlequin Enterprises ULC.

Harlequin Enterprises ULC
22 Adelaide St. West, 41st Floor
Toronto, Ontario M5H 4E3, Canada
www.Harlequin.com

Printed in Lithuania

MIX
Paper | Supporting responsible forestry
FSC® C021394

JoAnna Sims is proud to pen contemporary romance for Harlequin Special Edition. JoAnna's series, The Brands of Montana, features hardworking characters with hometown values. You are cordially invited to join the Brands of Montana as they wrangle their own happily-ever-afters.

Books by JoAnna Sims

Harlequin Special Edition

The Brands of Montana

A Match Made in Montana
High Country Christmas
High Country Baby
Meet Me at the Chapel
Thankful for You
A Wedding to Remember
A Bride for Liam Brand
High Country Cowgirl
The Sergeant's Christmas Mission
Her Second Forever
His Christmas Eve Homecoming
She Dreamed of a Cowboy
The Marine's Christmas Wish
Her Outback Rancher
Big Sky Cowboy
Big Sky Christmas

The Montana Mavericks: Six Brides for Six Brothers

The Maverick's Wedding Wager

Visit the Author Profile page
at Harlequin.com for more titles.

Dedicated to:

Miss "Deb" Pedraza

Thank you for your abiding friendship,
kindness and grace.

I love you always, dear friend.

Prologue

Hideaway Ranch
Big Sky, Montana
June 2001

Dean Legend walked slowly up the porch steps, trying to calm his nerves. His Western-style tuxedo felt a little bit too tight just about everywhere. And even though Rayna Brand, his high school sweetheart and prom date, had told him specifically to wear a gold-colored shirt, Dean felt like he was just wearing yellow. He imagined all of his friends were going to razz him and call him *buttercup* or something along those lines because he sure as heck would've done it to them.

At the front door of the Brand family's log-cabin home, Dean closed his eyes, took a deep breath in, let it out and then knocked on the door. He heard several voices, but Rose Brand, Rayna's mother, was the loudest of the bunch. Dean knew that the rapid, decisive footsteps toward the door also belonged to Rayna's spitfire mother.

The door swung open, making a bell attached to the doorknob jingle as it always did. Rose's bluish-gray eyes were shining with anticipation. Her hair had been freshly home-dyed her signature mahogany brown and was swept up into a simple ponytail. There was a small telltale smudge of dye on her left ear, but that didn't change the fact for Dean that when he looked at Rose he was looking at Rayna twenty years into their marriage. Rayna and her identical twin sister, Danica, were Rose's miniatures.

"Dean Legend!" Rose greeted him with so much genuine affection whenever he came to the ranch that he considered Hideaway Ranch his second home.

"Hi, Mrs. Brand," Dean said politely. "I'm here for Ray."

"Well, of course you are." Rose's face was alight with excitement. "You look so handsome."

"Thank you."

"Come in, come in." Rose stepped aside so he could enter. After she shut the door, she hugged him tightly.

"I got this for Ray." He showed Rose the delicate corsage he'd had made at the flower shop.

Rose looked down at the corsage and then hugged him again. "It's absolutely perfect, Dean. You are such a dear boy."

He was glad for Rose's approval of it; he hadn't heard of a corsage prior to getting prepared for the prom. His mother, Nettie, had walked him through the preparation and he'd thought most of it had been a real waste of time, but for Rayna, who had dreamed of going to prom since she'd become a teen, he needed to get all of these details right.

"Rayna!" Rose stood at the bottom of the old creaky stairs. "Dean is here."

"She'll be down in a minute!" Danica called back.

Rose tilted her head and smiled at him. "You heard it. In a minute."

He nodded. "Yes, ma'am."

"Let me put this lovely corsage in the fridge to keep it fresh while you join Butch in his study." Rose took the plastic container from his hand. "And relax, Dean. You look like someone starched *you* inside of that getup."

Dean had always gotten on well with Ray's father, Butch Brand. Butch wasn't a classically educated man, having hardly made it out of high school, but he could've had an honorary PhD in ranching and homesteading. The man was a genius in those areas, and he appreciated young people who'd had the work ethic instilled in them at an early age, and Dean fit that bill. His father, a third-generation cattle rancher, expected Dean to know every single job on the ranch just in case anything were to happen to him. Just like Rayna, he would be up before sunrise helping with the ranch chores before heading off to school.

"Hey, Mr. Brand." Dean walked into Butch's study at the back of the house.

"Hey there, D.L." Butch put his newspaper aside, pushed his reading glasses on to the top of his head, groaned as he stood up and held out his rough, strong hand to Dean.

After they shook hands, the elder looked him up and down with a discerning eye. "You don't look half bad for a cowpuncher."

"I'm not much for it." Dean rolled his shoulders forward, trying to get more comfortable while he tugged on the bottom of his jacket. "But Ray…"

Butch chuckled as he sank back into his brown recliner that had been patched in several places by Rose's crafty hands. "Yeah, buddy. Ray is her mother's daughter, and she is mighty particular about those fiddly diddly details."

He lowered his reading glasses, grabbed the newspaper off of the table, jerking it to get it sorted out so he could read it. Butch looked at him over the edge of the paper and said, "If you didn't want to deal with all of that, you should've cut Charlie from the herd."

Butch and Rose had triplet daughters: identical twins Danica and Rayna and a third fraternal triplet, Charlotte. Charlotte "Charlie" Brand was her father's daughter through and through. Charlie was a tomboy who had better cowhand skills than most full-grown men; she could rope, brand, wrangle and birth-assist before her twelfth birthday. She didn't mind mud or dirt or sweat, and if the conversation didn't revolve around horses or homesteading, she wasn't interested. Charlie would one day make the perfect rancher's wife, but his heart belonged to Rayna.

A minute later, Rose came scurrying in with a delighted expression on her face. "They're ready."

She waved her hand at them to follow her. "Come, come."

"Well, let's go see what all the fuss is about." Butch stood up again, tried to close his paper neatly but then folded it haphazardly and tossed it onto the seat of his chair.

Dean walked down the narrow hall filled with frames of all finishes of the family. Rose had marked every occasion with the triplets and had made three giant photo albums for each of her girls.

Rose was waiting for them at the bottom of the stairs; she smiled at them and gestured for Dean to stand on one side while Butch was directed to stand on the other.

"Okay!" Rose called up the stairs. "We're ready!"

Danica appeared at the top of the stairs in a formfitting black vintage gown that had a scoop neckline made of ruffles and an eyelet corset that emphasized her tiny waist and a thick velvet sash that was tied into a large bow at the back. She had worked several jobs to save up enough money to purchase it, and with her wheat-blond hair in a perfect chignon, she looked as regal as Grace Kelly.

"Wait! Wait!" Rose said. "Daddy doesn't have his camera."

"Shoot," Butch said on his way back to his study.

He returned moments later with his Nikon digital camera, and once he was ready, Rose gave the signal for Danica and Rayna to make their entrance. Once again, Danica appeared at the top of the stairs; she waved her hand with a dramatic flair and said, "May I present to you Miss Rayna Brand!"

Dean felt his entire body break out into a nervous sweat; his heart was beating so fast and so hard in his chest that it was making him feel light headed. At the top of the stairs, Rayna appeared, a vision in a gold chiffon floor-length gown with a unique square bodice, cap sleeves and a natural waist. The gown was covered in hand-embroidered delicate wildflowers. Her long waist-length hair was sleek and unbound.

When their eyes met and she smiled at him with the sweetest, slightly self-conscious smile, his knees tried to buckle on him. She was so beautiful and kind and intelligent that Dean couldn't imagine a day in his life that he wouldn't love Rayna Brand.

Beside him, he heard Butch rapidly clicking on his camera as Rayna reached the bottom of the stairs. Dean held out his shaking hand to her and she took it.

"You have never looked more beautiful," he told her, feeling for a brief moment that they were the only two people in the world.

"Thank you," she said. "You look handsome. Thank you for wearing the gold shirt."

Rose raced to the kitchen, grabbed the corsage and brought it back. "Get a picture of him putting it on her wrist, Butch," she said, opening the plastic container for Dean to take out the corsage.

He slipped the corsage onto Rayna's wrist, and he was pleased with how well the corsage matched her dress—he was beginning to see the point of all of the preparations. This was a life highlight that deserved a gold shirt, a snug tuxedo and a corsage for his sweetheart.

Butch and Rose fussed over their girls, and the way that they still looked at each other, the kindness that they showed each other always left an impression on Dean. After twenty-five years together, Butch and Rose were still in love.

Danica broke free from the group and looked out of the kitchen window.

"Scott is here with the limo!"

Scott Johnson was one of his best friends, and Scott and Danica had an on-again, off-again relationship. For the prom, they had decided to be "on again."

Rose hustled her husband out of the front door so he could grab candid shots of the prom party as they walked down the steps.

"Charlie!" Rose yelled for her eldest daughter, who was riding her horse in the adjacent field. Tim Harris had planned on taking Charlie Brand to the prom, but an emergency at his family's hay-and-grain operation had forced him to back out.

"Charlie!" Rose waved her arms in the air. "Get over here! I need you in the pictures!"

Charlie turned her buckskin gelding and galloped across the field, jumped over a log and then barreled into the clearing in front of the cabin. The eldest triplet—dressed in jeans, a faded Wrangler T-shirt, a cowgirl hat and boots—halted the horse a few feet from the limo. Smiling with her face flushed, Charlie swung her left leg over the saddle horn until she was sitting sideways in the saddle and then jumped down. She patted her horse on the neck, pulled the reigns over its head and looped the reigns over a hitching post nearby.

Scott had gotten out of the limo and was now being photographed with Danica while Rose directed Butch.

"Why don't you come with us?" Rayna asked her older sister.

Charlie wrinkled her nose and gave a quick shake of her head. "Spare me. When Tim had to cancel, my prayers were answered."

"Charlie Brand!" Rose turned her attention to her wild-child tomboy daughter. "Couldn't you at least have put on a clean pair of jeans?"

Charlie looked down at her jeans, "These are clean."

Rose sighed at her eldest child; then she waved her arms to her daughters and herded them back onto the top steps of the porch.

They lined up eldest to youngest: Charlie on the right, Danica in the middle and Rayna on the left. They hooked arms as they had always done—arm in arm, side by side.

"Smile, my beauties," Butch said.

Dean stood next to Scott while they waited for their dates.

Dean felt something different in that moment, something more deep than he had ever experienced in his life up to that point. He was enchanted by Rayna and knew that what he felt for her was genuine, lasting love. The kind of love Rose and Butch shared.

"One day, I'm going to marry Ray," Dean said quietly to his best friend.

Scott had his hands in his front pockets. "Yeah. I know."

Chapter One

"Ma'am?"

"Ma'am?" the man said. "You're next."

Rayna Brand had drifted off in her mind, but the person behind her in the airport security line brought her back to the present.

"Oh," she said, "I'm sorry. Thank you."

She stepped up with her carry-on bag on her shoulder, but then something in her gut, something that hadn't yet reached the analytical part of her brain, made her stop, step aside and let the line move along without her. After a minute of her standing and staring at the passengers moving through the security point Rayna turned around to walk to the cluster of seats nearby. She sat down, carry-on in her lap, and looked at the overhead digital board for flight information. Her flight back to Connecticut had arrived, but they weren't boarding.

"What are you going to do now?" she asked herself in a whisper.

She had just visited her twin boys, Ryder and Rowdy, at college in Oregon. Back in Connecticut, her divorce from her husband of nineteen years was nearly finalized and the contract for the sale of their family home had been signed two weeks ago. The majority of her belongings were in storage, and she had been bunking at her friend Zuri's house until she figured out her next steps. Once the second mortgage on the house was paid, there wouldn't be much money left for them to split. Her decision to be a stay-at-home mom had limited her prospects in the job market, and her life back in Connecticut seemed…

"Impossible."

Her flight switched to *Boarding* on the screen.

Rayna hadn't realized how long she had been sitting in a waiting area; her mind was busy with her introspection. The only thing that broke her internal dialogue was her name being called on the intercom. "Rayna Fortier. Please come to gate seven. This is your final boarding call. Rayna Fortier."

She heard the message, but it didn't inspire her to move.

It was strange—she had thought of herself as "Rayna Fortier" for half of her life, and now she only thought of Fortier as her sons' last name. Rayna Fortier seemed like a woman she used to be a long time ago; that name didn't fit her any longer, and there was an open question in her mind—*Had it ever really fit?* That was the reason why, as part of the divorce, she had opted to change her name back to Brand.

The flight personnel made a second final boarding call, and then her flight changed from *Boarding* to *Departing*. A couple of minutes passed, and then Rayna stood up and hoisted her carry-on over her shoulder. She felt disconnected from her environment, and she supposed it was shock—she was soon to be a divorcée and an empty nester with no real plan for the rest of her life. On one hand it was, at times, exhilarating, and on the other—absolutely terrifying. Rayna slowly walked back to the main entrance of the airport, where she spent some time reading information on a kiosk.

"I love road trips," she said. "I've always loved road trips."

Rayna followed the signs to the car-rental area, walking in a meandering fashion as if she just hadn't deliberately missed her flight. Her luggage was on that plane. But she wasn't completely devoid of resources; in her carry-on she had a thick sweater rolled up tightly, a change of clothes including undergarments, some toiletries, her prescription medicines and her large assortment of vitamins, her wallet and her laptop. Perhaps from an outside perspective—to her friends, children, sisters and soon-to-be ex-husband—an impromptu cross-country drive might be a sign of an emotional breakdown. But in her gut, and at the core of her being, Rayna felt that this trip would help her sweep the clutter out of her brain and allow her mind to see her path forward.

She rented an SUV and called her friend, Zuri, to let her know that she wouldn't be crashing at her place tonight. Zuri was always exploring ways of self-improvement, so it wasn't surprising that her long-time friend had a positive response to the idea of a "finding myself" road trip. Now inside of the SUV, Rayna mapped a course home, made reservations along the route back to Connecticut and then sent a group text to her sons that she had missed her flight and would be driving back to Connecticut. Within seconds of receiving her text, Ryder called.

"Mom. What are you doing? How'd you miss your flight? Why are you driving all the way back to Connecticut?"

"This road trip is a gift I'm giving to myself."

"Why can't you give yourself a gift of a yoga retreat or a

girls' trip like a reasonable person?" Ryder asked and then suggested, "I think you're having a midlife crisis, Mom."

"Maybe I am. Don't worry about it. Focus on your studies instead of worrying about me. I did manage to navigate my life before you came along, Ryder."

There was a pause at the other end of the line before she heard her son sigh in frustration. "Well, at least download a tracking app so we can check on you."

She agreed, and after she downloaded the app, she asked, "Do you feel better now?"

"I guess," Ryder said. "At least now if you drive off a cliff and are rendered unconscious, we'll be able to send help so you won't be covered by snow and found once the snow melts in spring."

"Well, that was unnecessarily dramatic," she said. "Let Rowdy know what's going on. I need to get on the road."

"We love you, Mom," Ryder said. "Please be careful."

"I love you too—both of you."

After the phone call with Ryder, Rayna felt even more secure in her decision. This was the right path for her, and for the first time in quite a long while she felt *excited* about the adventure of it all. She buckled her seat belt, touched the Start button on the dashboard map and then turned on a Fleetwood Mac playlist up loud. Rayna turned onto I-84 East, toward her overnight stop in Boise, Idaho.

Three hours into the first leg of the road trip, and after replaying Fleetwood Mac's "Landslide" ten times while she'd sung along off-key—this song always made her cry— Rayna felt as if she was emerging from a dark mental tunnel when she arrived at the hotel. After checking in and getting settled in her room, she texted her boys and Zuri while eating two nutrition bars from a stash she carried in her backpack. Then she showered, changed into a white cotton T-shirt with a brightly colored lotus flower that had a stem looped into cursive words reading *Namaste* and a black pair of yoga pants, and put herself through a simple routine of poses that were perfect for getting the body and mind ready for sleep. Unfortunately, it didn't work this time. Instead of sleeping, she lay on her back, her head sunk into a soft hotel pillow, staring up at the ceiling. And there was one question that her mind returned to her time and time again…

"Is Connecticut still my home?"

She had only moved to Connecticut because her nearly ex-husband had been accepted into the University of Connecticut medical program. She had stayed in Connecticut because that was where her ex had been accepted as an intern and then offered a full-time job. Connecticut had felt like home to her because that was where she had built a life with her Ben, made a home and raised her sons. She had a small group of core friends who shared her passion for yoga and clean eating; she knew that she didn't have to live in Connecticut for those friendship bonds to persist.

Rayna tossed and turned all night, drifting in and out of sleep, contemplating the subject of *home*. With all of her pondering, she awakened with a big question mark floating above her head. She packed up her few belongings, stopped off to have a complimentary breakfast of scrambled eggs and a small cup of green tea, checked out and then headed to her rental. She sat behind the wheel for quite a long time, her hands resting on the steering wheel, her mind racing. Finally, she turned on the SUV and pulled up the route.

Rayna pulled off of the highway and parked so the headlights would eliminate her path to the closed metal gate. She left the engine running and the vehicle in Park while she jumped out, walked quickly over to the closed metal gate and fumbled with the latch. The metal gate was covered in ice, and her ungloved fingers started to burn and feel numb with only a short exposure to the cold. Her thin jacket only provided the smallest of protections from the cold.

"Open, damn it," Rayna cursed as she fought with the latch while her words turned into curls floating up from her mouth.

Finally, she managed to fight through the cold, unstick the latch and then push the wide metal gate. The gate creaked open slowly while she carefully picked her way back to the rental over the snow and patches of ice in her path. Once inside, she put her hands up to the vent in an attempt to warm them. Then, she turned on the four-wheel drive and pulled through the gate. She had driven in snowy, icy conditions as a teenager in Montana, but years of nice salted streets during winter in Connecticut had spoiled her.

"Whoa, whoa, whoa." Rayna searched for the road through snow flurries that were coming down harder now. She hit a patch of ice that sent the back end of her vehicle sliding to the right. Some of her training from her father, Butch, kicked in, and she left her foot off of the gas and gently guided the car back to the center of the road. She leaned forward with a gentle foot on the gas and did her best to follow the snow covered gravel road while the wipers, set on high, wiped away the snow from the windshield.

"Easy, girl," Rayna said to the car as the tires hit another slick patch of ice.

Visibility only went a few feet past the headlight beam. A herd of deer—mothers and babies—crossed the driveway and she was able to brake quickly, barely missing them. That near miss got her heartbeat racing and her still-cold hands gripping the steering wheel to the point of hurting.

She closed her eyes, let out a calming breath before she continued her slow journey to the house that only had dim yellow lights to guide her way.

She felt her shoulders relax as she drove through the arch and gate that had thankfully been left open. After shutting off the engine, she grabbed her carry-on bag from the front seat and then quickly got out of the car. She had just used the remote to lock the car when she heard a menacing male voice yell at her, "This is private property!"

"Charlie?" Rayna called out in the dark. "Wayne?"

"Ray?" She heard her eldest sister's voice. "Is that you?"

"Yes!" she called out to them. "It's me!"

Rayna stood by the car while the figures of her sister and her fiancé materialized out of the shadows of the night.

"What are you doing here? It's past midnight! We could have shot you!" Charlie gave her one of her famous bear hugs. "She's shivering," she said to Wayne while she put her arm around Rayna's shoulders. "Let's get her out of the cold."

Wayne took her carry-on bag off her shoulder. Together, the three of them walked the short distance to the main house.

"I'm so sorry I woke you," Rayna apologized as they walked the short distance to the main house. "I thought about texting so many times, but all along the way I thought of turning back. And then I found myself here."

"Home," Charlie said. "You found your way back home."

Wayne unlocked the door, turned on the inside lights, put her carry-on just inside of the front door and then headed to the kitchen.

"Put on a pot?" Charlie asked him.

Rayna slumped gratefully into a seat at the new butcher-block island; the entire house had been renovated to turn their family's once cattle farm into an Airbnb. Charlie pulled a quilt out of a nearby hall closet and put it around Rayna's shoulders. "This will help get you warm."

"Thank you." Gratefully, Rayna wrapped herself up into the quilt that had been made by their mother's hands several years before her passing.

Charlie sat down next to her and searched her face closely as if she could decode her thoughts. "I love that you're here, Ray," she said sincerely. "But…?"

"Why now?"

Her sister nodded.

It was a valid question. The morning she had awakened in Boise, Idaho, and only after she had gotten into her rental car had Rayna arrived at an answer to the question that had made it impossible to sleep the prior evening. Was Connecticut still her home? No, it wasn't. And reaching that conclusion had made driving the rest of the trip to New Haven seem like a complete waste of precious time. Instead, she had programed Hideaway Ranch, her childhood home, into the navigation system and started to drive toward Big Sky, Montana. For her entire married life, she had never thought of the ranch as her home and she certainly hadn't believed that it was somehow baked into her DNA. But it was. The fog had cleared in her mind, and what had come into view was the glaring fact that the only home she did have now was the land where she had been raised.

"I was visiting the boys in Oregon," Rayna explained in a voice that she recognized as a bit detached and monotone. "I flew in, but for some reason, I thought it would be an adventure to drive back to Connecticut. When I was younger, I used to love road trips. Do you remember that about me?"

Charlie nodded. "Yes, Ray. I do remember."

"So, I rented a car. But when I reached Boise, I realized…" Rayna warmed her hands around the hot mug full of coffee Wayne had put in front of her. She thanked him and then took a sip of her coffee before she said, "I guess… it was time for me to come home."

"Well past time." Charlie hugged her again, and Rayna felt the love and the acceptance in her sister's hugs. "Welcome home, Ray. I'm so happy that you're here."

Her sister and she drank coffee and caught up while Wayne snored lightly in a recliner chair in the nearby living room. Although Rayna had felt exhausted when she'd arrived, the coffee and the excitement that her sister felt for her unexpected visit had given her a burst of energy that lasted several hours before the inevitable crash came.

Still wrapped up in the quilt, Rayna rinsed her coffee cup in the sink and then put it on the drying rack.

"I'm beat," she said, her eyes trying to droop shut.

"I bet." Charlie put her coffee cup in the sink before she grabbed the carry-on bag. "Let's get you set up so you can get some sleep."

Rayna yawned loudly, nodded her head and followed her sister down the narrow hallway to the room that had been hers until she'd graduated from high school and left for college.

The house felt both familiar and foreign. The main cabin had gone through a massive renovation overseen by middle sister Danica. Most of the furniture was new, with the exception of family antiques that gave an authentic farmhouse flair for their guests. But many of the walls were decorated with enlarged photographs of the ranch going back five generations.

After their mother, Rose, had died, the ranch had been left to her triplet daughters; together, they had turned their family ranch into a destination short-term rental. Their very first guests had booked the ranch for late December. Between now and then, Rayna was sure that seven weeks was ample time to figure out her next steps and put her new life plan into action.

"Do you want to stay in Mom and Dad's room or your old room?" Charlie asked her as she led the way down the hall.

"My room," Rayna said sleepily. She just wanted to crawl into a relatively familiar den and hibernate.

Just before reaching her old bedroom, Rayna stopped to look at a framed photograph taken by their father of the three sisters on the day of high school prom. The expression on her face was so innocently happy, and her eyes were shining bright with love. He wasn't in the picture, but he was standing behind her father, and she had been looking at him when her father had taken the picture: James "Dean" Legend.

Charlie had put her things in her old bedroom and then rejoined her in the hallway.

"That seems like a lifetime ago," Rayna said, and as she did, unshed tears broke free. The Rayna in that picture was long gone—never to be seen or heard from again.

Charlie wrapped her arms around her again. "You're going to get back to yourself again, Ray. I promise. Now that you're home, you will."

A week after her arrival, Rayna had begun to feel like she had some energy. She had spent much of her time sleeping, sitting on the front porch of the house bundled up in layers of flannel, and she had gotten into the routine of yoga practice that made her feel more like herself. And helping Charlie with the care of the animals was a wonderful distraction while she tried to untangle her past as she figured out her future. Charlie had rebuilt the barn, putting in many features that kept the horses and donkeys warm and safe during the winter months. Rayna had found solace in the company of the horses, donkeys and goats. Her time mucking out stalls, refilling water buckets and feeding twice a day had made the major muscles of her body sit up and take notice. In a short time, she actually felt stronger both mentally and physically.

"I love you." Rayna knelt down beside the two miniature donkeys named Vincenzo and Grazia to give each of them a daily hug. Their stall was the last that she had mucked and put fresh bedding into. Now she was going to take a well-deserved break with the goats. She loved all of the animals, but she had to admit to herself that the goats were her favorites—they were loving and comical, and their little horns were adorable. She had attended a goat yoga class at a farm near New Haven, and that crazy, chaotic, thoroughly enjoyable experience had stuck with her.

"Hi, my beloveds." Rayna opened the gate to the larger stall that was plenty roomy for three Nigerian Dwarf goats by the names of Persephone, Beatrice and Eloise.

She closed the gate behind her and found a good spot to sit while the young goats clamored for her affection, each trying to beat the other onto the most coveted spot—her lap. Beatrice was the winner and curled up happily. But Rayna gave Persephone and Eloise hugs and kisses and was happy to have them lie down on either side of her. These moments cuddled up with the goats while the quiet barn noises— horses blowing their noses, drinking water, chewing with an occasional donkey bray—made her inexplicably happy in a way she had forgotten she could be.

Rayna had unintentionally dozed off, and she was awakened by the large, metal door to the barn being pulled open;

metal on metal made a high-pitched sound that jolted her awake. She checked her Apple watch—it was too early for Charlie and Wayne to be back from Bozeman, and during the winter months, most of the skeleton crew of cowboys was off-site picking up supplies in Ennis. It had been a slow, easy day to herself on the ranch, and she found that the peace of this land suited her in a way she had never experienced as a child. But the fact that she was supposed to be the only person on the property shocked her awake, put her body on high alert and her hands shaking from shots of cortisol and adrenaline released from her brain. Rayna stood up quietly and peeked around the corner; she saw a truck and trailer backing into the wide barn aisle. The frigid outside air began to overtake the warm air in the barn generated by the animals. On the side of the trailer she read, *J. Dean Legend, Farrier, Big Sky Montana.*

Rayna's inhaled deeply, pressed her back against the wood of the stall and put her hand over her heart that was beating as rapidly as hummingbird wings—still from fear, though not because of an unknown intruder but from the idea of seeing her first love again. Yes, she had kept tabs on him through Facebook, but they hadn't seen each other face-to-face since his mother's funeral and that was more than a decade ago. And she was pretty sure that she wasn't ready to break that record.

Rayna was still contemplating her situation when she heard the door of the truck open and shut and then, a moment later, the squeaky barn door being pulled closed. The only way she could get out of this barn was by encountering Dean. From her vantage, she could see Dean without him seeing her. When he walked around to the back of the trailer and opened the doors to access his equipment, the memories of their past love flooded her brain. Dean, who had always been tall and thin like a reed of prairie grass, had filled out—he was burly now, with broad shoulders and a scruffy beard covering most of his face.

Rayna closed her eyes tightly, and when she opened them again, she moved out of her hiding spot and into full view.

"Hi, Dean."

Dean pulled up to the refurbished horse barn at Hide-away Ranch. For years it had been falling apart one plank of wood at a time, but now, after Charlie had tried to tran-sition their family's ranch from a working cattle ranch to a corporate retreat or an Airbnb for families, the barn looked like it had when he'd been a kid. He drove in a circle until his farrier trailer filled with every tool he would need and parked for a minute while he walked over to the closed barn door and pulled it open so he could back his rig in. After he backed his truck into the barn, he shut the doors to keep the warmth generated by the animals from escap-ing while he worked.

Dean opened the door to his supply trailer, grateful for the diversion of work. Caring for his ailing father, raising his two young daughters and managing the day-to-day op-erations at Legend Quality Cattle felt like the weight of the world on his shoulders. Farrier work helped to keep him sane, and when Charlie Brand had brought a herd back to Hideaway Ranch, Dean had been happy to take care of their hooves. But every time he drove onto Brand prop-erty, the feelings he had always harbored for Rayna broke through the dam he had built around her memory and bub-bled up to the surface. He missed her. He'd always missed her. Perhaps, upon reflection, this was one of the reasons his marriage had failed: he'd never gotten over Rayna. He thought that he still loved her, and now that he was forty, he understood as fact that part of his heart would always belong to her.

"Hi, Dean."

He heard his name spoken in a voice that for many, many years, he had only heard in his dreams. But this wasn't a dream. Nipper in one hand, Dean turned toward the voice—there, standing in the goat pen, was Rayna Anne Brand dressed in so many layers that she looked as if she had prepared to climb Mount Everest.

He was so caught off guard that he took a step back, tripped over his hoof stand and was knocked right off of his feet and landed smack dab on his backside.

"Oh!" Rayna exclaimed, opening the goat pen and rushing over to his side—but her thick layers of clothing made her waddle, and that made him laugh out loud.

Dean sat up and rested his arms on his knees, shaking his head and chuckling at the fine pair that they made. He'd imagined their reunion so many times—those thoughts kept him company when he felt lonely—but none of those reunions had him tripping and falling, that was for darned sure.

"Let me help you up." Rayna held out her hand.

"Well, why not," he said, more to himself than to her. He took hold of her hand and let her help him up. Once upright, he dusted off his jeans and then looked at Rayna.

"What happened?"

"What happened?" He repeated her question while he busied himself getting his tools together. "*You* happened."

Chapter Two

Dean felt blindsided and embarrassed. After all of these years, he was still literally and figuratively falling for Rayna Brand. She looked at him with those cornflower-blue eyes and that sweet, shy expression on her pretty face, and for him, the years between them melted away. But she was a married woman. That boundary was one that he would never cross.

"Don't sweat it," he said, doing his best to cover up the gut punch he'd suffered by her barging back into his life.

Dean did have a pretty bad bruise on his pride for falling like he had, but he did his best to cover that up. He walked over to the spot where he would trim the hooves of the horses and the donkeys. He was always grateful for the work, but today he felt an extra dose of gratitude. The work would keep him focused so he could stop his brain from heading down roads that were best left untraveled.

"It's been a minute, hasn't it?" he asked her.

She leaned against one of the stall gates while she gave some attention to a muscular gelding with blue eyes and a white face.

"Ten years," Ray said quietly. "Your mother's funeral."

That pain he'd felt after his mother had died was still an ache in his body that he figured would be with him for the rest of his life. That pain kept his mother front in his mind so he could let his girls know about her.

Skirting the issue of his mother, he said, "I didn't know you were in town."

He strapped on his weathered half chaps to protect his thighs while giving him pockets for easy access for his nippers and his large file.

"Well, I didn't exactly know that I was coming to town," she said with a small shrug.

"How long you stayin' for?" he asked.

It was a casual question, but his gut was all twisted up when he asked it. Part of him wanted her to go away quickly and never come back; the other part of him wanted to end the distance between them, take her into his arms and never let her go again.

When he glanced over at her, he saw a dark cloud pass over her face. There was a fleeting frown, and then she wrinkled her forehead and gave the slightest shrug—yes, the years had passed, but he could still read her pretty face like a favorite book. This wasn't just any ol' visit to her childhood home. It ran much deeper than that—but he knew it would be best if he didn't wade into that murky water. He had too much on his plate with his two girls and his ailing father.

She walked over to the donkey's stall, reached over to give each of the donkeys some love. She finally said simply, "A while."

"Are you ready, pretty girl?" Dean put a halter on a petite chocolate-brown mare that bore the name of Rayna's late mother: Rose.

The mare nuzzled his hand, and he gave her a pat on her neck before leading her out to the crossties where he had set up his equipment. He hooked her halter to the crossties, and then he started at the left front hoof and would work his way to the back hooves.

"It's good to see you back to trimming again," Rayna said.

He pulled the mare's left leg gently forward and hooked her hoof onto the green stand that had a hydraulic component to adjust quickly to the horse's height.

"It keeps me sane. Gets me off the property and the horses don't expect me to talk much," he said, taking the nippers to trim some of the growth from the hoof before he used his file to smooth off the rough edges. Dean inspected the hoof, felt satisfied with the work and then moved on to the next front hoof.

Ray took a step closer to him to give some attention to a tall Thoroughbred-Quarter mix named Cash. "I bet your daughters keep you plenty busy."

Dean smiled; they'd had his heart in their hands and he had spent every single day since they'd been born working to be the best father he could be for his girls.

He chuckled while he worked. "That's for darn sure they do."

"Paisley and…?"

"Luna." He filled in the name for his youngest. Paisley was thirteen going on thirty-two, and then there was his sweetness and light—Luna was ten. They were the best part of him, and he was so grateful to have his girls with him in Montana—he wanted his girls to understand the roots of their family before they went off to do amazing things like their jet-setting mother.

"Luna!" she said. "Sorry."

"No need." He finished the second hoof and took Rose's hoof off of his stand, putting it down slowly and gently.

Dean stood upright and gave his back a break—trimming

hooves was more of a young man's game. But he loved it and it gave him some much-needed time on his own a couple of days a week.

"And your boys?"

That was when he finally saw that free and easy beautiful smile that lit up her face at the mention of her boys.

"Ryder and Rowdy…"

"Pure back-country names." He smiled. "Can't imagine there are too many of them in Connecticut."

"No." She laughed. "None, I should think."

"Charlie told me they were off to college," he said. "Hard to believe. Years just flyin' by."

"And they get faster as we go."

"True that. Raw deal there."

There was a pause between them before she said, "I'm sorry to hear about your father. A stroke, was it?"

"At first. Last year he was diagnosed with emphysema and lung cancer."

Her mom and Dean's dad had often smoked together after dinner; sometimes they'd borrowed cigarettes from each other. In the end, that habit had taken years off their lives.

"I'm sorry."

"Thank you." He caught her eye and held it. "He still adores you. He'd be tickled to see you again."

"I'd love that," she said simply.

After another pause, he said, "Well, I'd best be getting back to work."

Rayna nodded and was about to turn away when she stopped herself. "This is so awkward, Dean. We're acting like we're strangers. We've always been friends, haven't we?"

He nodded wordlessly.

"Is it okay if I give my friend a hug?"

When he didn't protest, she took that silence as a yes, crossed to him and then wrapped her arms around him.

After the hug, Dean gave her the once over. "God bless it, Ray! Are you actually in there somewhere? How many layers of clothing *are* you wearing?"

Rayna left the horse barn and walked as quickly as she could back to the main house; the heavy layers of clothing did make her feel like she was waddling more than walking. The cold and snow in Montana just seemed wetter and colder. While she walked, her mind mulled over her reunion with Dean. It was a strange mixture of really awkward and oddly familiar. He had seemed cordial and aloof. Before today, those were two words she never would have used to describe Dean. But he had lived in New York, and he had married a high-profile designer. He still resembled her Dean from years gone by, but he wasn't that boy anymore. Yet she felt hurt that he didn't seem to remember or care about how important that barn had been to them when they'd been in high school. That was where they'd shared their first kiss; that was where he'd first told her that he loved her; this barn was where he'd asked her to prom.

Looking back, she had to admit to herself that she had been starstruck by Benjamin Fortier the Third, "Ben" to his family and friends. The fact that he was the third in his family line and she was a triplet had seemed like kismet to her. She'd been a freshman fish out of water at Princeton, a Montanan born and bred with a full-ride scholarship and awkward in every way a person could be awkward. Ben had been handsome, self-assured, the guy that everyone wanted at their party. He'd been captain of the field hockey team, president of his fraternity, and whatever he'd wanted, he'd gotten. And for some reason, Ben had wanted her.

Her new roommate, Zuri, had dragged her out one night to a frat party, and that was where she'd met Ben. And just like Ben had been one hundred percent convinced he was going to follow in his father's footsteps and become a doctor, Ben had been one hundred percent convinced that he was going to marry her and she would be the mother of his children. And ultimately his certainty had become a reality.

"Gosh darn it!" she said as she grabbed a hold of the icy railing of the front porch steps with her thick mittens that provided a less than desired grip while she fought against her clothing to get up those steps. "Why is *everything* so hard here?"

Once inside, she used her teeth to pull off one mitten and then tugged off the other. Even with the mittens, her fingers felt stiff and cold. She jerked at the zipper on her jacket again and again, cursing with each failed attempt. Finally, she got the zipper down, yanked her arms out of the jacket sleeves, roughly put the jacket on a hook by the door before she quickly stripped off layers of winter weather clothing. Once she was free of them, Rayna put on a pot of coffee to warm her on the inside.

Her relationships with Dean and Ben seemed to be intertwined and overlapping inside of her mind. Her personal truth—the truth that she kept in a vault in the recesses of her mind—was that Ben and she hadn't ever been compatible. Not really. He had been attracted to the naive, sweet, shy girl in the crowd who hadn't immediately thrown herself at him. The frat house had been crowded and hot and filled to the gills with drunken college students. There'd been a live band that was truly terrible, and their "covers" of songs had been horrible and every room had smelled like sweat and beer. She had found her way to an outside patio to breathe in the fresh air. Then, as if from a dream, Ben had been by her side, asking her if she was okay. That was the moment that had changed the course of her life.

Rayna poured herself a cup of coffee and sat down at the kitchen counter. She realized that she was in a midlife crisis that had been forced onto her by Ben's decision to divorce her. The unvarnished truth was the fact that Ben's parents had never accepted her; they were an influential, high-profile family that called Washington, DC their home. And when Ben had decided to marry her against their wishes, they'd cut him off financially. This fracture in his family was deep, and even though things had improved when the boys had been born, Rayna had known that this emotional wound always had and always would put a strain on their marriage.

"Doomed from the start." Ray sighed after a sip of hot coffee.

This was the major reason she had worked two jobs to fund med school. But now the boys were grown and off to college; Ben was ready to turn the page.

"Why didn't I see this coming?" she asked aloud. The only things that they truly had in common were their sons.

Rayna was on her second hot cup of black coffee, and her mind drifted easily from Ben to Dean. When they'd been in high school, he had been slim as a string bean and always the tallest in any school photo, gangly and endearing. He wasn't skinny now—he looked burly and manly, and she couldn't believe how handsome she thought he was with a full bushy beard that had some gray hairs in it. And of course, his Van Halen concert shirt he'd been wearing under his unzipped thick winter coat made her smile. He'd always been such a metal head, and that hadn't changed.

Rayna was still ruminating about Dean's large, capable hands and his strong, masculine appeal when her phone rang. She looked at it and frowned when she saw it was her ex-husband.

"Hey, Ben." She answered the phone with a neutral tone. "How's Connecticut?"

"Cold," Ben replied with forced cheerfulness. "Busy."

There was a short pause between them. It struck her as odd that her relationship with Ben after over two decades together had been reduced to bland small talk. They covered her trip to see their sons, and then Ben asked cursorily, "So, how's Montana?"

"Cold. Busy."

"Good. Nice." Ben made a noise in his throat that grated on her nerves and let her know that he was only half listening to her. "So, Ray, the reason I called…"

"I signed the papers electronically this morning." She cut him off in a tone that was terse. "Check your email or text messages."

A second later, Ben said, "Okay. I see it now. Good! Well done. Thank you."

"You're welcome."

Today seemed to be the day of many uncomfortable pauses with her first love and her first husband. Several moments ticked by, and then Ben said, "Well, time waits for no man."

"Or woman."

"True. True." Her ex-husband bantered back, "Clever girl."

She closed her eyes, shook her head for a brief moment and realized that she didn't need to indulge Ben's misogynistic quips any longer. She wished him well, and they hung up. It was the first time that they had said goodbye without a perfunctory *I love you* attached. Even while they'd been in the divorce process, they had held on to that one tiny thread that had kept them connected as spouses. And of all things, that last snipping of the frayed thread made her cry.

She stood up, walked over to the kitchen counter, pulled some tissues out of a box and wiped the tears from her face. She didn't love Ben as a wife should love a husband—but they *had* loved each other once, hadn't they? And after a couple of clicks of a mouse on DocuSign it was over. Twenty years, two sons, years of playing the part of doctor's wife, perfecting the role of happy homemaker and host for hospital administrators and colleagues—all of that effort, all of that life building gone just as easy as a snap of her fingers.

Rayna blew her nose loudly several times, leaned her hip back on the kitchen counter and brushed some strands of hair that had gotten loose from her ponytail holder back off of her face.

"Well, Ray?" she asked aloud with a shrug of her shoulders. "I keep hearing that forty is the new thirty. So what's next?"

"Hey, Legend."

Dean was packing up his equipment in his trailer when he heard Charlie Brand's voice.

"I just finished," he said as he put his tools in the toolbox so he could shut the trailer door and bolt it shut for safe travel.

Charlie Brand was the eldest of the Brand triplets. She was muscular from work on the ranch, and the skin on her face was both chapped red from the cold wind and tanned from spending most of her time out in the elements.

"How are they?" she asked about her horse herd that had been on the ranch for less than a year.

Dean grabbed an invoice pad out of the passenger side of his truck. He made some quick notes in the margins before he totaled the bill and handed it to her.

"Dusty has a stone bruise, so keep an eye on that."

Charlie nodded. "I'll watch for any signs of abscess."

"Rose is a doll." He leaned back against his truck. "No issues there."

He reviewed the hoof health of the herd, and when he got to her draft-quarter mix, Atlas, he said, "That boy has soup plates instead of hooves. He's got so much weight on those hooves, he's gonna need shoes."

Charlie laughed. "They are heavy! I have to take a minute to rest between each hoof. Luckily Wayne takes care of him most of the time. I'll let him know about the shoes."

Dean nodded. Wayne was a seasoned cowboy who had helped Charlie convert Hideaway Ranch into a destination for guests. He'd also had the good sense to put a ring on Charlie's finger.

"If you're going to work any of them this winter, we'd better talk about shoes and pads to protect their hooves."

"Okay." Charlie folded the invoice and tucked it into her coat pocket. "All of them will have a job, so we may as well get that going next time."

"Okay. When do you want me to come back for that?" Dean pulled the squeaky barn door open, getting a blast of snow flurries in the face.

Charlie said, "Can you squeeze them in next week?"

Dean nodded, checked his schedule and then pulled an appointment card out of his front pocket, scrawling on it quickly before he handed it to the elder Brand.

"And I'll get this invoice to Danny," Charlie said, and

then teased him affectionately: "You know, you'd get paid faster if you would embrace technology. PayPal, Zelle."

Dean shook his head. "My system works just fine for me. Thank you for the unsolicited advice."

"Okay, grumpy bear." Charlie followed behind him. "I swear you get more prickly as the years go by."

Dean walked around to the driver's side of his truck, opened the door and then kicked the snow off of his boots before he climbed behind the wheel.

"You're the only one who ever says that," Dean retorted before he closed the door to the truck in a signal to Charlie that he was finished with the conversation.

"I'm the only one who isn't scared to say it!" she said loud enough to be heard easily through the glass. Then she tapped on the window with her knuckles to get him to roll it down.

After he cranked the engine, he rolled down the window. "I do have more clients, Charlie. You know that, right?"

"I'm almost done," she said. "And if you'd just let me tell you what I want to tell you instead of interrupting me, you could be out of here a lot quicker. Honestly, you're the one dragging this out."

Dean breathed in deeply and then let it out, his breath white and billowy. "You use a lot of words."

"Says the father of two daughters. You're in for a bumpy ride, my friend." Charlie smiled at him broadly. "Better buckle up."

"Okay. More unsolicited advice." He started to roll the window back up.

"Wait!" She put her hand in the way of the glass. "I wanted to share some news!"

He stopped rolling up the window and waited for her to continue.

"We got our first booking! A professor and his family are going to spend Christmas *and* New Year's here with us! Not too shabby, right?"

Dean knew that the Brand family had struggled financially for years, but Charlie had never given up. And the fact that she had switched gears and adapted to changing times in order to keep Hideaway in the family meant that she had gained his respect as well as the respect of all of the old-timer ranchers in the area.

"Congrats, Charlie. I mean it," he said sincerely. "You didn't sell out—you were smart enough to adapt, evolve. It's the Jason Newsted effect."

"Who in the world is Jason Newsted, and why do I care?"

Dean raised his hands off the steering wheel in disbelief. "Who is Jason *Newsted*? Hello? Metallica? He cut his hair and—this is just my opinion—led his band to a new era when big hair bands were becoming irrelevant. I mean, can you say *Poison who?*"

"First of all, I can absolutely say *Poison who?* because I seriously don't know who they are. Secondly, you took this to a really strange place, Legend," Charlie said. "You need to switch to a country music station ASAP and then ask Dolly Parton for forgiveness."

Dean shifted into gear. "You go ask Ray about Metallica. She'll understand the spot-on analogy I just made."

The minute he mentioned Rayna, he knew he'd made a mistake. Charlie was more quick-witted than most—all of the Brand sisters were, and he could see Ray's older sister putting the pieces together one millisecond at a time.

"Whoa! Whoa, whoa, whoa!" Charlie raised her voice in excitement as if she had solved the biggest mystery. "You've spoken to Ray!? That means she must have come out to see you, right?"

"Damn it, Charlie," Dean snapped. "Mind your own business, and I'll mind mine."

"I *knew* something was fishy with you, Legend!" She pointed her finger at him in a playful accusatory manner. "Whenever you're being weird, your left eye twitches. And it's twitching right now!"

"I'm running late." Dean started to roll up his window with her arm going for a bit of a ride.

Charlie pulled her arm back just before it reached its destination. She wrapped her knuckles on the glass again. "Did she tell you why she's here?"

"That's her business, not mine," he said as he crept his truck forward.

"Ask her!"

"I'm rollin', Charlie," he hollered back. Before he put his foot on the gas, he said, "Mind your toes!"

Dean drove forward and kept his eyes trained straight ahead instead of looking into the main house's windows for a possible glimpse of Rayna. He wasn't running late in all honesty; he just needed to put some distance between Rayna and himself. So many unwanted feelings and memories of her—a jumble of good and bad—had risen to the surface. He knew that he would always love her—any doubts of his love for her had been vanquished, and all that was left was a newly opened wound on his heart. The *real* reason they had broken up and sought out other partners had been Ray's desire to make a life as far away from Big Sky as possible. She hadn't wanted to be a rancher's wife, and he'd known that his heart would always be in Montana.

He had always known, no matter how much time he'd spent on the East Coast, that his attachment to the land and the obligation he had to take care of his parents in their old age and take the reins of Legend Quality Cattle would eventually lead him back home. He had loved two women in his life, and both of them could not and would not adapt to ranch life—his girls' mother had hoped to change him, but Ray had known the deal right up front from when they'd still been school kids.

The way Charlie was acting, Dean's mind raced with possibilities—could Rayna be back in Big Sky to stay? That singular idea had sent adrenaline to every place in his body and lit up his heart and mind that could only be compared with the feeling he had when he held each of his beloved daughters in his arms. And *that* fact had scared him straight. He needed to lock up the deep love he still had for Ray in an impenetrable safe where no sunlight could give nourishment to that love for her to grow.

Rayna watched Dean pull his rig out of the barn until he was out of sight. She had wondered if he would look over at the kitchen window where she was so plainly in view and wave, but he hadn't. And that absence of such a simple gesture had broken a place in her that she had gone to for comfort in her private dreams—she had sincerely believed that Dean would always love her in the same hidden place she had kept memories of him in her heart.

She was still processing her interaction with Dean when she saw Charlie marching purposefully toward the main house wearing only a soft shell jacket to keep her warm.

Charlie opened the door, kicked off her rubber boots, left them on the porch and walked into the house with her socks on. The left sock had a hole in it.

"Boy, is it a *mess* out there." Her sister slipped out of their father's brown coat and hung it on a horseshoe hat rack just inside of the front door.

"Do you want a cup of coffee?" Rayna asked, and there

was a waver in her voice that was a telltale sign that her emotions on the inside were leaking to the outside.

"Lord, yes," Charlie said. "And then I want to hear all about your encounter with Dean."

Chapter Three

Rayna worked hard to stop new tears from forming. Everything balled up into one—signing the divorce papers and then Dean turning back up in her life was too much to handle. Her heart felt like it was shattering into thousands of shards, and she couldn't imagine that it would ever truly be patched back together. And if it could be repaired, it would never be the same innocent heart that it had been before.

Rayna put a mug on the counter where Charlie was sitting. She brought the pot over to the mug, head down, trying to hide her puffy eyes from her sister. But it didn't work.

"Have you been crying?" Charlie asked in a tone that let Rayna know that she was actually realizing it in that moment.

She could barely nod yes to her sister when new tears began to break through her will to not cry one more tear. Charlie got up, rushed to her side and then wrapped her arms around her body in a wonderful bear hug. Out of the triplets, Charlie always gave the best hugs.

"Do you need a hug?"

"Yes." Ray closed her eyes and nodded pitifully; Charlie wrapped her arms tightly around her. Charlie had always been steady—she had always been a strong shoulder to lean on, even when they'd been kids.

"Do you need chocolate?" Charlie asked her.

That made her laugh. "No. The hug was enough."

"Okay," Charlie said, "but that's a standing offer. I have my own private stash for just this sort of occasion."

Charlie brought a tissue box over to her. Ray blew her nose loudly. She had always been the type of person who wanted to fix things. Yet she hadn't been able to fix her own marriage, and that stung. The most important fix of her life and she had failed.

"Come sit down with me, Ray." Charlie took a seat on one of the new bar stools. "I want to know everything that's bothering you."

She held out the tissue box again so Rayna could dry the tears off of her face and blow her nose one last time.

"What's wrong? Besides everything." Charlie always managed to throw something into her words that made Rayna laugh in spite of her pain.

She laughed a quick laugh before she said, "It's official—we're divorced. I signed the papers today."

"Oh, Ray," Charlie said, her blue eyes were the same as Rayna's, and at the moment, they also held the same sadness. "I'm so sorry. Truly I am. Of course, I always thought that Ben was—how can I put this while still being fair to my nephews' father?"

"Don't hold back, Charlie," she told her triplet. "This is a safe space."

"Well," her sister said, "he always reminded me of milk toast."

Rayna laughed at the unexpected comparison, and it came from a genuine place.

"He's like soggy sour-dough bread—no real crust or taste or appeal in the looks department." Charlie pulled a disgusted face as if she had smelled and tasted something terrible.

"Well, that will never be said in front of my boys." Rayna smiled at her. "But I have to admit, and upon reflection, he is a *little bit* like milk toast."

"Well, my nephews skipped a generation and took after Butch, thankfully," Charlie said. "How are they both taking all of this?"

Rayna got up and brought the coffee over to refill their mugs. When she returned to her spot, she said, "They're so different in who they are as people on the inside, and their outside appearance is even *more* different. In a side-by-side comparison, I believe most people wouldn't mistake them for identical twins."

"Like Danny and you."

"Yes! Exactly," she agreed. "Rowdy throws himself into sports to push down any signs of emotions other than anger, frustration and impatience. But I know that all of that roughness is covering up pain, and he won't let me in enough to even attempt to help."

"And then there's Ryder—he's always been my sensitive guy. He takes after me with the long hair and involving himself in the causes of the day. He's really struggling with the divorce and trying to understand the changes in my life. I seem to be quickly evolving, and that's understandably difficult for him. Ever since he first noticed that I had taken off my wedding ring his world…my world, *our* world has been flipped upside down."

"And the mom he has always known wouldn't skip a flight, rent a car and end up in Montana instead of Connecticut."

"No. I was always consistent, steady, the parent they could always count on. I hate how our failure is hurting our sons." She sighed. "I guess I really needed a place to lick my wounds."

"This is *your home*, Ray. You can stay as little or as long as you want." Charlie had deep tenderness in her eyes. "All of this works both ways, Ray. You have no idea how much you being here has already helped me find some balance. I have always believed that I could accomplish anything alone and on my own." She paused and shook her head. "But I might actually be in over my head with this Airbnb deal."

"No, you're just getting cold feet. But if you think I can be of some help to you, I'll stay on for a while. We all rise together, and we all fall together."

Charlie's eyes widened with surprise mixed with relief. She held out her fist for a fist bump as she said, "Well, then, Ray. Let's damn well rise."

Soon after her discussion with Charlie ended they both went on with their days. The conversation had been so focused on the end of her marriage with Ben that Charlie, whose mind was almost always focused on ranch work, had forgotten to delve in to Rayna's first meeting with Dean. Of course, she knew this was only a short reprieve—Charlie would be back on the hunt sooner than later when it came to the topic of Dean.

"Mmm." Charlie came through the door several hours later, full of the energy that kept her fueled up for ranch work, her cheeks and nose wind burned. "Something smells awesome in here!"

Ray smiled at the compliment. "I cook my way through my tears."

Her sister gave her a bear hug and then peeked into the pot of stick-to-your-ribs stew Ray was making. "Mom's stew."

"Perfect for warming you up on a cold day from the inside out."

Charlie had taken a tablespoon from a nearby drawer, scooped up some of the simmering stew, blew on it and then tasted it. "Mmm!"

"Good?" Rayna asked but already knew from the expression on her sister's face.

"Incredible!" Charlie said, putting her spoon in the sink. "You made a pretty big batch."

"I made enough for ten!" Rayna laughed. "Let Wayne and anyone else who's interested know that there's supper in the main house."

Charlie texted her fiancé and then sat down on the bar stool she tended to consistently choose.

Ray leaned her hip against the kitchen counter. "What?"

Charlie's eyes were wide, her face reading excitement and her body language following suit. "I can't believe that I hadn't thought of this before!"

Ray waited for her sister to continue.

"But then again, I didn't know you were coming here. And even if I *did* know, until today I didn't know that you were open to staying on at least until we get through the holidays," she said as if talking only to herself.

"Charlie!" Rayna interjected. "What are you trying to say?"

"You can cook!" her sister exclaimed.

Rayna took a pause, not sure how to respond to that. She had been cooking since she'd been old enough to turn on the oven. This wasn't exactly a revelation or worthy of all of this suspense.

"With Aspen in Texas for the foreseeable future, we need a cook!" Charlie said, still excited with her epiphany.

Wayne had three younger brothers: Waylon, Wyatt, and

Wade. Wyatt who had fallen in love with Aspen, a dear friend of the Brand family, and after they'd married, she had announced that they were expecting. When Wyatt had taken Aspen home to Texas for an extended visit, she'd experienced some symptoms that had later been deemed to be high-risk enough to stop her from flying home to Montana. And until her doctors gave her the green light, driving home was also out of the equation.

Rayna began to chew on the side of her nail. She had just promised her sister to "rise together"—on the other hand, she had imagined playing a supporting role rather than a starring role.

Charlie was always disappointed when others didn't react to her many plans with the same enthusiasm she had delivered them. She crossed her arms in front of her body and prepared to battle.

"Charlie Brand! Don't look at me with that attitude," Ray said to her sister. "Give me a minute to mull it over. I didn't say no."

"First, I don't have an attitude…"

"You are *all* attitude nearly all of the time!" she interjected good-naturedly.

"And *secondly*, yes, you are trying to say no! I can read you like a book, Ray!"

"Maybe you need to get a new book!" Rayna said. "I actually think it makes sense. I'm here, and I'm actually the logical choice to fill in."

Charlie had a habit of tuning others out when she was in full-on *I'm going to win this battle at all costs* mode. "You literally worked oven glove in oven glove with Aspen on the winter menu! Who better to cook while she's in Texas? I was going to limp along, do my best and royally screw it up for all of us. But now—" Charlie opened her arms wide in excitement "—I have you!"

At this point, Rayna was just going to hold her ground and wait for Charlie to get it all out of her system.

Her sister continued, "Our first *ever* guests want to experience a classic American Christmas with all of the traditional decorations, desserts and cuisine, and that's what you do! No one does Christmas like you do, Ray. No one. You are the queen of traditional American Christmas—the foods that you can prepare, the way you decorate! The job that's in front of us was tailor made for you. I didn't realize it until just this moment," Charlie added with a deeply reflective tone.

"I've been worried about this, Ray. So worried. I've tried my best to keep a positive attitude, but underneath it all, I've been..." She didn't finish her thought, instead said, "We have one shot to make a good first impression and give these guests everything that they requested and then some. But with Aspen off the roster, I thought we were sunk because I really believe that the success of this ranch is hinged on this one first booking."

"Are you serious, Charlie?" Rayna's tone changed when her sister's worry, which was news to her, churned up worry inside of her. "You're that concerned?"

"Yes, I was," Charlie said. "But not now, Ray. Not anymore. I believe—scratch that, I *know* that it isn't a coincidence that you're here. You have a huge role to play in our success. You were the missing secret ingredient."

Rayna was taken aback by Charlie's obvious concern. When she'd arrived, she had been seeking solace in a place that had been, at one time, her home. It was difficult to rectify in her mind that she wasn't overly concerned with the first guests *or* the gravity of this initial booking. But looking at her sister now, with her usual *think you can, know you can* attitude replaced with real fear for the successful transition from a working ranch to an Airbnb, she felt selfish and out of touch. The burden of their aging parents and the cattle ranch that was hemorrhaging money had all been laid at Charlie's feet. Rayna supposed she had gotten too comfortable with that dynamic. But that was wrong, and she needed to fix it.

"And you didn't tell me all of this because…"

"You had enough on your plate," Charlie said. "But I can't cook—not really—and I don't decorate cookies or anything else for that matter. I can chop down a real nice tree for them, devise a pulley getup to get it into the house and set it up like it should be, but decorate it? That's not my deal."

"But it is my deal."

Rayna sat in silence with her mind rapidly flipping through her current situation juxtaposed with the current situation of the ranch. Every year she looked forward to Christmas; she loved the decorating, the music, the baking and making Brand-family traditional fare for her friends and relatives. She loved to go shopping and search for the perfect gift for everyone that she loved, and she loved to sip eggnog and sing along to carols while she wrapped those presents and put them under the tree. She loved to fill the stockings she had made by hand before hanging them on the fireplace mantel.

She had been rather depressed about the approach of Christmas—this would be the first year that she wouldn't decorate her home with all of the Christmas decorations she had collected. During her divorce process, she had worried that she didn't have skills that would fill one page of a résumé; in her mind, employers wouldn't be impressed with *stay-at-home mom for twenty years.* But in a twist of fate or by grand design, her particular skillset was needed in order for the ranch to put its best boot forward for the guests.

"Well?" Charlie prompted her.

"I don't know," Rayna said seriously, doing her best to fight a smile from breaking through. "What kind of benefits do you offer?"

Dean had tossed and turned for a couple of hours the night after he'd come face-to-face with Rayna. He knew he had residual feelings for her, and yes, he had always believed that he held her in a very special place in his heart. But he hadn't considered the full force of his emotions when it came to his first love. He didn't want to dwell on things he couldn't change or emotions that he wasn't ready to address, so he did what he had done for the last twelve years—he focused on work and his daughters.

"Good morning, Dad." His eldest daughter, Paisley, was in the kitchen cooking eggs. She was on the verge of turning thirteen. Before the divorce and the move to Montana, Paisley had been a carefree, curious, bright child who was full of energy and a zest for learning. But after the divorce, Paisley had taken on the role of big sister *and* mother to her younger sister, Luna, two years her junior.

He dropped a kiss onto her head. "Smells good."

"Thanks, Dad." Paisley took the spatula and moved the scrambled eggs as they cooked, then put some bacon in a hot pan.

No matter how often he told Paisley that it wasn't her job to raise Luna and take care of him, she just kept on doing what was in her heart to do. His father, Buck, had told him to leave her be. This was how she was coping with the reorganization of their family.

"Would you make sure Luna gets her hands washed before she sits down at the table?" Paisley asked while turning wide strips of bacon. "She's in her room playing with her iPad. I think she's getting way too much screen time."

"Aye, aye, Captain." He saluted his daughter.

That always elicited a rare smile from his eldest child. In fact, if she didn't rebound to her normal, carefree, playful, artistic self, he'd already decided that family counseling would have to be explored. She hadn't unpacked her sewing machine or her sewing materials since they'd moved to Montana several years ago. Dean had become a single parent, something that had not crossed his mind as a possibility when he'd married the girls' mother, Catrin.

His ex-wife had emigrated from Cambodia with her family when she'd only been four. She had a genius-level IQ; she was creative, strong and determined. All of those traits, plus her undeniable beauty, had made him the bee seeking out that honey. But she had been his date to Ray's wedding to Ben; Catrin had seen his heart being broken in real time, and she had fallen in love with that vulnerability.

They'd truly had been an opposites-attract union, but that type of attraction had turned out to have an expiration date. Truth was they'd both wanted the other to give them something that neither one of them had to give. They had eventually decided to divorce amicably and focus on being co-parents to their children. Dean had been awarded full custody because Catrin's clothing brand was taking off and she was traveling all over the world, with an open invitation to come visit their daughters at the ranch.

Dean snuck up to Luna's bedroom door. As noted by Paisley, Luna was sitting on her princess-themed canopy bed with her eyes glued on the screen of her device. He ran into the room, jumped and landed on the bed next to his youngest child. Luna screamed, then giggled when he scooped her up into his arms, rolled over so his feet touched the fuzzy pink rug by her bed and then stood upright.

"Dad!" Luna wiggled in his arms while reaching for her tablet. "I'm not done playing!"

"Well, I have to disagree, munchkin face. I bet you've already had two hours of screen time while I've been out in the cold feeding livestock."

Dean playfully threw his slight daughter over his shoulder like a sack of potatoes and walked toward the kitchen while she giggled and wiggled and reached back for her iPad, all the while yelling, "Nooooo!"

Luna was growing like a weed, and these were the last days that he would be able to pick her up like this. He wanted to remember it always.

Dean carried her across the hallway to the bathroom, put Luna down gently and then turned on the water before he reached for the soap. He looked at his daughter in the mirror while she pouted as she washed her hands. People always commented on how much his girls resembled him, but he saw Catrin's exquisitely beautiful face in his daughters' faces—they had round faces and noses that were petite and straight, but he had to admit that the tawny-greenish color of their eyes and the unruliness of their bronze-golden locks were all thanks to the Legend genes. They'd also gotten his curls—unlike Catrin's pin-straight locks.

After Luna was done with her hands, Dean picked her up again, tucking her under his arm like a football.

"Look what I found," he said to Paisley.

"Oh, good," she said, sounding like a full-grown adult checking off an item on her checklist. "I'm ready to plate."

The three of them sat at the enormous table his mother and father had had custom made for the room by a local artisan at the time. It always struck Dean as a sad state of affairs that there were only three of them sitting at the table that over the years had seen family meals, celebrations, feeding of ranch hands and honoring those who they'd lost after the funeral. How times had changed. How *they* had changed.

They all held hands while he lowered his head and said a quick prayer before they began to eat the breakfast that Paisley had made for them.

"You get better and better every time." He smiled at his eldest with a wink.

Paisley, who was sitting with her slender legs crossed, dabbed her mouth with a napkin and said in her most mature voice, "You say that every time, Dad, and statistically, it doesn't make sense. Eventually, just as a matter of probability, I *will* cook an unsuccessful meal."

Luna nodded her head in support of her sister while she stuffed two large pieces of bacon into her mouth. Dean was onto this routine—she was trying to eat as fast as she could so she could finish her game.

"Baby girl," Dean said to the chef, "sometimes you could just say thank you when someone gives you a compliment."

Unsmiling, she said seriously, "Thank you, Dad."

Luna grinned at him with new teeth that were coming in crooked with a big gap. "I don't think she meant it."

He wiped his mouth off with a napkin and dropped it onto his empty plate. "I kind of thought the same thing, squirt."

After, Dean helped the girls clean up after breakfast, and then he allotted Luna thirty more minutes for *Minecraft*.

"I'm going to check on Grandpa, and then we're going to go into town to pick up some supplies," he told his daughters.

"I want to see Chi Ta." Paisley used the Khmer word for *Grandfather* as she shut the door of the dishwasher.

Dean nodded his head in agreement. The years hadn't been kind to his father, especially after the loss of his beloved Nettie. He often thought that his father had become a shell of his former self when Nettie had passed away. When he was awake, he was often sad and mournful. Dean did his best to take care of his father, and he had to be grateful that he'd made a massive amount of money during his time on Wall Street so he could easily keep his father at home. Buck had round-the-clock nurses and a hospital bed that they had decided to set up in the downstairs library. Even though the house had an elevator, it wasn't big enough to get everything Buck needed to the second floor.

They walked across the grand entryway with a double staircase meant to impress, then headed down a hallway with pictures of the ranch's history, a nostalgic walk down memory lane for his father. They walked past the grand library stuffed in every nook and cranny with books. His mother had loved reading, and his father had always wanted his wife to have what she loved. Now it seemed fitting that his father spent the majority of his time in this room. It was big enough to accommodate his hospital bed and the recently unused physical therapy equipment, and his father often said that it made him feel closer to his beloved wife. Every day Buck prayed to be reunited with his wife, and it was difficult to watch his father suffer in what was supposed to be his golden years. Buck often said that he could handle the pain of cancer without giving it a second thought, but his broken heart? That was an unbearable pain.

"Chi Ta!" Paisley broke into a run and leapt onto Buck's bed.

Buck's eyes lit up whenever his granddaughters entered the room. "Sweetie pie!"

She curled herself in a way that allowed her to perfectly fit her body next to Buck's body. "Chi Ta, I love you."

"I love you." Buck's voice was weak and raspy—barely recognizable from the hard-working, resilient man his father had been when he'd been a boy. Dean could remember that he'd thought his dad was a giant both in size and in the respect he always garnered when the ranchers in the area came together. The only man who could've rivaled Buck had been Rayna's father, Butch.

"How is he today?" Dean asked the nurse on duty while his oldest daughter talked excitedly to her grandfather about everything and anything.

"He's good today," Greta said.

Greta was a painfully slender woman in her early sixties. She had a freckled complexion, blue eyes and reddish-blond frizzy hair clipped back at the nape of her neck.

"Thank you, Greta," Dean said, "For everything you do for our family."

"Yes, sir." The nurse nodded. "Thank you."

"It's good to see you, Dad," Dean said and leaned down to hug his father.

"Good to be seen." Buck put his hand on his arm.

"We're going into town." He asked, "Do you need anything?"

Buck perked up a bit and said, "The usual."

Chapter Four

The day after seeing Dean for the first time since his mother's funeral, Rayna awakened with a sense of new resolve to help Charlie make the ranch a huge success right out of the gate. If her parents had bothered to ask her while in utero with Danica and Charlie, she would have taken a hard pass on Montana. But Hideaway Ranch was the place where she had worked out the kinks of youth, and it was where she had fallen in love for the first time. And now it would be the place where she figured out her post-divorce life.

What made it different this time was the fact that a shopping and gathering hub had been built in the Meadow Villages for tourists, skiers and Big Sky residents to shop, to gather and to play. There were quaint storefronts with lights strung overhead; there was an outdoor ice-skating rink and special events for every season. For Rayna, it felt like civilization had come to Big Sky. She would bet that the core families who had been in the region for generations had most likely objected to the housing and commercial boom, but she loved the energy and excitement that came with new residents and tourists. And even Charlie would have to admit that this growth could only help their efforts to be an Airbnb option for folks who didn't want to stay at the resort or overflow when, during the winter months, everything was already booked.

After she turned in her rental car, Rayna decided to roam around the town center with Christmas on her mind. Her brain had already begun to whirl with ideas. The Hideaway Ranch canvas on which she could paint her Christmas ideas was so much vaster than she'd ever had before. She was a classic-Christmas girl all the way, so she was certain she could apply her decades of decorating experience to the ranch and to allow their maiden clients to feel as if they had just stepped into a Norman Rockwell painting.

After she had window-shopped, taking her time and taking mental notes for gifts she wanted to buy and decorations she wanted to use, she then decided to warm up with a cup of coffee. She gravitated to the industrial big-city vibe in a coffee shop called Cowboy Coffee. She found a nice "hang out" place and spent time texting with friends and her sons while she drank her first cup of coffee. After she finished adding some pictures to her social media, she leaned back in a comfy chair with her second cup and took the time to relax and enjoy the ambiance. She was so relaxed there that she closed her eyes, she began to imagine how she would like to decorate the ranch for Christmas.

"Hello, Ray."

The familiar deep timbre of the voice that had spoken her name sent wonderful chills across her body as she opened her eyes.

"Hi, Dean."

He was standing in front of her flanked by two lovely girls who were each holding on to one of his hands. The girls looked like replicas of each other, just at different ages. She could tell instantly by the body language that Dean had built strong attachments with his daughters. She stood up so she could make the acquaintance of her first love's daughters.

"This is Paisley." Dean looked toward the taller girl.

"Hi, Paisley."

"Hi." She waved her hand in a small movement in front of her body.

"And this is Luna."

Dean's youngest dropped his hand and ran over to Rayna, threw her arms around her and squeezed tightly before she ran back to Dean and retook possession of his left hand.

"You don't have to do that to everybody, Luna," Paisley said to her younger sister with a disapproving furrow in her brow.

"It's okay," Dean gently corrected his eldest before he said to Rayna, "Luna is a hugger."

She smiled at the girl, "I'll tell you a secret—I'm a hugger too."

After that warm hug from Luna, Rayna said sincerely "They are beautiful, Dean."

"Thank you. Luckily they take after their mother."

"I see you in them too."

After a small lull in the conversation, he said, "It's good to see you again."

"It's good to see you again too."

Ray could see in Dean's eyes that his words weren't just a perfunctory social exchange—he meant it. She also meant it; she was happy to see him on a level that reached the innermost part of her soul.

"I didn't expect to see you," he said. "Again. Are you following me?"

She gave a smile that reached her eyes and her heart. "You wish."

"I do wish." A light of humor came into his eyes, and he said, "A man can dream, can't he?"

Whenever he was near her he couldn't seem to keep his feelings close to the vest. Look at all he had just given away with the *I do wish* comment to a married woman! He suspected Rayna was back in Montana because of a rift in her marriage but as far as he knew, Rayna was still very much married.

"Dad…" Paisley began to tug on Dean's hand. "We need to get Chi Ta's coffee!"

The eldest daughter's tawny-green eyes held a newfound suspicion—Paisley sensed something between them, and she didn't approve.

"I have to go," he said. "Dad loves his coffee."

She laughed. "I remember."

"Well…" Dean said, and she could read his expression as not wanting to leave her.

"Go," she said easily. "I was just about to call for a ride."

Paisley had raced Luna over to the bags of coffee, won the race, grabbed two bags and then handed them to Luna with a directive: "Go put these on the counter while I get Dad."

She ran back over to her father, grabbed his hand again and tried to pull him toward the counter.

"Paisley," Dean said in a fatherly tone that brooked no argument, "please go to the counter and wait for me."

"Okay," she grumbled while shooting Rayna an unhappy, disapproving glance.

"Sorry," Dean said and then added quietly, "*This* has been hard on us. We're still figuring it out."

"I totally get it, Dean," she said. "I really do. No worries at all."

"Thank you."

"Of course."

She could feel Paisley's laser-focused gaze on her in her peripheral, and that made her want to wrap up this conversation with him.

"So, goodbye for now?" she asked.

"Yes." He nodded. "Goodbye for now."

Dean had been contemplating his unexpected reunion with Rayna Brand. She had always had a small part of his attention from the first time they had met as children. He'd always wanted to tag along with her and help her with any peace-loving thing she was doing, and he hadn't even cared when other boys had teased him about it. All he'd wanted to do was be near Rayna. The fact that they were star-crossed lovers, meant to travel different roads hadn't really registered fully until college—and even then, he'd held a micrometer of hope after she'd announced her engagement to a dude named Benjamin Rafferty Hamish Fortier the Third, which had seemed so out of the realm of his reality that it simply hadn't fully computed. *His* Rayna would *never ever* be interested in the literal antithesis of her life in Montana. So he'd turned into a very good loser, an excellent friend, and waited until that relationship imploded. But it never had. He'd been invited to the wedding between his soul mate and "Ben," and he'd invited an up-and-coming clothing designer to be his plus-one to the wedding. Catrin had later turned out to be the mother of his two incredible daughters.

And when he'd decided to take Paisley and Luna to the town center to get some of his father's favorite coffee and give Paisley a chance to shoot some content for her newly created YouTube channel, *Pretty Cool Paisley*, running into Rayna had not been on his radar. The fact that he had run into Ray two days in a row made him feel as if he had meditated on her so deeply that he had made her appear.

"Dad!" Paisley pulled on his arm again just when he was about to turn back to Rayna. "Come on!"

Luna was twirling in the middle of the store, which also attracted the displeasure of his eldest. Paisley let go of his hand and quickly and authoritatively marched over to Luna, grabbed her hand and grumbled to her that she should stop twirling.

Dean did turn back to Rayna, who looked up from her phone, and then he held up the bag of coffee. Without any reason, he decided to give the coffee a verbal thumbs-up: "A taste of the Old West."

Rayna looked at him and then the bag of coffee, and then she returned his thumbs-up. His girls were already waiting at the front door, and Dean was happy for a way out of that weird "exchange" with his first love. Once he rapidly reached the door—and after he had resisted the urge to look back at Ray—he seemed to lose all coordination, and instead of opening the door, he bumped into the glass while he pulled on the door handle.

"Dad?" Paisley said, exasperated. "You have to push out to get out."

"Yeah, Dad," Luna said. "*Hashtag* You Have to Push Out to Get Out!"

Dean followed the simple instructions from his daughters, pushing out, and then he got the holy heck out of there. The brisk winter air slapped him in the face, and he felt more clear-headed for it.

"Luna," Paisley directed, "hold my phone! Do not shake it! And when I say *when*, push the record button."

Yes, Luna was younger, but she wasn't a pushover for her sister. Paisley got into position by the front door of Cowboy Coffee. Dean watched on as his nearly thirteen-year-old had enough poise and emotional intelligence to face the camera, natural in her delivery, and provide a clear, succinct review of the shop in general. He was always amazed by his daughters, loved them deeper every day and looked forward to awakening just so he could be a front-row-seat spectator as their lives unfolded before them.

Paisley concluded her review, walked over to Luna and asked, "Did you get it?"

Luna looked at her sister with an impish smile and handed the phone back to her. Paisley looked at the phone and then said, "Luna! You didn't record it!"

She shrugged and smiled in a way that allowed her sweet dimples to appear. "You didn't say the magic word."

"Dad!" Paisley gave him a frustrated, pouty look. "She didn't get it!"

"Good help is hard to find," he said to her.

"Just say *please*," Luna said, "and I'll record this time."

With a roll of her eyes, Paisley said, "Please, Luna, will you record it for me?"

She nodded, took the phone back, determined the correct angle to show Paisley in the best light, and then began to record. Right when the record button was hit, Rayna opened the door to the café, interfering with Paisley's second attempt to record content.

"Oh!" Rayna said. "I'm so sorry!"

His daughter's shoulders dropped in frustration.

"It's fine, right, Paisley?" he asked her in a way that was more of a strong suggestion.

Paisley nodded her head, but she was less gracious than he liked. Still, he always struggled to find the balance between enforcing some basic manners with giving them some leeway while they healed the open mental and emotional wound the divorce had caused.

"She's so polished," Rayna said of his daughter. "The camera loves her."

"She gets that from her mother," Dean said. "All of that creativity and poise."

Rayna leaned close enough for him to smell the clean fragrance of grapefruit and lilac, and she whispered, "Catrin is amazing. I actually own two of her dresses. They aren't just another garment—they are pieces of art."

"She's a genius when it comes to clothing design," he said. The woman he'd married had been fighting her way to the top of the high fashion word; now Poem, her brand, had global reach and she was a celebrity in her own right.

When Paisley was reviewing the footage Luna had shot, Dean noticed Rayna looking down at her phone and then looking around.

"What's wrong?" he asked.

"Oh, nothing, really," she said, still looking around. "I dropped my rental car off, and I called for a ride."

"Are you going back to the ranch?"

"Yes." She nodded, still occupied with the app on her phone. "Charlie and Wayne are working so hard—I didn't want to make them stop what they were doing just to drive into town to get me when I could easily Uber."

"No need to call them. We're heading home. I can give you a ride."

"I wouldn't want to impose."

"Impose in what way?" he asked. "I have to drive by your place in order to get to mine."

"Okay. If you don't mind…"

"I don't."

"Then, sure. Why not? Thank you."

"My pleasure," Dean said, happy with the idea of spending more time with Rayna. Yes, he felt awkward around her and unsure of himself in a way he hadn't experienced in decades. And yes, her reentry into his life had unearthed too many feelings and emotions that had been buried inside of him. Rayna made him *feel*, and feeling again had made him realize that he had been numb. How was that fair for his daughters? They deserved much better than a shadow of a man; they deserved a father who was present for them.

"We finally got it," Paisley said in an exasperated tone.

"Good teamwork, you two." Dean hugged his daughters. "Ready to go home?"

His daughters raced over to the Range Rover parked nearby. Paisley stood by the passenger door while Luna went to the back door behind the driver's side.

"Back seat, Paisley."

She tilted her head back as if he had just crushed her dreams. "But I'll be thirteen in twenty-eight days!"

"And on the twenty-ninth day you can ride up front." Dean put his arms around her, kissed her on the top of her head and then guided her to the back passenger-side door, making room for Rayna to sit up front with him.

Paisley begrudgingly pulled open the back door, climbed into the vehicle and buckled up. Once he knew his daughter was secure, Dean closed the door behind her and stopped Rayna from opening the passenger door herself.

"Okay, Mrs. Fortier," Dean said as he opened the door for her. "Mom raised me up to be a gentleman, so just sit back and enjoy it."

Rayna smiled at him, and that smile reached her cornflower-blue eyes and then ricocheted straight back to his heart. Yes, he had loved his first wife, but there was a part of his soul she could never touch. That part belonged only to Rayna.

Dean returned her smile before he shut the door and jogged around to the other side. He made sure that Luna was buckled in right before he climbed behind the wheel.

Softly, and with a tinge of embarrassment, Rayna said, "Brand. I'm Ms. Brand now."

He met her gaze, any suspicion he had about the state of Rayna's marriage was confirmed. He felt a deep sadness for her with a small dash of hope that he might be able to win her heart for a second time.

He could see plainly in her eyes, fresh pain from the divorce so he gave her a quick nod of understanding and cranked the engine.

"This is pretty fancy," Rayna ran her hand over the finely tooled leather of the passenger seat. "You must've done pretty well for yourself on Wall Street, Mr. Legend."

"Well, I don't want to brag…"

"But of course you do," she interjected playfully.

"My colleagues used to call me Quick Draw."

Rayna laughed happily, and her laugh hit him in the gut like a sucker punch. That sound was what he had been missing for too many years: Rayna's laughter and Rayna's lovely eyes and Rayna's open heart. Yes, the boy who had been Dean Legend had fallen in love with teenage Rayna Brand, but this was the moment that Dean Legend the man had fallen in love with the woman she had become—deeply, completely and undeniably.

Rayna couldn't have predicted another impromptu meeting with Dean, but how she felt was also completely unpredicted. After the undeniably awkward first "meet-cute" in the barn, she had prepared herself that perhaps she would never recapture that comfortable friendship they'd had when they'd been teenagers.

Ray sighed and looked out of the window, then said out loud when she'd actually meant to say it only in her mind: "Everything changes."

"What?" Dean asked as he headed in the direction of her home.

"Nothing, really. Just thinking about all of the changes here. With all of the development around the resort, it's starting to feel like an actual town."

He nodded. "With all of this residential and commercial development around the town center, I think Big Sky will become a town in its own right."

Rayna nodded. She had mixed emotions that were surprising to her—she loved the fact that Big Sky was a draw for visitors and that they had events around the holidays. She loved the fact that she could get away from ranch life and spend time soaking in the ambiance of a café. And yet there was an unexpected longing for the past and the innocence of her youth.

As if reading her thoughts, Dean asked, "How'd you find the pop-up town? Civilization knocking on our door?"

She smiled faintly, still soaking up the scenery outside of the window. "I have mixed feelings, honestly. I thought I would love it without reservation, but I find myself longing for the raw beauty of the land. It's so bizarre to be nostalgic about it—all I wanted to do when I was growing up was to escape the drudgery of ranch life. I must be more fickle than I thought."

Dean said to her, "We all change over time. I wouldn't sweat it."

There was a lull in the conversation, and then from the

back seat, Paisley asked him, "Don't you remember when Mom was here and we all went skiing?"

He looked at his daughter in the rearview mirror and smiled at her. "We found one thing that Mom couldn't do well right off the bat!"

Paisley laughed, and then father and daughter said at the same time, "Skiing!"

"But don't forget," Dean said, glancing back at his eldest child, "by the end of our vacation, Mom had mastered the slopes!"

After her laughter faded, Paisley said to Rayna, "My mom is a designer."

"I know!" she said with genuine enthusiasm. Rayna twisted her body around as much as she could and spoke to both girls: "Can I share a secret with you?"

Luna looked up from her tablet with a smile. "It's not nice to keep secrets."

"It's not a bad secret." Rayna started to scroll through the pictures on the phone, found a picture she was searching for and then used her fingers to zoom in on the photo and held it up for both girls to see.

"That's Mommy's dress!" Luna's gold and green–flecked eyes widened with surprise.

"It is," Rayna said. "I wore one of your mother's dresses to my sons' graduation."

"Mom dresses too many celebrities to count. She shows her collections in Paris, Milan and New York. She's a social media queen, and one day I'm going to be just like her," Paisley told her with a look of deep pride on her face and resonating in her voice. "She's in Paris now."

Rayna turned her body back to facing the road ahead. "Your mom *is* incredible. So beautiful and talented."

Dean had glanced at the picture of her in his ex-wife's dress. "You looked beautiful in that dress."

His unexpected compliment made her feel simply wonderful; it was a feeling that had started on the inside and manifested as a shy, pleased smile on the outside. "Thank you."

Then Paisley said, "I do like your hair better in the picture, though. You look so much older now. I think you should try red, actually. A darker red, not a lighter red—your gray hair will look like sorrel highlights. It would be good for your skin tone and your eyes. You have nice eyes, I suppose."

"I hadn't really considered red before." Rayna reached up to touch the top of her head; over the last year, gray hairs had begun to sprout everywhere, and she hadn't had the motivation to cover up her roots while she'd been figuring out her next moves in Montana. The animals in the barn didn't care one iota about the gray in her hair.

"Paisley can be too blunt—that's something she got from me I suppose."

"I think the word was *older* not *old*, and it's okay," Rayna said quickly to smooth things over. "I think she has a good idea. I've been wanting a change, and maybe henna is the change I should try," she said to Dean and then to Paisley, "Thank you for the suggestion."

"Sure," Dean's oldest said flippantly with a shrug, her attention turned back to her phone.

Dean mouthed the word *Sorry* again, and she shook her head in response. The last thing she wanted was to be the cause of any sort of rift in Dean's relationship with his daughters.

"I have plenty of gray hair in my beard, and you've never told me that I look old," he said to his daughter.

Luna didn't lift up her head, still focused on the tablet, but she said, "She tells you that all the time."

"This morning," Paisley added.

"She also tells you that you need to clean up your beard and your eyebrows are tragic."

Paisley said, "There's so much going wrong that it will take too much time that I don't have right now or in the foreseeable future. I have a life." She held up her fist for Luna to bump and said to her sister, "Speak truth to power."

"Wow!" Rayna laughed. "Tough crowd."

"I don't think that my eyebrows are *tragic*," he said, looking at his reflection in the mirror, and then asked Rayna, "Do you think they're tragic?"

"They are," Paisley said in a monotone while still fixated on her phone.

"You already cast your vote, Paisley. Now I'm asking Rayna." Dean glanced over at her and then asked, "*Are* my eyebrows tragic?"

She started to laugh and had to turn away, cover her smile with her hand and take a moment so she could answer in as normal of a voice as she could muster she said, "Not really."

"I'm hurt," Dean told everyone in the vehicle. "Truly hurt. That's it! I'm pulling over, and everyone can walk!"

"They're fantastic, Dean," Rayna said after they laughed together. "So smart, so talented. I wish I had a fraction of their self-esteem."

"Thank you, Ray. It isn't always easy, but they make me as proud as peanuts."

When Dean pulled into the long drive to Hideaway Ranch, flashing images flooded her mind of days and nights and school days and weekends and summer vacations that were all connected to Dean. When he stopped his vehicle, Rayna said goodbye to his girls. Luna smiled at her in the sweetest of ways before getting back to *Minecraft*.

Paisley rolled down her window and said, "If you do decide to move forward with the color, go to Hairology in the town center. If you say I referred you, you'll get a discount. And make sure you snap a selfie, hashtag PrettyCoolPaisley, like and subscribe to my YouTube channel. I'll tag you if you tag me." Then she rolled the window back up and returned to business on her phone.

Rayna exchanged a look with Dean and then said, "You've got a mini mogul in the making."

"An *influencer*," he said with a roll of the eyes. "There was no such thing when we were young."

"There was no such thing as smartphones either." She laughed good-naturedly. "Have we just become our parents? Do you find yourself turning off all of the lights in your house while grumbling about electricity costs?"

"Absolutely I do! Electricity *is* too expensive."

"*And* money doesn't grow on trees."

Chapter Five

Dean had dropped her off with a promise that she would come over to the house to visit with Buck. They'd exchanged cell numbers, and that had reminded them each of a time when life had been simpler and he had asked if he could call her. They had been such close friends when they'd been younger than Paisley and Luna. But there'd been a moment when feelings had changed.

The Brands and the Legends had always planned an end-of-summer shindig at a watering hole that was shared between the two cattle giants. Any fish caught had been cleaned and cooked right on the spot. She remembered that summer so clearly—it had been the first time she'd had to worry about wearing a bra. She was by no means a busty girl, but she'd been able to fill out the cups in her new navy blue one-piece bathing suit that had had a brightly colored flower on the side.

She remembered so clearly how embarrassed she had been about the way her body had been changing, but Dean had managed to make her feel comfortable in a way that her sisters and Rose had not managed to do. She had pulled her crocheted bathing-suit cover over her head and ventured out toward the area around the lake that had a small pebble beach where she could access the part of the lake designated for swimming.

No one had seemed to be paying her any mind, and she'd been happy to fade into the background. Even though Danica was her identical twin, she'd always garnered more attention—she was confident, gregarious and so full of life and energy that it had been natural for Ray to hide in the shadow of her identical twin. And that day, the day that had changed everything, had been another day of her life in the shadows. When she'd finally reached the pebble beach, Dean had materialized by her side. He'd helped her pick her way over the pebbles and then said, "You look mighty pretty in that new bathing suit, Ray." She remembered looking into his eyes and seeing love and total acceptance reflected back. And that had been that. One tiny moment and their relationship had changed forever.

After Dean had dropped her off, and as she went about her day, Rayna's mind was occupied remembering details of her first-love romance, many that she had thought were long-since forgotten. She felt dazed and disconnected and it hadn't gone unnoticed by Charlie or Wayne.

"Are you still with me?" Wayne asked her.

His question did the trick of snapping her back to the present moment.

"Yes. I'm sorry."

"So what do you think? Is it workable?"

Rayna looked around the mini camper that Wayne had used to crisscross around the western seaboard of the United States for the last part of a decade until he'd finally found a place where his heart felt at home—here on Hidden Ranch. The camper was compact, but it did have all of the essentials plus an unexpected king-sized bed at the end of the camper.

"I think it's definitely workable," Rayna said. She was occupying the main house now, but their guests were going to arrive mid-December, so eventually she would have to move. But more importantly to her, now she would be staying at least until Aspen's return from Texas, Rayna wanted to feel settled in her own space and the cozy camper seemed to be the perfect cubby for her.

"Well, you're welcome to it." Wayne gave a nod of his head and said, "When winter breaks, we can build you a log cabin—if you decide to stay on. I know Charlie would feel real happy to have you stay on, and I'd be happy not to have her chewing on my ear about it."

"Thank you, Wayne. And sorry about that ear-chewing thing."

Wayne took off his cowboy hat, smoothed his shoulder-length salt-and-pepper hair back from his forehead and then placed the Stetson back on his head. He was a handsome man, tall and lean from years working outside. The goatee he wore was a nice mixture of white and dark brown.

"We're family now," Wayne said. "Charlie just wants what's best for you."

"I know she does." She sent him a faint smile. "And yes, we are. Family."

He gave her a quick tutorial of the trailer functions before they headed out the door into the cold. A blast of frigid air and large chunks of hardened snow broke loose when the door was opened and landed on Rayna's nose.

"Gosh darn it!" She brushed the snow off of her face.

Wayne was smiling behind his bushy facial hair. "It's gonna take a minute to wake up that cowgirl muscle memory. Once it does, you'll be all right."

She pulled the hood over her head and crossed her arms tightly around her body so little to no air was able to weave its way through weak barriers to send a chill through her skin to her innocent bones. "I'm not sure I ever had many cowgirl muscles to begin with. That was more Charlie's department."

Wayne shut the door tightly behind him. "You hail from Connecticut, don't you?"

"Yes, I do," she said with a small nod of the head. "I know what you're getting at, Wayne. Connecticut does get cold. Connecticut does get snow. But Connecticut's winter lasts three months—" she held up three gloved fingers "—three and a half at the most. *Not* nine! *Nine!* And in Connecticut, they have salt and snowplows. It snows, and then civilization as we know it continues.

"Here," she said, pointing to the icy, snowy ground at her feet, "there's nine months of snow, melting snow, mud everywhere, hidden patches of ice! Animals still need to be tended, so instead of drinking a hot cup of cocoa in front of a fire, I'm out in it many hours a day out of sheer necessity. I never really feel warm. I'm cold all of the time," she complained. "Then, as a bonus, that awesome three months of summer is often fraught with drought and fires."

"You've given this a lot of thought, haven't you?" Wayne asked with a chuckle.

She lifted her arms up as high as they would go given the stiffness of her Michelin Man puffy coat she had borrowed from Charlie. "I've thought about this for a lifetime. I couldn't wait to get out of here when I turned eighteen."

"Well, maybe you're due for a change," the cowboy said.

"You just want her to stop gnawing on your ear!" she accused playfully.

"Yes, ma'am. My woman is a pit bull with a bone." Wayne put his hands into the pockets of his weathered coat.

"Well, she's just going to have to understand that this—"

Rayna waved her arms around stiffly to point to all of the land around them "—is temporary."

"Montana can be a hard lady to love, I'll grant you that," Wayne said with a faint smile, "but she can get under your skin mighty quick."

"Not mine," she said. "I like to be warm."

"Well, I suspect those summer fires could heat you up good and quick." Wayne tipped the brim of his cowboy hat to her with a quick wink of his eye. "I've got to get back to work."

"Thank you for the tour and letting me crash in your camper. I just want to burrow into a space that's mine."

"Glad to help."

Charlie had told her that they were building another guest cottage when the weather was clear enough to work, and she supposed she could bunk there after it was built if the camper was too much of a life downgrade.

She thanked Wayne again before they parted ways, and she was about to walk as quickly as she could safely manage back to the main house when she heard him whistle loudly. She looked back over her shoulder out of curiosity, and that was when she saw Bowie, Charlie's one-hundred-and-twenty-pound Rottweiler–pit bull mix, barreling toward her at full tilt through the snow, his bluish tongue dangling out of the side of his mouth, his heavy paws kicking up snow as he forged a direct path to where she was standing. Knowing that she could not run across the yard without landing on an icy spot, she turned around and yelled, "Don't you do it, Bowie! Don't you do it!"

The next few moments were a blur. She heard Wayne's voice calling out the "Leave" command, which Bowie ignored as he launched himself into the air. His front paws landed on her chest, and he pushed her backward into the snow.

"Damn it, Bowie!" She tried to avoid his tongue as he licked her face with all of the love he had for her. "Quit licking me!"

Bowie's muscular, heavy body was pushing her down into the pillow of soft snow, and she could feel the saliva on her face freezing. Rayna had two super active boys who'd wrestled in high school, and she had picked up a few tricks. She wrapped her legs around the dog's lower body and at the same time gave his upper body a bear hug. In one motion, she rolled to the side, and that was when she gained the advantage. While she still had him in her control, she kissed the dog several times on his lovable face.

"Bowie! Leave it!" Wayne had crossed the yard to join them.

Bowie whined at the reprimand from one of his most favorite people. Rayna sat up, tried to brush melting snow from her pants and the sleeves of her borrowed puffy coat. It was a useless attempt; the snow had melted and she was wet everywhere. Wayne offered her a hand, but she brushed it away.

"Thank you," she said to soften the rudeness. "Thank you. But I've got it."

She rolled to the side and got onto her feet. When she looked at Wayne he seemed to have a new found respect for her.

"Did you put Bowie in a figure four?" He had a surprised expression.

"Yes. I did. My sons wrestled in high school," she said while she gave Bowie a scratch on the head. She answered Wayne's question, but she was also telling Bowie, "I watched and I learned."

Bowie wagged his tail happily after carrying out his plan to show her extra special love.

"I love you too, Bowie."

To Wayne she said, "Now, if you'll excuse me, I'm going to change my clothing and wash this frozen dog saliva off of my face."

Rayna took a long, hot, soothing shower. She had hoped this tactic would work to calm down her mind, but she couldn't seem to shrug off the deep feeling of loss and sadness that had become her daily companion. Even when she was smiling outwardly she had a belly full of glass shards that cut at her on the inside. And seeing Dean again had blown a hole right through her heart. He was just as kind and funny and caring as she remembered him to be, and he was an amazing, involved father. The whole package, really.

As if Dean had heard her thinking so hard on him, he sent her a text.

Are you free this afternoon? Dad is anxious to see you.

She stared at that text for a long time. When she had made a detour to Montana instead of heading back east, she hadn't taken a deep dive into all of the fallout from that decision. There would be relationships formed and fractured relationships mended. Those were the binding ties that would make it difficult for her to leave, and she would also hurt people along the way.

After several more moments mulling over the invite to see Buck, she decided that seeing Dean's father was more important that any future pain it might cause. Nettie wasn't the only Legend who had treated her like a daughter—Buck had too. She agreed to come over in an hour for a visit.

After a quick yoga stretch to relax her tense muscles and ease some of the stress she was feeling about her life in general, she went into the bathroom to fix her hair and put cream on her face. She stared at her reflection while she ran her fingers through her hair. She used to have a thick, luxurious mane of hair; it had been one of her best features and it was one thing that she had been confident about. Now, after such a stressful year, her hair had started to shed heavily, and the loss of hair made her feel sad. She had started using products to help salvage the hair left and regrow strands that she had lost.

She shook her head as she looked at the brown-and-silver roots. Paisley was right—it did make her look "older." And it made her *feel* "older."

Ray pulled her shoulder-length hair back into a pony-tail, and used a light touch with makeup to enhance her lashes, high cheek bones and her lips. After pulling herself together, Rayna made an appointment with Hairology, and she did mention Paisley; if it would make her feel better to get her hair done, then that was what she was going to do. She had survived the divorce—now it was time for renewal, self-discovery and building a new life.

She let Charlie know that she was going to take their father's old farm truck over to the Legend ranch. She made a solemn vow to fill in her sisters on the details during their weekly triplet catch-up video chat. She managed to squeeze herself behind the wheel of the old truck with the many layers of clothing she had put on in order to feel comfortable. Once inside, she fought with the door to get it shut and then fought with the gearshift to get it into Reverse and then in Drive.

"Why is every single tiny thing so difficult here?" She asked this question aloud again.

She drove toward the main entrance of Hideaway Ranch, the steering wheel hard to grip with her gloves. The heat did not work in the truck and hadn't since she had been a kid, and the driver's-side window only went up halfway. She could see her breath when she cursed at the truck when it refused to steer straight and insisted on fishtailing when it encountered the smallest amount of ice. She managed to get herself to the closed gate, leaving the truck running because it might not start again if she didn't. She hit the door several times with her body to get the driver's door open and then swung her body to the left and carefully climbed out into a slippery, slushy puddle and gingerly stepped one cautious foot after another until she reached the gate.

"I did it!" she exclaimed aloud as if she had just beaten a foe.

After she opened the gate and was about to head back to the truck, a gust of wind caught the gate in the exact right spot, and it began to move and take her along with it. One foot stayed behind while the other foot slipped forward while she held tight to the gate. If it weren't for her yoga practice, she would have fallen and landed on her hind end in a half-frozen dip in the ground.

"Gosh darn it!" Rayna slowly readjusted her feet into a secure stance while she pulled herself upright.

Then she used her "cowgirl fortitude" Wayne had talked about, opened the gate and got back into the truck. Rayna shifted back into Drive all while feeling a sense of accomplishment. Maybe she did have some hidden cowgirl stuff inside.

There was a lot of play in the steering wheel, which made the truck difficult to steer, but she drove the short trip to the Legends' ranch entrance without much trouble. When she turned onto the paved drive leading up to Dean's family home, she put her foot on the brake and stopped. She suddenly felt anxious about reopening old wounds; everyone in her family and in Dean's family had been devastated with their breakup, but perhaps no one save Dean had taken it harder than Buck. He had always held on to hope even after she had gotten married and even after she'd had her twin boys.

Rayna squeezed her eyes shut tightly, gripped the steering wheel hard with both hands and then took several deep breaths and blew them out slowly. After calming her nerves, she opened her eyes and put her foot on the gas. In the expansive pastures on either side of the drive was a rather desolate scene with spots of brown grass revealed after some snow had melted and black cows lying down closely together to share warmth. Halfway up the drive, Ray saw an enormous red metal structure that had been built. After she spent time with Buck, she was curious to see inside of it.

She drove around the circular drive until she could pull into one of the parking spots. While Butch Brand had been satisfied to keep the rustic feel of Hideaway Ranch, Buck and Nettie had brought a more grand aesthetic to their ranch as their wealth had grown. Rayna parked the truck, cut off the engine, climbed out and then fought with the door to get it shut all the way.

Packed snow from the roof of the truck fell through the open window and onto the driver's seat. She cursed under her breath and then discovered that Dean had put salt on the walkway and glorious deep red brick stairs that led to the double-wide veranda complete with porch swings and handmade rocking chairs. On her way up the stairs, the large front door made of thick carved wood and stained glass opened. And there, in the doorway, stood Dean. He was wearing a green plaid button-up shirt tucked into darkwash jeans. He had trimmed his beard and had taken the time to brush his unruly wavy hair. Just as she had taken some few extra minutes to spruce up her appearance for today's visit, so had he. That knowledge touched her in a secret place in her heart that had been reserved for Dean, and when their eyes met and held, the lost years between them melted away, and she could only see the gangly teen that she had loved so deeply and completely.

Luna had followed Dean to the bathroom that was en suite to the main bedroom. It felt uncomfortable to be occupying his parents' room, but when the need for more equipment and more caregivers for his father had grown, the library had seemed the best option. And the fact that he was on the first floor made sense should a nurse need him quickly.

"What are you doing?" Luna had climbed up onto the large white marble bathroom counter.

"I'm going to trim up my beard a bit."

"Good idea."

While Paisley was a very serious, introspective child, Luna was inquisitive and full of positive, happy energy. She sat cross-legged in her jeans that had sparkly unicorns on them and a matching shirt.

"So I shouldn't look like an old grumpy grizzly bear?" Dean leaned over, growled like a bear and cocked one eyebrow at her and gave her a silly look. He loved Luna's infectious laugh, and he made a point of making her laugh every single day. His ex-wife had rightly said that Luna had come into this world laughing.

Luna watched him with fascinated eyes as he carefully shaped his beard into a more presentable version. He moved his face back and forth and examined his reflection. When Rayna had come back into his life, he'd begun to pay more attention to his appearance, and he was shocked to notice that he looked a bit worse for wear. While he'd watched TV with his girls, he had suddenly been researching creams for men to help with lines around the eyes and dye that could cover up some of the gray in his beard.

"What do you think?" he asked Luna.

"It's better," she said pragmatically. "What about the eyebrows?"

He raised one eyebrow and lowered the other. "What about my eyebrows?"

His daughter laughed again, swung her body sideways so she could lean down and rummage through the drawer, and didn't sit upright again until she had a pair of tweezers in her hand.

"Sit down," she said. "Your eyebrows make you look weird."

"Gee, thanks," he said while she plucked his brows. "Where did you learn to do this?"

"Paisley. TikTok." She moved back so he could look at himself in the mirror. "They really need wax, but it's definitely better. I got all the white hairs too."

"Thank you," Dean said. The brows did look better; he wasn't at all sure he was going to let anyone get anywhere near his face with *wax*.

"What about your hair?" Luna asked. She was sitting cross-legged, and her head was tilted to the side as if she were truly trying to figure out how to improve his appearance but was having a challenging time. "It's, like...*shaggy* I think is the right word."

Dean took another hard look at himself in the mirror while dragging his fingers through his hair that had always been difficult to tame. When he'd worked on Wall Street he'd made regular visits to the barber, but since he'd been back in the saddle, he hadn't bothered with it this much. He just put on a hat and got on with his day.

Luna jumped down from the counter this time and told him to sit back down on the stool his mother had used to put on her makeup. She grabbed a brush, fought her way through the tangles, searched in a nearby drawer to find some product, found a bottle, put the product into his hair despite his objections, took the ponytail holder from her hair and then pulled it tightly back off of his face into a ponytail.

"Okay." She stepped back so he could see his reflection.

"No, ma'am," Dean said emphatically in less than one second. "I'm not doing a manbun, a mantail or any other trend you saw on TikTok."

Luna scrunched up her impish face. "*Mantail* isn't an actual thing, Dad."

"This! This is a mantail," he said, working his hair out of her ponytail holder. When his hair was free, he noticed it looked greasy from the product his daughter had shellacked onto it.

"That's not a real thing, though," his daughter told him, stuffing the ponytail holder into her front pocket.

"I just invented it! Okay? Now, what am I going to do with this?" he asked. "It's greasy, and it's…poufy!"

Luna nodded her agreement but didn't seem to take any of the responsibility for his current appearance. "You should have left it in the mantail."

Dean ducked into the adjacent closet and returned to the mirror wearing a ball cap with the Legend logo on it. "I don't wear hats in the house."

She was perched on the counter again. "No, it's a rule."

He looked at her. "It is a rule. It's Mom's rule."

And even though Nettie wasn't alive, all of her rules

of conduct persisted and would persist as long as he took breath.

"Do you love Rayna?" Luna asked out of absolutely nowhere with her eyes focused intently on his face. At times, he very much believed that Luna was an old soul by the look she had in her eyes.

"What?" he asked even though he had heard her perfectly well. Stalling for time.

"Do you love Rayna?"

"Why would you ask that?"

She shrugged one shoulder and played with her long strands of hair that fell over her shoulder. "Intuition."

Dean looked at his daughter as if he hadn't seen her before. "Intuition?"

"Mom says that all of the women on her side of the family have intuition."

After a moment of silence, he asked, "And what if I do?"

"I'm cool with it." Luna gave him a sweet smile and another little shrug. "It's *Minecraft* time."

"Set your timer!" Dean reminder his youngest as she disappeared around the corner to go find her tablet.

After his daughter left, he realized that the only solution to his current problem was to shower for a second time, which he did. He showered, dried off again and then spent a good amount of time finding ways to flatten his shoulder-length wavy hair. He worked with it for more time than he had in the past year and finally gave up on it cooperating. He put his green plaid button-down back on—Ray had always liked him in green—tucked it in nice and tight and then cinched his belt. He gave himself a hard look and decided that this was the best he could do for now. He loitered around the aftershave and cologne area of the counter. One was too strong, and the other smelled spoiled, so he tossed it into the garbage.

When he emerged from the master bedroom, he headed for the library.

"Is she coming?" Buck asked in a weak voice. He wasn't the only one who had decided to spruce up for Ray's visit; his father had been bathed, his snow-white hair slicked back off of his gaunt face. He was dressed for the first time in months, and he was sitting in his wheelchair instead of lying in his bed.

"She texted me that she's on her way."

"Good," Buck said, looking out of the floor-to-ceiling windows that brought natural light into the library. Nettie had strategically placed those windows to let in the light without harming the old leather-bound books in their expansive collection.

When he saw Ray drive into sight in her father's old truck that was thirty years old and had clocked over 300,000 miles, Dean had to force himself to remain some sense of calm.

"I'm going to greet her," he told his father.

"Bring her here right away." Buck coughed several times, but his voice held a ring of fortitude that Dean hadn't heard in a long while. "Right away."

Dean opened the door and waved at Ray. He was immediately taken back to a place in time when Ray had been his girl and she'd been pulling up to the house in that very truck when they'd been seventeen. And all of the threads that had stitched over a wound deep in his heart blew apart, leaving nothing but deep abiding love for Rayna Anne Brand.

Chapter Six

"Hi!" Rayna waved back at Dean. "So much new to look at!"

"I've kept myself busy." He smiled. "Lots of upgrades and renovations."

"I can see that!"

When she reached the top step where he was standing, there was an awkward moment between them, acting out the *do we hug, or do we shake hands?* dance. They decided on a hug, and she had to admit for the second time in the last couple of days that Dean Legend gave the best hugs that beat Charlie's hugs by a nose.

"Dad's waiting for you." Dean opened the front door for her to walk in before him. "I haven't seen him this excited since Luna agreed to join the 4-H club."

"It's been so long." Ray began to unzip and unbutton layers of outerwear, handing each one to him. "I feel kind of nervous."

"It's just Dad," Dean reminded her. "He always loved you just a touch more than he loved me."

He knew how to make her laugh, and she did, but it didn't take away the nerves. When she'd chosen to make a life on the East Coast, she hadn't known at the time how deeply it would impact Dean's father, and she had carried guilt over that pain she had caused Buck.

"Bless it, Ray," Dean said with an amused smile on his face. "You act like you've never experienced winter before."

"Does that mean that I'm a snowflake?" Rayna asked playfully before she bit down on the fingers of her gloves to pull her hand out. She put the gloves on top of the stack Dean was holding and said, "It's a colder cold here, okay? I'm not a meteorologist, so I can't tell you *why*. But I can tell you that it just *is* colder."

Dean's smile widened, and now that he had trimmed his beard back she could see his front teeth, with one just slightly over the other and those lips she had kissed so many wonderful times. "You look good, Legend."

"I was just thinking the same about you."

She helped Dean hang up her winter gear in a nearby hall closet, and then she had a moment of silence, just soaking up the world that Nettie had built.

"You haven't changed it," she said. "So much is changed on the outside…"

"But never on the inside," Dean told her. "I want my girls to know her."

"And she is *here*," she said. "Her energy, her spirit, her sense of humor. Her love. All here."

"Still Mom's domain."

Rayna walked over to the Wall of Family Fame, as Nettie had put it. It was an entire wall filled with frames of her favorite family moments. Rayna had seen so many of her formative years on this wall. She felt emotion well up in her body and form as unshed tears in her eyes. Every picture of her as a young girl and as a teenager touched her in a way that she imagined everyone felt to some degree when they saw themselves as children and looking back on them as an adult. That Rayna—a flowerchild who'd loved horses and cats and swimming and holding hands with Dean.

"Oh." She pointed to a picture. "That's us!"

They'd been at the last Legend-Brand shindig and off in the distance at the very back of the picture. The two of them had been caught holding hands and walking back toward the woods.

"You were the subject of many family moments."

"What we didn't know back then," she said in a quiet voice. "What we didn't know."

The pain that was rising inside of her made her turn away from the pictures. Maybe later—maybe one day— she would be able to look back on that Ray without feeling so much loss that a failed marriage and so many years wasted on trying to get her husband to love her had caused her. Maybe one day.

"Dad's in the library now."

Ray had her arms crossed in front of her body as they walked down together. It would have been so natural to reach out for Dean's hand, but she didn't. This already felt surreal and familiar and unfamiliar and nostalgic and tragic all rolled up into one.

The library had been transformed into a hospital room at home for Buck. She had known from Charlie that he had emphysema and lung cancer; the lung cancer had started in the right organ and had spread to the left.

Dean stopped her before they reached the library.

"He's very thin," he said in a hushed tone.

"I understand."

"He's refused all treatment. I'm surprised he's still eating."

That was when Ray stopped trying to keep a safe distance from Dean; she wrapped her arms around him and hugged him as tightly as she could. He was devastated—she could see it so plainly in his eyes because she *knew him.*

How could she ignore this pain in her childhood sweetheart just because she was afraid of falling for him again? She couldn't. It would be unbelievably selfish and uncaring, and she wasn't okay with embodying those two characteristics.

"I'm so sorry, Dean."

He held on to her a bit longer before he moved back, but he didn't in a way that broke their proximity to each other.

"I am too," he said. "But when you love someone the way Dad loves Mom, this world doesn't hold anything for you when they're gone."

Tears formed in Dean's eyes, and that shattered her heart. She reached up and wiped the tears from his cheeks.

"I'm here, Dean." She acted purely on emotion and not practicality when she made that declaration.

"Thank you," he said simply.

"And I'm ready."

Something new and rare entered her body just before she arrived at the end of the long hallway that led to the library; she felt a sense of renewed purpose and self-value. Whether it be God or the Universe or Destiny or Fate, the "how" of it didn't matter to her—she had been placed in this moment in time to be useful to the Legend family, and in return, the Legend family would help *her* heal her wounds. So when she went into the library and saw Buck for the first time in nearly a decade, she had a spine of steel that helped her overlook the shell of a cattleman that was Buck's current reality and remember the mountain of a man he had been for so many years of his life.

"Rayna!" Buck's weary eyes lit up when he saw her. He started to cough and wheeze, and the on-duty nurse quickly came over to make sure that he was getting enough oxygen.

Buck swatted at the nurse. "Quit."

The patriarch of the Legend family had lost half of his

body weight, and his voice sounded hoarse, breathy and raspy in between coughs.

"Dad." Rayna hugged him tightly, ignoring the tubes and machines and the wheelchair and the scents of medicine that hung in the air.

"Daughter." Buck reached out for her.

She knelt down by the wheelchair, his fragile hand in hers, his free hand touching the back of her head. She hadn't imagined shedding tears today. She felt like that spine of steel was going to make her into a super woman who could face any challenge with quiet confidence, but perhaps being a super woman also included being a kind-hearted and compassionate woman who felt.

"I've missed you so," Buck said in between coughs.

"I've missed you," Rayna said with tears flowing down her face.

"Do you believe God can answer prayers?" he asked her.

Nettie had been the God fearing of the two of them; Buck would placate his beloved now and again, but he had set foot in a church for very certain events like a marriage or a christening or a funeral.

"Yes, I do, Dad."

"This is one of mine—right here, right now."

"Thank you." Rayna rested her cheek on his hand, mourning the loss of the hands that had once been so strong and capable, but feeling incredibly grateful that God's grace had led her to this moment. God's grace had led her to *this* home, a home that had been as much as her home as Hideaway Ranch, and to her second father who had considered her to be his daughter as much as Dean was his son.

Dean came over to them and quietly handed her tissues while finding her a chair that she could sit in. Rayna smiled at him but then returned her attention to Buck. "I'm sorry it's been such a long time between visits, Buck."

"No, daughter," Buck said in a voice that reminded her that he was still Buck Legend. "You were growing up. You were forging your way through life. That was your path. And now, thanks to God in heaven, your path has led you back here—back to me."

She wiped the tears from her cheeks and smiled at Buck. He smiled back at her and said, "Wouldn't my Nettie be on her feet praising Jesus that I'd finally come around to her way of thinking?"

"Yes, she would, Dad." Rayna laughed through fresh tears. "She certainly would."

Dean stood in the background, letting Rayna and his dad have their reunion. He was so focused on the scene unfolding before him that he didn't hear Paisley walk up beside him.

"Why is Chi Ta crying?"

He put his arm around his oldest child and hugged her to him. "Because he considers Rayna to be his daughter."

Unexpectedly, Paisley pushed away from him with a hurt look on her face. "Is that why Chi Ta never accepted my mom?"

Paisley's words slapped him hard in the face. He turned his attention from Rayna and his dad to his daughter. "Why would you ever think that my dad didn't accept your mom?"

"Mom always felt that way. And she told you! You just didn't care!"

Dean felt blindsided and shocked—Paisley had never said anything like this before. Rayna was occupied with his dad and he was occupied with her; Dean wouldn't be missed at the moment. Tears were streaming down Paisley's normally stoic facade, and the look in her eyes was filled with so much pain and hurt and shattered pieces of a lost family.

Dean held his daughter's hand tightly in his as he led her to a home office he had been occupying since he'd moved back to Montana. It was private and close by.

He shut the heavy door behind them, pulled a chair with rolling casters over to his office chair and gestured for her to sit down. He took some tissues out of a nearby box and dabbed her face for as long as her independent nature would allow.

"Sweet girl," Dean said to her, "tell me what's wrong."

"I already told you." Paisley raised her voice in frustration. "Mom never felt like Chi Ta accepted her. I heard her say it, so don't say that I didn't!"

"Okay, I won't." His mind tried to flip though the memory files in his brain labeled *Divorce—Do Not Open Under Any Circumstances!* He did have a vague recollection of Cat feeling jealous about his family's embrace of Rayna. It was something that they'd struggled with for years, but it hadn't been the main cause of their divorce. Their differences were just too broad to bridge; he'd been ready to return to Montana, and she'd wanted to be on the world's stage. She had worked for her entire life for this chance, and it had been a chance he couldn't let her pass up. They *had* contemplated long distance but ultimately decided on building a co-parent partnership, always striving to put the girls ahead of any issues, so they could both go in the direction of their disparate dreams.

Dean took Paisley's hands, pressing them together inside of his. He leaned his body toward her and his head down so he could look into her eyes. "Listen to me, sweet girl," he said. "Chi Ta loves your mother. He loves her as much as he loves you. Do you understand? One love can't happen without the other. Don't ever think that he doesn't love your mother. It hurts me to know that you've ever felt that way."

Sitting in the chair, Paisley looked slight and vulnerable and more broken than he cared to admit. She had always braved the divorce with bravado and ease that he had hoped was sincere. But now he knew that it had been a facade made out of the most fragile bone china. And he felt ill equipped to fix it. In truth, he couldn't claim to be completely healed. How long could this pain last? How long could it take to build two whole worlds out of one shattered nucleus? He had been so lucky; his parents had been happily married for decades. So much so that his father had refused treatment for his cancer so he could rush to the end of his life to be once again united with his beloved Nettie.

"How do I make this better for you?" he asked.

"Why can't you get back together with Mom?" Paisley asked. "I liked how it was before."

Dean's shoulders dropped as he let out his breath slowly. He had wondered if this question of a reunion would ever arise. And here it was.

"Come here, lovebug." He coaxed her onto his lap, wrapped her up in his arms and rocked the chair back. She was a mite too old to sit in his lap any longer, but enveloping her in a tight hug was the best reassurance he could think to give her.

He sighed again, buying time while his mind raced through soothing options for Paisley, but none came to mind. Not a single one. "I wish that I could give that back to you, Paisley. I really do. But I can't."

Paisley sat up a bit so she could see his face. "But you always talk about Mom like you still love her."

"That's the thing. I *do* still love her as a friend and as

your mother. She is a part of you, and I am a part of you. And we both love you."

"But you won't get back together," his daughter, said returning to her own chair.

"No," he said. "We can't."

The silence that followed didn't produce any words of wisdom; maybe he was looking at this problem from the wrong angle.

"Paisley—are you happy here in Montana?"

She shrugged, but she seemed to be getting her emotions more under control. "I like it. But I miss the city and I miss Mom. She says that I'm a big-city girl just like her."

He nodded his understanding; ranching was a life filled with long spaces in between conversations. And maybe that was why he'd worked so hard with building a large equestrian barn, picking up clients as a farrier and tending to the purposefully shrinking herd of cattle. It was his hope that one day Luna would get her footing as a cowgirl in 4-H and then take the reins of this ranch and continue the Legend family legacy. But he already knew that this would not be the path for Paisley. Like her mom said, she was his big-city girl.

"Your mom travels too much during the school year," he said. "You mom and I agree that you need to be here with me so you can focus on your schoolwork."

"I know," Paisley said with her chin jutted forward. "But I could be homeschooled, and that way I can be with Mom anywhere in the world."

"She can't have you with her, Paisley. She just doesn't have enough free time to help you with school. This is just the way it has to be—you with me here in Montana."

In a low, sullen voice, Paisley said, "She could hire a tutor."

Dean breathed in deeply and let it out on a long sigh. These conversations with Paisley made him feel woefully lacking in skills that would help him through these times when she came up with perfectly acceptable solutions that would allow her to travel with her mother. The problem he had was skirting the real issue without bending the truth so far that it broke into a thousand pieces. The truth that he was hiding was the fact that Catrin didn't want the girls with her when she traveled. They distracted her, and Catrin was well aware that a rising star could fizzle out if they missed one beat. For Catrin, the girls would be a distraction that she couldn't afford.

"Look, sweet girl, if you want me to ask Mom if you can be with her on the holidays or long weekends, I will."

Everything in Paisley lit up, just like a flower suddenly finding the sun. "Do you think Mom will say yes?"

"I do," he said, hoping that he was more right than wrong on this front. "We can talk to her about it tonight, look at our calendars and figure something out. Okay?"

Paisley threw herself into his arms, hugged him tightly as if to comfort him as much as herself. She stood up and said with a very mature and serious expression on her adorable face, "You'll still have Luna here to keep you company. And I'll video chat with you every day so you won't miss me too much."

"Thank you." He accepted that hug and put a mental notch in the "win" column for this crisis. "I love you a little bit more each and every single day."

"I love you too, Dad."

Buck was holding court with Rayna on one side and with Luna draped all over him. When he saw Paisley walking into the library, he waved at her with a shaky hand, coughed several times and called out to her in a breathy, raspy voice, "Where have you been, Parsley?"

Early on, and before Nettie had realized that Buck needed hearing aids, his father had thought they had named his first granddaughter after an herb. And the nickname had just stuck.

While Buck was occupied by the loving attention of his granddaughters, Rayna slipped away to speak with Dean.

"Everything okay?"

"Sort of," he told her. It was the only short version of Paisley's emotional crisis over Buck's reaction to seeing Rayna again, revisiting the divorce and finally crossing the finish line in one piece by offering more time in civilization with her mom.

Rayna had always been sensitive in the way that she noticed the minutest of details from how someone held their body or the intonation of their voice. Most people glossed over those tiny "tells" because they were necessarily focused on their own lives and duties, but not Rayna. She watched, she observed and she used that collected information to paint mental pictures of the people around her.

When she met his gaze he saw, reflected back to his eyes, an understanding that something important had occurred and that she also knew that this was the wrong time to address it. Paisley glanced over at him, and that was his cue to join his daughters with his father.

Buck was soaking up the attention, waving at Rayna to come back. All of the talking and laughing got him coughing, and when the coughing didn't stop, the nurse helped Dean get him back into bed with a mask over his mouth and nose for a more efficient means of getting oxygen into his lungs.

"Rayna…" Buck worked to get her name out from behind the mask.

She quickly went to him, taking his hand, and Dean was touched by how kind and attentive Ray was with his father. The parent-child relationship that had developed between Ray and Buck had been real, it had been strong, and it had just been rekindled.

"Promise me…" He pushed the words out in between coughs. "Promise me you will come back."

"I will, Dad," she promised and then kissed him on the cheek. "I promise."

Paisley and Luna both kissed Buck, and then they all left the patriarch of the family to rest and recover from the big visit he'd just had.

The four of them walked toward the main entrance of the rustic mansion. Paisley nodded to them as she broke off from the group and disappeared into a hallway that led to a back staircase to a rather secluded mother-in-law suite upstairs, where she resided.

"Do you have time to see the stables?" Dean asked Ray.

"Yes. I'd really like that." Rayna started the process of suiting herself back up in layers of winter outerwear.

"That's, like, three jackets." Luna watched Ray curiously.

"Well," she said, "two jackets because the other one is a sweater not a jacket."

Dean told Luna to go get her winter coat, hat and gloves that were still on her bedroom floor from her morning riding lesson. By the time she returned, Ray was still trying to zip up the zipper of her last layer.

"Let me do it," Dean said after watching her struggle for what had seemed like an eternity to him.

"I've got it!"

"Rayna! Will you stop and let me do it?"

"Fine!"

"Okay," he said. "Release the zipper."

"Fine!"

Dean had to smile at Rayna's reaction while he tugged on the zipper, sometimes pulling her forward or upward on the tips of her toes.

"What's taking so long?!" she asked with all sorts of attitude. "I'm starting to sweat."

"So am I! I'm sweating trying to get you into this get up."

Finally, Dean gave one hard yank on the zipper and it gave way.

"There," he said.

After a few sullen moments, Rayna said, "Well, I guess I should thank you."

Dean took note of the fact that the actual thank-you never came.

Then she asked, trying to hold back a smile, "Would you be so kind as to hand me my gloves? I don't currently have full range of motion with my arms."

After Luna and Dean took a couple of minutes to put on barely any sort of protection from the overcast early winter day, they all walked toward the enormous equestrian complex he had installed. Luna had already seemed to accept Ray as one of the family, and Dean's youngest was happy to be in the middle holding her hand and her father's hand.

"Wow." That was the only word that came to her mind as they grew closer to the complex. "It's huge, Dean."

The outside materials used were matched closely with the aesthetic of the main house that included stone accents, cream-colored hardy board, dark wood pillars and doors, and a distinctive white metal roof to deflect the sun. Without seeing the inside, Rayna estimated that this had easily been a one- or two-million-dollar project.

Dean let go of Luna's hand so he could do the gentlemanly thing; he opened the door for them to walk through ahead of him. That door led into a lounge that was decked out with comfortable seating, climate control, showers, lockers and a small kitchenette stocked with all blends of coffee, tea and hot chocolate.

"Wow," she said again, already beginning to sweat and then steam the sweat inside of her outerwear bubble.

"Twenty oversized stalls, indoor riding arena, tack room, this lounge, four wash racks, rubber pavers throughout and two offices."

Dean kept on talking and walking, and then out of the blue, she started to get really hot and claustrophobic. She could feel heat prickles making her want to itch all over her body. Her face and neck felt hot and her heart was racing making her feel faint.

"Rayna?" He had turned around to see why she hadn't gone through the door he was holding open that led into one of the main aisleways. "What's wrong?"

"Hot!" she shouted. "Dizzy!"

"Damn it, Ray! I told you this was too much!"

Luna pointed at him and said, "Curse word! Swear jar!"

Dean reached for the zipper of Rayna's coat and, after some tugging, managed to get it moving down. "Quit being the word police and help me unwrap her!"

Luna worked her gloves off of her hands and then helped her dad strip off the first coat. Layer after layer, they finally reached the end of it, leaving a large pile of Ray's clothes on the polished wood floors.

He led her over to the nearby couch, helped her sit down and then got a water out of the fridge and tossed it to Luna to give to her while he ran some cold water on a dish towel to make her a compress.

After the cool water and cold compress, Rayna began to feel better. Luna sat down next to her, leaned on her a bit and stared up into her face worriedly.

"Are you better?" Dean's youngest asked.

"Yes." Rayna put her arms out to Luna and hugged her. "Thank you."

Dean also had a worried look on his face. In that moment, she took the time to really look at her first love. Yes, he was older now, with some gray hair pushing through. He wasn't a string bean anymore, but she actually preferred him with a little meat on his bones. Right now, as always, Dean Legend was simply handsome to her.

Chapter Seven

Luna proudly finished the tour of the incredible equestrian facility; everything was topnotch and high-end—a dream for any horse owner. She was proudest of her two-barrel racing ponies, Duke and Duchess.

"Are you showing?" Rayna asked, petting Duchess's umber neck.

"Not yet," Luna said. "But I'm practicing a whole lot. Did *you* ever show?"

Rayna shook her head while she stroked the Duke's soft black nose. "No. My sister Charlie was a bona fide rodeo queen."

"What are you talking about, Ray? You had a great seat when we were kids. We used to race bareback with nothing on the horse but a halter and a rope. You'd win those races plenty, if I recall correctly."

"Your memory is just fine, and so is mine. The last time I rode, Bear, he got spooked by a log. When I posted up, he swiped right, and then the next thing I knew, I was flying through the air without my Supergirl cape, landed on my belly, bounced, and when I did finally get up, it felt as if every single bone in my body was held together by muscles and ligaments that had been stretched beyond their normal capacity," Rayna said. "Now that I'm older and wiser,

I think, now, why in the world did I voluntarily strap myself onto the back of an animal that may become irrationally petrified of a leaf blowing by and, as they are built by God to do, *bolt* and ask questions later? Doesn't make a hill of beans of sense to me."

Luna and Dean were both staring at her as if she had morphed into an insect. Then Luna looked up at her dad and asked, "Is she okay?"

"She's fine." Dean gave his daughter a side-hug. "She just needs a little more time to find her inner cowgirl."

"Oh." She scrunched up her face. "Okay."

"Luna, go up to the house and ask Paisley to let the dogs out," he said, and then said to Rayna, "The pack has grown substantially, and they're not as trained as I'd like. I didn't want you to get run over on what I hope won't be your last visit."

"I promised Buck that I'd be back."

Before Luna left, she asked, "Do you want to come back and see me ride?"

"Of course I do."

"Okay. Good," Luna said. Then she hugged her dad, then Rayna before trotting off toward the main house.

"She loves you already," Dean said. "She takes after me in that department, I suppose."

"I feel the same way," Rayna said. "I love her already."

He smiled, and in that moment, when his face was lit up with love and pride for his daughters, she had this nervous, undeniable sensation that she could absolutely fall for Dean Legend again.

"This place is so incredible, Dean," she said. "But what is it all for? Are you thinking about boarding?"

"I am," he said. "Luna loves being in the barn, taking care of the horses, and she's a natural barrel racer. If I could get some kids out here to join her, this place would pay off in spades. And I'm slowing down the cattle here."

"What about your farrier work?"

"I'll have to let that go if I want to give this place an honest chance," he said. "But don't worry—I know a great farrier, Katie Stankiewicz, who's actually better than me when it comes to barefoot trimming. But, you don't need to advertise that."

She smiled at him faintly. "So I have the goods on you?"

He returned the smile a bit sheepishly. "Haven't you always?"

They stood in each other's presence in a silence that seemed to be filled with so many unspoken words between them. Rayna's return to the Legends' home, her reunion with Buck, and her experiences with Dean and his daughters had taken their toll. She was emotionally drained and on the verge of tears thinking about Buck's decline. It was heartbreaking and incredibly poignant and special at the same time. And then when she added her own major life changes, she just felt like she needed to get into bed with a box of tissues and binge-watch Hallmark holiday movies. But there wasn't really any time to feel sorry for herself— she had a heck of a lot of work to get herself ready to play chief cook and bottle washer for Hideaway Ranch's first guests!

"Well… I'd better get back. With Aspen in Texas on bed rest, I'm going to be doing all of the meal planning, grocery shopping for supplies, cooking—all that fun stuff. And I've got to take care of the chickens and the donkeys and then the goats, God love their playful souls, so that will keep me super busy."

Dean was watching her so intently, and she blushed. It had been decades since she had blushed, and she wasn't altogether sure she liked it that much. "Can I show you one more thing before you go?"

"Okay."

He led her over to his well-appointed office in the inner sanctum of the facility. Once she was inside, he pulled a key card out of his pocket, held it up against the wooden wall and then the bookcase began to open.

"Dean Legend! A secret door?"

Dean had always been fascinated by secret passages in European castles. It seemed totally "on brand" for him to build his own secret passage. Of course he would.

He took her hand and guided her into the small space behind the bookcase before he shut it, leaving them in darkness until her eyes began to adjust to the light coming from the top of a hidden staircase.

When they were alone, out of sight and out of earshot, the calm facade she had been maintaining crumbled. Her hands went up to her face, and she began to cry.

"It's okay, Ray," Dean said as he gently took her hands in his and guided her arms to wrap around his back. "I've got you."

As natural as breathing, she accepted the hug and the comfort, and she leaned her head against his chest and let all of the sadness she had been holding in since seeing Buck out.

"Dad…" she said in a broken voice.

"I know, Ray. I know."

"I've been gone for too long."

"You came back just in time."

"Why won't he do anything? Nettie wouldn't want this. She wouldn't want this!"

"No, she wouldn't. But then I think that it makes total sense…she was his heart—she was his reason for getting up when the sun rose, and she gave him a reason to sit down on the porch swing and enjoy the sunset. Mom was his sunrise and sunset. How can he go on without her?" Dean tightened his arms around her and kissed her on the top of the head.

He moved back a bit so he could look down at her face in the sparse light. "You've made him so happy today. I hope you will come back."

"I will. I promised him." she said, using her hands to wipe the tears from her face.

"Good." Dean took her hands into his. "There's no distance between how he loves you and how he loves me or my girls."

He kissed each of her hands and then brought her back into the security of his burly arms. Dean had always had a way of making her feel accepted, protected and loved unconditionally, and a moment to release her sadness over Buck *and* her divorce had been the exact thing she had needed at the exact time she had needed it the most.

Quietly, she said, "I'm divorced. You might have already suspected."

"I'm sorry, Ray. Divorce cuts to the bone."

"Yes. I does."

With one finger he lifted her head gently so she could see the features of his face and the light in his eyes when he said, "You'll get through this, Ray. It can be rough going— real rough going, but you're strong…"

Ray rolled her eyes and made a sound of denial in the back of her throat.

"And you will find footing on a new path. I promise that you will."

Standing so close to a man who was moving toward her emotionally and physically instead of pushing her away made something very real, very raw, rush over her body. She lifted her head and Dean lowered his, and it felt as if their lips might touch for the first time in two decades when Luna's laughing and giggling echoing in the hallways just outside of his office and the barking of several large dogs running behind her broke the moment.

Naturally, both of them stood stock-still and held their breath until they were sure that Luna wouldn't find them out. When they were out of the woods, they both started to laugh.

"When we were young, we had to hide from our parents," Rayna said, laughing and a bit breathless.

"And now we're hiding from my daughter!" He joined in laughter with her. "Some things never change."

"Nope." The laughter did a lot of good, and she could feel her spirits start to rise after releasing the sorrow that had built up in her body.

Her eyes fully adjusted, she could see Dean raise and lower his eyebrows in a satirical way when he asked, "And may I take you on a tour of my lair, tasty little morsel?"

For all of their childhood, whenever she was sad or hurt, Dean would do everything he could to make her laugh, and she supposed he never lost that desire to make things right for her.

"Yes," she agreed. "But only if you *never* call me a tasty morsel ever again."

After they'd almost shared a kiss in his secret stairwell, Dean had taken Ray up the stairs and into a hideaway that he had always imagined as a boy. At the top there was an open room that was hidden in the large copula at the very center of the barn. It looked like copper embellished with slender vertical stained glass from the ground; behind those slivers was a private room that during the day looked like a magical kaleidoscope.

"Is this where you take all of your hot dates?" she had asked.

They had laughed together about her overheating in her winter clothes; not the kind of hot date he had hoped for.

It had only been one *near* kiss, but that moment in time was often in the forefront of his mind. He had wanted to kiss Ray—he always *had* wanted to kiss her, and he proved that twenty years, two daughters and one failed marriage later, he still *did* want to kiss her. But the stakes were high for him now. Rayna's boys were young adults, while his daughters were school-age, and they had already been put through so much. Yes, their mother and he had done their very best to be amicable during the separation and subsequent divorce, but it *had been* a divorce.

"How are you?" Cat had called him now on video chat to touch base with him in advance of her visit. She planned to stay at Big Sky Resort and take the girls skiing. Her dark sable-brown hair was razor-sharp blunt cut in line with her chin with blunt-cut bangs creating a perfect frame for her lovely face. Her makeup, as always, was flawlessly applied to make her appear to *not* be wearing makeup, but her skin looked dewy and youthful and ready for any unguarded moments when she might be photographed by the European paparazzi. Cat never left the house without having been styled to perfection.

"I'm good. You?"

"I am good as well, Dean, thank you for asking." She smiled fleetingly.

"The girls are bouncing off the walls with excitement to see you."

"I feel the same. I've missed them deeply."

Because her family had fled from their country when she'd been just a girl and English was her second language, the syntax she used was more formal. And because of the poverty she had endured after moving to the US and the bullying all throughout school she had suffered, Cat had built an almost impenetrable armor between her and the rest of the world. The only time he saw more emotion from her was when she talked about Paisley and Luna or her passion for her clothing line, Poem, which was the meaning of her name in her first language, Khmer.

Another pause and Dean decided he needed to breach an uncomfortable subject with her. He tugged on his beard, and Cat said with a fleeting smile on her pretty bow-shaped lips, "I see you worrying your beard. It's always easier between us if you just get to the point, Dean."

"Well, I just wanted you to know before you hear it from the girls…"

"Rayna."

He dropped his head, shook it and blew out his breath, "Blast it. I'm sorry I wasn't the one to tell you."

"You still procrastinate."

"I hate to admit it, but yeah, you're right. I guess I do."

His difficulty getting things done as quickly as Cat wanted had been a big deal in their marriage—he'd thought she was controlling and she'd thought he was unmotivated. He guessed they'd both been right, looking at it in hindsight.

"I do truly want you to be happy," she said. "Is Rayna available?"

That question made Dean smile a bit because Cat was always so black and white, with little need for the gray areas that predominately greased the wheels of human interactions.

"She's fresh off a divorce. Real fresh."

"Perhaps with time."

"I can't say one way or the other right now. Dad wants her here, and I want Dad to have everything he wants right now. He deserves that."

"Yes, of course. But I should think that you also want her back in your life as well."

"Yes, I do. Absolutely. But I'm not in the market for an engagement ring, if that's where your mind is heading."

"Well, I could make an argument that you've been in the market for an engagement ring for Rayna for decades."

That barb hit, and it hurt. Dean caught a tiny crack in her perfect visage and saw, in a flash that only lasted a second or two, the real pain she carried about the failure of their marriage.

"I'm sorry, Cat."

"No." Cat kept looking down until she had recovered her composure. "I'm sorry. And as long as Rayna is good with our daughters, I could have no objection if you should wish to pursue it. How *is* she with the girls?"

"Couldn't be better. But Paisley is being a tough nut to crack. She's older and remembers the good times we had as a family."

"I do want you to be happy, Dean." She reiterated.

"Thank you," he said. "I feel the same about you. If you find it, grab it."

A rather lengthy silence reigned before Cat said with a tone that she would use to tell her maid items on a grocery list, "I have been wanting to share something with you, and in light of the current topic of conversation, I think this may be an opportune moment to inform you that I have met someone."

He got mental whiplash and felt like one of those cartoons that got clobbered followed by a growing knot on its head, with stars and tweeting birds circling, tongue hanging out with its eyes rolling around.

"I'd like to tell you about him, if you're open."

Dean felt only able to nod because the words that might've come out of his mouth would most likely be inappropriate for the peaceful co-parenting agreement that had become their new normal.

"You know I've been spending so much time in Monaco for my business."

Now he was imagining Cat's new beau as an overly pampered poodle. That image gave him a moment of joy that made him lift the corner of his mouth in half a self-amused smile.

"Nico and I have been moving in many of the same circles, and then quite unexpectedly, we fell in love on a mutual friend's yacht.

"He is a humanitarian, an entrepreneur and the eldest son of a very influential family, so he does have many obligations and I have mine, so we do think it's time to sync our calendars."

"It all sounds incredibly romantic."

"Maybe not for you, but for us it is." She addressed his sarcasm and then added, "He has asked me to marry him, and I have accepted."

One more round of whiplash and Dean asked, "Did he propose to merge companies, or did he propose marriage?"

"Don't be ridiculous, Dean. I would never merge my company with anyone for any reason. And as an heir of the Othonos fortune, Nico will not be squeamish about a prenuptial agreement."

"And you don't think this is quick?"

"It's not quick for us."

"Oh." That made Dean pause while he tried to refocus

his thoughts that were scattered all over the place. But that news helped him focus in on that point. "Okay. So, this has been an ongoing deal?"

"Yes. For quite a while now," she said. "And now that he has proposed, I would like for him to meet the girls. Would you have any objection to me bringing him on this next trip?"

"God bless! What is all this urgency about, Cat? Seriously?"

Her lips pursed slightly, and then she confessed, "I wanted to keep this relationship private until I knew, without a doubt, that it is serious. And there is the matter of us having been photographed on a beach on the French Riviera."

The sudden urgency of introducing this new love interest to the girls made more sense now; Paisley was a whiz kid when it came to searching for her mother on the internet.

"How do you want me to react to this deal, Cat?"

"You could say congratulations, I should think."

"Congratulations."

A lengthy silence followed that half-hearted attempt, then Cat said in one of her best diplomatic tones, "You don't even know, Dean. This could be a very good thing for them. They will have a new family to love them, and it will help Paisley accept our divorce. After all, that is reality, is it not? She can help me plan the wedding—you know how incredibly creative she is. And Luna is a light for all of us. As she has accepted Rayna so easily, I think she will also accept Nico. He doesn't have any children, but he is up for the role of stepfather."

"You've given me a lot of grizzle to chew."

Cat frowned. "What does this mean? I have never heard this before. You see?! You've become a mountain man again and you string words together that don't make sense. Do not teach these bad habits to my daughters."

"My roots are country, Cat, which means that Paisley's and Luna's roots are country, and there's not a darn thing wrong with it."

When his annoyance was breaking through his cordial veneer, Dean knew he needed to get off the call. They had worked so hard to keep their interactions, behind the scenes as well as in front of their daughters, cordial and supportive. He sure as heck didn't feel cordial right then, and he was sure as all get-out not supportive of her marrying a guy—a playboy jet-setter, from her description—who he'd never heard about before today.

"Let's table this," he said.

"Of course," she agreed. "We will continue this in a day or two. Just like you wanted to tell me about Rayna yourself, I would like to tell our daughters about my fiancé before they see it online or in print."

Cat managed to get one perfectly crafted barb in before they hung up. With the girls in town with Miss Minnie, a stout woman in her sixties who had been with the Legend family since he was a boy, he was alone in the kitchen, stewing over the conversation with Cat. He stood there basting in anger and frustration and feeling like he'd just gotten steamrolled by his ex-wife.

"Damn. Damn." Dean dropped his head down, kept on shaking it and hooked his thumbs on his jean pockets. "Damn it all to hellfire and back!"

He marched over to one particular part of the kitchen counters, pulled out his wallet, took out a one-hundred-dollar bill, crumpled it in his fist and stuffed it into the swear jar that his mother had placed there to collect one heck of a lot of money from Buck. The words *Swear Jar* were written in Nettie's stylish cursive on paper beneath clear tape that had yellowed with age and had started to chip around the edges. His mom had been a God-fearing woman, and she had not taken any mess when it came to cursing in her home. Buck had paid a pretty penny for every curse he'd said within earshot of his wife.

"May's well get a tab started, Mom," he said. "More's to come."

Several days after her first visit and the poignant moments she had shared with Buck and Dean, Rayna still wasn't able to successfully unravel the big tangle of mixed emotions that had resulted. So she did what she'd been raised to do: focus attention on the job at hand. Work, her parents had always taught, was the way to salvation, and she decided to give that theory a big ol' try.

She moved out of the main house and into the modest accommodations of a mini travel trailer, worked with her friend to get some boxes in the storage unit to move to Big Sky along with a car that was the last present that Ben had given her. She wished that he hadn't. With that chore done, Rayna divvied up her time between taking care of the animals—this was her joy—and getting everything set up for their guests. She had managed to establish a bit of a routine, and that made her happy because she loved to make order out of chaos. And it was a real possibility that Aspen would want to stay at home with her newborn when they were ready to travel back to Montana as a new family—that time with a newborn was such an incredible bonding time between parents and baby that Rayna would be completely supportive of that choice. With that in mind, she had to factor that in when getting the food end of the ranch sorted.

She was also mulling over her idea of taking a lease in the town center to start a yoga business once things were set up on the ranch. To be able to turn what she loved in a venue to support herself while helping others feel physically and emotionally better was a dream. When she had been a teenager, Montana had seemed like an albatross holding her down, and now Montana seemed like the land of possibilities. It didn't hurt Montana's case that she had begun to reconnect with Dean as friends—where they had started as kids was where they were picking back up as adults.

Rayna was giving love to all of the animals in the barn before she was going to head back to the main house for more meal planning when her phone rang.

"Hello," she said.

"Howdy."

"How did you know I was just thinking of you?"

"Lucky for me," Dean said.

"What's going on?"

"Dinner. Seven sharp. Invitation came directly from Buck."

"Hmm. Are you sure about that? Why wasn't he the one who called me?"

"He's got people for that sort of thing." Dean laughed good-naturedly. "How should I tell him that you replied to his invitation?"

"Tell Dad I'll be there early with an appetite."

Chapter Eight

Rayna managed to get a walk-in appointment at the salon in town, and just as Paisley had said, she got a discount when she mentioned the girl's name. For years she had worn shoulder-length, no-fuss, no-muss blunt cut bob. It had been easy and chic. When she'd been growing up on the ranch, she had always been a throwback from the nineteen sixties' flower child, and her hair had had a wave in it and reached all the way down past her lower back. The first time she'd cut a significant length of hair off was when she'd gone off to college. Then the next big change had occurred when she'd found out she was pregnant—she'd cut her hair into a blunt bob and had kept that same signature hair style until Ben had asked for a divorce, she had begun to grow out her hair and pull it up into a ponytail.

Now she walked out of her hair appointment, climbed into her dad's truck and took another look at herself in the rearview mirror.

"Not too shabby, Ray!" She smiled at her reflection before she cranked the engine and headed back to the ranch.

Tonight she would be having dinner with the Legend family, and while she hadn't gotten her hair done for Dean per se, she did feel excited butterflies at seeing his reaction to her new look. She parked the truck outside of her tiny abode, grabbed two overly stuffed shopping bags from the clothing store right next to the hair salon and rushed to the door.

Once inside, she quickly stripped off her outerwear and then made a direct line to the bathroom. There she turned the light on, staring at her reflection and turning her head one way, then the other to see how her hair moved. To the touch, her hair felt smooth and silky and healthy. Some of her lost hair was starting to sprout.

"She's a magician!"

She put on a pot of coffee to help get the chill out of her bones while she took the new clothes out of the shopping bag and hung them up so they didn't get wrinkled. Then she took a large boot box out of the second bag, took the top off and admired her new cowgirl boots. This was her first pair of western boots since high school, and she had to acknowledge that being back at Hideaway Ranch had already begun to change her inside out and outside in, and it had only been a short while since her arrival. She was finding herself again, and she was sincerely excited to see who Rayna Brand would become in this next phase of her life.

Ray had just stepped out of the shower, her hair tucked into a shower cap to protect it, when her phone rang.

"I'm coming, I'm coming!" She searched for her phone and found it inside of the boot box.

"Hey!" she greeted Charlie once she'd managed to get that green button pushed after fumbling the phone with slippery wet hands.

"Hey," her sister responded. "How's everything going?"

"Good." She put the phone down so she could slip on her terry cloth robe to help dry her body off. "How's Helena?"

Charlie sighed, and she sounded exhausted. Wayne and

her sister had traveled to the state capital to find some much-needed building materials for their new project.

"Honestly?" Her sister sighed again. "I wish we had just decided on the prefab tiny house. The supply chain hasn't rebounded since the pandemic, and everywhere we go it seems to be a brick wall."

"No." Ray sat down on one of the bench seats on either side of the small dinette table with a cup of black coffee. "Quality over quantity. It was unanimous."

"I know it was. But Danica is micro-managing me from California, especially after we had to turn down another group that wanted to book in December because we just don't have the room yet."

"Growing pains."

"I'll let you tell that to your sister," Charlie said. "She thinks she can snap her fingers and things magically happen."

"I love how she's my sister when she's being a pill." She laughed. "Just remember she's under a lot of stress."

"Aren't we all?" Charlie countered. "Anyway, let me tell you why I called. Turns out we've got kin all over Montana…"

They had discovered that the Brand family in Bozeman were relatives, and now that family extended to large landholders just outside of Helena on a large cattle spread called Bent Tree Ranch.

"Coming out of the woodwork."

"Well, they're our last-ditch effort," Charlie said. "I took a long shot and sent a direct message to a Sophia Brand, and she responded!"

"You're kidding!"

"And she invited us out to Bent Tree tomorrow. Turns

out they have some building materials stockpiled, and they may be willing to work a deal with us."

"Now, see there? It really pays off to have a philandering great-great—I don't know how many more *greats*—grandfather! We got great horses from the Bozeman Sugar Creek Ranch Brands and now perhaps building supplies from Helena Brands."

That actually made Charlie laugh, and it was a pretty rare sound, Ray noticed. Charlie had been trying for years to save the ranch that had been in their family for over one hundred years, swimming against the current, going it alone while two thirds of the triplets had been focused on their lives on either coast. Now Charlie had their support, but Ray could see that years of bailing water out of a sinking ship had taken a very big toll on her.

Ray heard Wayne's voice in the background, and then Charlie said, "My fiancé is going to take me out for a prime-rib dinner for two."

"Go. Have a great time!"

"Thank you, but hold on. Don't hang up!" Charlie said. "Dr. V. is coming tomorrow for biannual shots. We're coming back a day late—can you help her out?"

"Of course. Don't worry. I've got this."

They hung up, and Ray refocused her attention on getting ready for dinner. She rubbed a sweet-smelling lotion onto her body—winter was turning her skin scaly. Then she slipped on a pair of Ariat jeans. She had a lean physique from years of yoga practice, and these dark jeans with a unique stitching and rivets were designed for cowgirls who lived their lives in the saddle. Even though she wasn't all that sure that she would ever find interest in getting back into the saddle, these jeans fit her well-formed glutes like a glove.

She slipped on a gold and brown–palate button-down western-style shirt with pearl snaps. "Embracing my inner cowgirl. Or at least dressing like one for now."

Lastly, she stepped into a pair of brown distressed leather boots and pulled the bottom of her jeans over them. These boots were the exact thing needed to pull the outfit together. She was in the process of applying a minimal amount of makeup when her cell phone chimed. She checked it and saw that Dean was texting, asking her if she was on the way.

Almost, she typed.

The very last piece of this cowgirl puzzle was running a hairbrush through her hair. The way the stylist had cut it made the best of her baby-fine hair with subtle layers and precision-cut ends. Ray stepped far back in the narrow trailer so she could get as close as she could to a head-to-toe reflection. Out of nowhere, an emotion hit her, and she felt tears welling up in her eyes. Three steps forward, she got her hands on two Q-tips and pressed each one into her tear ducts. After a moment or two, her makeup was saved and she had fought back the tears.

"Huh. What do you know? It actually worked."

Another text from Dean came through. She pushed the microphone button and said, "I'm coming! Hold your horses!"

Ray wrapped up in her winter gear and headed out of the door. The fact that Dean was anxious for her to arrive made her smile; it reminded her so much of their lives together before. She did tend to run late, and that really hadn't changed. Dean was always waiting on her; it was odd, but nice, that he was still waiting for her to arrive. The thought did cross her mind—maybe all of this time, Dean had been waiting patiently for her to finally come home.

* * *

Dean had made a concerted effort not to appear anxious while awaiting Ray's arrival. After their time together the last visit, he was impatient to spend more time with her. He was well aware of Ray's history with cutting bait and leaving and that he could get hurt again—perhaps this time more deeply. He was in his right place at the right time; the prodigal son had returned home. Ray was a long shot—she could stay, she could leave, and she could break his heart. His desire to have her back in his life in any capacity spoke to the deep connection he had felt for her that had spanned decades. Even when they hadn't been actively a part of each other's lives, Dean had felt connected. Had Ray also felt that unbreakable *thing* between them? It could be damaged, it could be bruised, but not broken.

"Son," Buck said in his raspy voice, "a watched pot never boils."

Dean had been standing in front of the floor-to-ceiling windows on the side of the library that faced the front of the house, hands in his pockets, rocking back and forth on his heels.

"She's always late," Dean said. "Some things never change."

"And some things change completely."

"Finally!" he said when that old truck from wonderful years passed appeared on the horizon.

"Son." Buck waved him over to where he was sitting in his wheelchair. Dean didn't want to take a detour, but his abiding respect for his father made him divert his path.

Buck reached for his hand. "You have a second chance, Dean. Don't squander it."

He didn't bother to set the history record straight: Ray had been the one who'd needed something more than to live her life by his side, as his wife, and deepen the connection between their two families with as many children as they could love.

"I won't, Dad."

It did strike him as disloyal to his beautiful daughters that he looked back to his breakup with Ray as anything other than a divine appointment meant to allow Paisley and Luna to be brought into this world. He would never—could never—regret how events had unfolded because to do so would be to deny his children. But nothing in life was ever that cut and dry, particularly when it came to matters of the heart.

Buck was holding on to his hand with shaky fingers, and when he let go, Dean took that as a sign that his father was finished.

"Dean. Wait."

Dean turned back to his father, who was sliding his wedding band off of his finger and holding it out to him.

"Put this in the safe with your mother's wedding set. It is my wish that you use these rings when you remarry."

Dean held the ring in his palm, stared at it with a pain in his gut that had been with him since his father had decided unilaterally to refuse cancer treatment. After a second, he closed his hand over the ring, leaned down and kissed his father on his cheek.

"Promise," Buck said.

"I promise, Dad."

Not wanting to lose the precious ring, Dean slipped it onto his ring finger on the right hand while he walked with a broad stride to the front door. He made short work of the front steps and managed to get to the truck in time to wrestle the driver's door open. The Rayna that accepted his offered hand was not the Rayna of the first visit. Very few times in his life had he been rendered speechless—prom, the birth of each of his daughters, the day Cat had asked for a divorce and now—today.

"Rayna." Dean said her name with the same surprise that he felt. "You look…"

Ray looked up and met his eyes, and he could plainly see that his reaction mattered to her.

His mouth went dry, and he had to clear his throat several times to get his voice back in line. "You're a vision."

"Thank you." She smiled up at him with happiness alight in her bright blue eyes. "I went to the salon suggested by Paisley."

Wordlessly, he took her hand in his and spun her around so he could admire the whole picture. Rayna's hair was a deep sorrel red with bangs swept to one side and long layers; she didn't have nearly the amount of outer layers of clothes reminiscent of her first visit, and he could see a brand new pair of boots peeking out from dark-wash denim jeans.

"She's got her mother's gift for all things fashion," he said, offering his arm so he could escort Ray up the steps.

Dean opened the door, stepped in behind her and then helped her out of her coat. Beneath her ankle-length coat, his first love was wearing new clothing that could only be described as cowgirl chic. It was a sign, however small, that Ray was, at least in the short term, embracing her Montana roots. Her years of yoga had kept her trim with sinewy muscles. He had loved Ray when they'd been young, but he had to admit that this Ray was much more beautiful. The sum total of her life experiences was etched in her face with fine lines—that only made her more attractive to him. It was that experience that had allowed her to come into her own and created in her a womanly strength that Dean wasn't sure even Ray knew she possessed.

"I thought something was different about you!" Rayna said to him as she walked beside him on the way to the library.

She used her fingers to gesture on her chin. "This is new."

Dean rolled his eyes, wishing that the entire night had gone by without discussing his beard.

"Luna's idea," he said. "Semi-permanent gloss. The things I let my little ones do to me."

"I like it," Rayna said with a smile and tilt of her head, "but I'm not sure it's you."

"You know me well." He smiled at that. "Good thing it'll wash out in four to six weeks. I might take some extra showers to move this process along."

Buck wanted Rayna to wheel him into the dining room and into his spot at the head of the oversized table. Every visit seemed to elicit a new trove of memories from her childhood; each memory had an emotion attached, and they were some of the happiest of her life. Yet many of those lovely memories were now attached to a sadness that Nettie's passing had caused. Ray could hear the sound of Nettie's booming, infectious laugh; she could smell lavender, which was the only scent Nettie had used. Nettie's absence was a gaping hole in the hearts of everyone who had known her.

"Sit next to me," Buck said to her when she'd locked the wheels of his wheelchair.

At that very moment, Paisley walked in with a platter of hors d'oeuvres in her hands. The moment Dean's eldest daughter saw Rayna, she frowned and said to her grandfather, "That's my seat, Chi Ta!"

"I have two sides," Buck said.

"Luna always sits on your left, and I always sit on your right."

Not wanting to give either of Dean's lovely daughters a reason to dislike her from Jump Street, she quickly said to Buck, "I refuse to interfere with any family traditions."

It was unsettling to recognize that Paisley's demeanor toward her had changed, for the worse, in the span of less than a week. Rayna was just pulling out an undisputed chair when Luna came barreling into the dining room, her long hair wild and unkempt, her cheeks and nose red from being outside in the cold, and her clothing dirty and covered with dog fur.

"Luna!" Paisley's face registered as frustration. "Where have you been?"

The youngest of Dean's girls ignored her sister and rushed over to Rayna, threw herself into her arms and hugged her tightly. "Sit next to me!"

Paisley quickly circled to their side of the table, but Dean ran interference, put his hands on Luna's shoulders and told Paisley to focus on the food. Luna was determined to get a promise out of Rayna that she would sit down next to her, and Dean backtracked, pulled out the chair next to where Luna would sit, and once she was seated, that was when Luna agreed to go get cleaned up for dinner.

"What do you think of my granddaughters?" Buck asked Rayna, as they were currently the only two people at the table.

"They're very special, Dad," she said without artifice. "Very special."

Even though she had just been seated, Ray stood back up and served Buck a serving of Nettie's famous stuffed mushrooms. Ray took one off the platter and tossed it whole into her mouth. As she chewed, she made happy noises in her throat.

"So good!" Rayna popped three more mushrooms into her mouth before she sat back down. "Okay. That's it. I'll fill up before anyone else joins us!"

Buck slowly cut his mushrooms into smaller portions and seemed to struggle with the oxygen tube. Rayna almost asked if he'd like her help, but he managed it on his own and she felt relieved. It still didn't feel "right" to be helping Buck Legend with anything, much less cutting up his food.

"Miss Ray? As I live and breathe is that you sittin' over there lookin' as pretty as a picture?"

Ray's face lit up with sheer joy when Miss Minnie C. Smith pushed a serving cart stocked with Nettie's silver bowls and platters. Miss Minnie had been as much of her history growing up as her own family. Minnie had never been slight, but she was now nearly as wide as she was tall now with her hair swirled on top of her head in a loose bun, dyed black, and her eyebrows were drawn on in two arches with black liner.

"Miss Minnie!" Ray's voice cracked. She was around the other side of the table in a flash and hugged the other woman.

Minnie touched Ray's hair, her brown eyes full of love as if Ray was one of her very own. "You look just as pretty as Naomi Judd, God rest her soul, with this fiery red hair. Are you here in Big Sky for a visit or for keeps?"

Buck waved a finger. "For keeps!"

Ray smiled down at the elderly housekeeper. "Whatever Dad says."

Minnie gave a nod of her head and winked. "Good girl."

Dean returned with a scrubbed-up Luna, but the very poor attempt from him to braid her hair made Rayna smile.

Paisley proudly took her spot next to Buck, Luna happily sat down in between Buck and Rayna and then Dean sat across the table from her. Everyone held hands while Miss Minnie stood in the doorway with a bowed head as Buck led the family in a thankful prayer. Everyone said a robust "Amen," and then the platters started to circulate, and not wanting to draw attention to herself, she quietly passed the platter of Legend steaks on to Dean. A couple of years ago she had made the decision to forgo meat and limit dairy so she could keep her numbers in line when she went to the doctor—someone, either Butch or Rose—had gifted her with genetic high cholesterol!

Tonight, as it was a special occasion, she filled up her plate with broccoli, mashed potatoes, more stuffed mushrooms and baby carrots cooked in bubbling brown sugar. If she ate like this on the regular, she would also have to add *pre-diabetic* to that list. For now, she was just going to enjoy eating backcountry stick-to-your-ribs, keep-warm-for-the-winter food guilt free.

Buck had periodic coughing spells and some difficulty chewing. His on-duty nurse was close but out of view and came in only when he deemed it necessary. After one such episode, Buck ordered the nurse back into the shadows, claiming that if the cancer didn't get him, the nurses would.

"Now, son! Doesn't our Rayna look like an angel tonight?"

Rayna winced inside because she saw this comment draw immediate attention from Paisley. Before Dean could respond, Ray said, "Well, I have Paisley to thank for my new hair."

The eldest girl frowned at her and remained silent.

"Paisley recommended a salon in town, and I got a discount just by mentioning her name."

"Well, I'll be," Buck said. "Luna will run the cattle and horses, and Paisley will keep the books and get the word out."

The lessening frown on Paisley's face was considered a big success, so Rayna doubled down. "I took a selfie in front of the wall and hashtagged PrettyCoolPaisley."

Paisley gave a side-glance to her father, shrugged one shoulder and said, "Thanks."

"Thank you," Rayna said. "You knew exactly what I needed."

"You do look better," she said.

"Paisley!" This comment drew a stern tone from her father.

"What?"

"You look really pretty." Luna leaned over and stared up at her with the sweetest expression on her face.

"Thank you, Luna," Rayna said. "And, you're right, Paisley. I do look better. And, more importantly, I *feel* better."

The rest of the dinner rolled along smoothly, and then Miss Minnie brought out her famous chocolate pie slathered with whipped cream, and Rayna could not, would not say no to this dessert. Dairy or no dairy, Miss Minnie's pies were their own religious experience.

Buck was just about to stick his fork into a thick piece of pie when he started to struggle to catch a breath. The nurse rushed in, did a rapid check and then took him away.

Paisley and Luna looked at their father with big, worried eyes. Dean said in a calm, assured voice, "It's okay. He's not going to miss out on this pie."

Everyone waited for Buck's return, and when he did arrive, he blustered, "I keep on jumping into God's boat so he can take me home to go see my best girl, but he keeps on throwing me back! One day, he's going to keep me in that boat."

Buck smiled at his family when he stabbed his fork into that piece of pie. "But I have to admit, I'm mighty glad to still be here to eat this big ol' piece of Miss Minnie's world-famous chocolate pie!"

After dessert, Ray wished that she could just grab one of Nettie's handmade quilts, head for the family room and sink down onto one of their enormous couches. She had had two slices of the pie and didn't feel one iota of guilt. Even though Miss Minnie didn't want them to help her clean up, everyone did. Rayna walked into the kitchen carrying a stack of dirty plates while Miss Minnie put on the coffee pot.

"Enjoying yourself?" Dean asked as they walked back into the dining room.

"I can't remember such a good time."

That brought a smile to his face.

"It's a clear night." He held the swinging door open while she walked through.

"Full moon."

"Would you like to join me for a walk? Say, after coffee?"

"Thank you, Dean. I'd really like that."

Chapter Nine

After drinking a cup of coffee to warm them on the inside, Dean helped Rayna into her winter gear, and together they went outside. Right before they walked out of the front door of the house, Dean saw Paisley, with a worried look on her face, come out from the kitchen to see them leave together. There was a real big part of him that almost rethought the idea of a moonlit winter walk, but he decided to move ahead. He knew that his feelings for Ray went much deeper than a revival of their childhood friendship. He also knew that Rayna wasn't, at least for now, open to anything more than just that: friendship.

Dean offered Rayna his arm before they navigated the steps that had slippery patches of ice. Once they had cleared the stairs, Rayna slipped her hand away, and he immediately missed that contact between them.

"It's so beautiful out tonight," she said. "Mom always loved a full moon. She would have all of us go outside with her. We all tilted our heads back, closed our eyes and got a 'moon kiss.'"

"I remember," Dean said with a smile. He had been included in some of these "moon kiss" moments.

Rayna stopped walking, tilted her head back, closed her eyes and said, "For Mom."

Dean did the same. He had always bent over backward to make Rayna happy, even if it was way out of his "rugged Montana cowboy" persona. If a "moon kiss" would make her happy, he'd do it a thousand times over.

"Thank you," Rayna said to him when she opened her eyes.

They walked together along the driveway, in the moonlight, with the sound of their boots crunching on the mixture of ice and hard-packed snow. In their recent reunion the silences between them had been awkward; but now, and so quickly, they could be quiet in each other's presence without feeling the need to fill the space with words. Even though his brain knew that a rekindling of their romantic relationship was a long shot, his heart rejoiced at having "his girl" walking beside him on a moonlit winter evening.

"Penny for your thoughts," he said.

Rayna hesitated, and that "blink of an eye" hesitation produced a chain reaction in his body. His muscles tensed as he waited for her to answer that question.

"Well," Rayna said slowly, "I was actually thinking about Paisley."

Dean stopped walking to look down at Rayna, who also stopped when he did.

"She doesn't like me."

Those words were hard to deny. His daughters had burrowed into his heart and expanded it in ways he had never imagined. They were his priority; they got the top slot in his life. On the other hand, the love that he now craved was not the love of daughters—it was the love of a good woman; a woman with a heart of gold, a woman who would take his daughters into her heart and love them as if they were her own flesh and blood. That woman was Rayna; perhaps it always had been and perhaps it always would be.

"Did you hear what I said?" Ray asked with a slight waver in her voice. He doubted anyone beyond her sisters or sons could pick up that change in her voice, but he did and it confirmed for him that Rayna had already taken his girls into her heart.

He put his hands in his pockets to warm them up. "Yes, I heard you."

She looked up at him with an expression that read *And what is your response?*

"I'm not sure exactly how to answer that."

"Truthfully. You answer it truthfully."

Dean took a deep breath in, blew it out through his nose and then said, "Paisley is having a hard time in general. The divorce, moving to Montana, watching her grandfather slip away…"

When Rayna continued to listen, he continued, "There's a part of Paisley that is holding out hope that Cat and I will remarry."

"And she thinks I'm an obstacle to that?"

"I think so."

After several steps forward in silence, Rayna said, "Well, then, tell her otherwise."

"I have told her that her mother and I are not going to get back together," he said. "What I haven't told her is that Cat is engaged to a man they've never even heard about."

"Oh."

"I'm running a tab on Mom's swear jar."

Rayna laughed, and it immediately made him feel lighter inside. If he could tell her his *truth*, he would tell her that just seeing her, just talking to her, just being in her presence made him feel better—more grounded and more capable of braving the rough waters ahead.

"Cat is coming to Big Sky to take the girls skiing opening day. That's become a big deal in these parts so the girls are as excited about that as they are on Christmas morning."

"Is opening day still right before Thanksgiving?"

Dean nodded, "Cat was going to bring her fiancé, but I couldn't get behind that. So we came up with an agreement that she would talk to the girls about Nico and introduce them on video chat."

Dean could see that Ray was starting to shiver even in her winter coat, so he turned them around and headed back to the house.

"Maybe it isn't such a good idea that I come over," Rayna said quietly. "I would never want to make things tougher on Paisley."

"No," he snapped more harshly than he had intended. "I won't give you up."

Rayna looked up at his face but didn't say anything.

"You've breathed new life into Dad, and you've breathed new life into me."

"Dean…"

"No. Don't say it. I already know," he said. "You're not ready for a relationship, you've put me in the friend zone…"

"That's not…"

"You can't see yourself living in Montana full-time, you can't see yourself as a cattleman's wife."

"I just want to…"

Dean stopped walking to face her. "I would do just about anything for my girls, but I'm not going to close myself off and give them half of a man. I'm not going to put this on blast with my guy friends, but I get lonely. I am lonely. I need someone to just share the mundane details of life, to hold hands, to ask for advice."

Rayna tugged his hands out of his pockets and held on to them with hers. "Can I speak now?"

"Sure. Go ahead."

"Well, that was rude, but I'm going to give you a pass on that one because you're 'nervous talking,' and I know that's what you do when you're..."

"Nervous," Dean filled in for her. She was right as usual—his tone had been less than gentlemanly.

"Dean, I don't know how long I'll be in Montana," she said. "Or when I will be ready to give love another try. But I was so busy with the noise of my own life—raising my boys, trying to find some common ground with Ben so we could be happy empty nesters together—that I had completely forgotten how much our friendship meant to me. And I don't want to give that up."

Dean's heart started to ramp up its beat while she continued.

"But I don't want to cause Paisley any more pain than she already feels," Rayna said and then suggested, "What if we kept some of our time together secret?"

"Secret rendezvous?"

"Sure. Why not? We're adults. We don't need to report all of our business to your family or my family."

"Damn straight."

Rayna laughed with her head tilted back, curls of cold air slipping up to the sky.

They began to walk back to the house, and he felt content when Rayna hooked her arm with his. "So how do we go about setting up these 'secret meetings'?"

"Text?"

"No go," he said. "Paisley set up all of my passwords for me, and she checks my emails for me."

"But," he continued, "I could get a Google number."

They reached the bottom of the steps leading up to the house, and Dean wished it could've lasted longer, but the completely unexpected suggestion by Ray to meet secretly had gotten his wheels turning. He already knew the first place he wanted to take her—it held many good memories for them, and he had to believe that Rayna didn't even know that, after all of these years, it had persisted.

"Let me work on it, and I'll send you a text when I get it set up."

Rayna held out her hand for them to shake on it.

"Operation *Keep Our Families Out of Our Business* starts now."

The next morning, Rayna started her yoga practice before dawn, then she went to the barn and got the horses, donkeys and goats fed and then took everyone out to their outdoor areas so she could clean the stalls. After that chore was done, she collected eggs from the chicken coop with a promise to come back later that day for some love and lap sitting, and then she stopped by the greenhouse that had been built over the summer to water the plants. The vegetables that they were growing would be one of the farm-fresh ingredients she would be using to cook for their guests three meals a day.

A text from an unknown number came up on her phone, followed by a picture of one hazel eye. When they'd all been kids, Dean had been forever getting sent to the principal's office because he'd been so busy getting his classmates to laugh that everyone had been distracted by it.

Guess who? A second text followed the picture.

She texted back, Tall, dark and handsome?

He sent her five laughing emojis, and then he called.

"Hello, Ray," Dean said with a smile in his voice.

"Hello, Dean."

"Can you meet me at noon near the creek?"

"Not today." She then asked, "Maybe tomorrow?"

"Maybe, or definitely?"

That made her laugh again, and it made her realize that she hadn't often laughed over the last several years.

"Definitely."

"This feels good, doesn't it?" he asked her before they hung up.

Yes. It did feel good. It felt fun and exciting. It reminded her of all of the times she had climbed out of her bedroom window to meet Dean after the rest of the ranch had gone to sleep. How often could a person truly plug back into a more innocent time in their lives when they'd been blissfully unaware of the rough roads ahead where they had to pay the bills, raise children, try to keep the fire lit in the marriage and face the reality of their parents' mortality?

"Tomorrow, then," he confirmed.

"Tomorrow."

They ended the conversation, and it was perfect timing on her end because the large-animal veterinarian, Dr. Tonia Vyslosky, drove through the gates in her super-duty truck. Dr. V. was a slight woman with bluish-green eyes and thick blond hair pulled back into a ponytail. She was dressed in slim-fit jeans tucked into just-below-the-knee brown boots that had thick tread on the soles.

"Hi!" Dr. V. greeted her cheerfully as she hopped down from the elevated height of her truck. She strode over, hand out, so they could shake hands. "Rayna?"

"That's me."

"So nice to meet you."

"Likewise."

Dr. V. looked around. "This is my first time here. You've got an incredible piece of land."

"Thank you," Rayna said, and she did feel a sense of

pride in this land of her forefathers. Charlie had always talked about that feeling of being grounded in tradition and connected to their ancestors who had first homesteaded on this property. "My family has been here for more than one hundred years."

"I love that." Dr. V. walked quickly back to her truck. "Where do you want to start today?"

"Let's do the horses first." The vet would be giving all of the four-legged family members health checks, and the horses would be getting their biannual shots.

Rayna grabbed Rose out of the pasture—she had really become one of her favorites. Her love for this compact muscular Quarter horse made her almost want to give riding another try. Almost, but not quite.

Once Dr. V. got started, she worked steadily and thoroughly. Even though the veterinarian was a petite woman, she commanded respect with all of the animals without being harsh or overly animated. She was kind and quietly assertive, and even Atlas, a giant draft horse, toed the line with her. It took two hours before the vet had worked her way through the horses, donkeys and goats.

Rayna accompanied Dr. V. back to her truck.

"Everyone needs the dentist," she said while writing up the tab. "I have a couple I let work on my horses. I can give you their names."

"Thank you."

While Dr. V. focused on her paperwork and they'd stopped speaking, Rayna heard the very faint mewing of kittens.

"Kittens?" Her ears perked up and tuned in.

The vet smiled faintly with a nod. "The last stop. I'd rather take them back to my office, get them healthy and up-to-date on vaccines, and then I'll try to find a good home for them."

"Can I take a peek?"

"Sure."

She opened up the back door of her truck and let Rayna hoist herself up into the truck, then shut the door behind her to stop the cold air from coming in. Dr. V. had put the kittens in a small box, lined it with clean towels and then put a clean towel over the top to help keep them warm. Ray lifted one corner of the towel—three kittens, their eyes not open yet, were curled up tightly together.

"Oh, sweet things," Ray said. She was an animal person in general, but she had always had a special bond with cats. Three black-and-white kittens, most likely with those wonderful tuxedo-cat green eyes. "I think we could make room for you here."

The minute she saw them, she fell in love. She couldn't keep them in the main house, and the camper seemed awfully small for three rambunctious kittens. Eventually they would be barn cats and earn their keep by taking care of any rodent issues. But as it stood, the barn would be too cold for the kittens that were so young.

The little kittens mewed sweetly as she touched them gently, and she just knew that they were meant for her. No, these little babies most likely didn't break Charlie's rule of "If they eat and make manure, we are all full up at the inn," especially since Ray was the one who would be taking care of them financially and physically.

"They're too adorable."

Dr. V. handed her a copy of the bill. "That they are. Two boys and one little girl."

"I'll send this to Danica, and she'll pay you from her end."

"I know you guys are good for it." And then Dr. V added, "They'll be up for adoption in about three weeks."

"I want them." Rayna said, and it felt as if her mouth had blurted that out before her brain had a chance to catch up. "I've got to figure some things out."

"Could be great barn cats."

"Yes." She nodded in agreement. "My thoughts exactly."

Dr. V. climbed up into her truck, waved and then rolled her window down. "Let me know if you want to adopt them."

"Consider them adopted," Rayna said. Yes, Charlie had banned her from bringing any other "surprise" animals on to ranch property after Donkey-gate—all she'd done was add some adorable miniature donkeys at the time of purchase for the goats, and Charlie acted like she had committed a crime! Rayna was pretty confident that the statute of limitations applied in this case. These kittens were sweet innocents and would eventually earn their keep as mousers.

Dr. V. smiled broadly and gave her a thumbs-up.

Rayna headed over to the chicken coop to fulfill her promise of a "chicken love" session. Once in position, her white Silkie Bantam named Marshmallow stole the position in her lap. While she pet the fluffy white Silkie Bantam and two black Silkie Bantams named Coco and Chanel waited their turns in her lap, she sang to them "The Twelve Days of Christmas," but instead of "three French hens" Rayna substituted in "three kittens playing," and this made her laugh out loud. Even though Christmas was still off in the horizon, Rayna loved Christmas carols and was known to sing them any time of year.

"Charlie may blow a gasket!" Rayna told her chicken companions. "But then she'll see the wisdom of having cats on the payroll. Just because she's been working tirelessly for years to save our family ranch doesn't mean she should lose her sense of humor. We can all agree on that, can't we?"

The three chickens clucked a couple times, so Rayna felt secure that the panel of one human and three Silkie Bantams returned a unanimous vote.

Rayna laughed happily. It was really hard to realize, and come to terms with, the fact that she hadn't laughed in years. She hadn't felt light-hearted or happy in such a long time and had become an expert at keeping the facade in place at all times. She loved being a parent; she was so grateful to have the wonderful boys that she did with Ben— two boys turning into successful, productive young men was a huge accomplishment. But while that was the truth, there was another truth and that was a marriage without intimacy—a marriage that had been filled with loneliness and the feeling in her gut that no matter how she changed to conform to the Fortier family, she would never be accepted. And ultimately, she had been correct on that front.

Dean hadn't been able to sleep the night before their first secret meeting. He'd lain flat on his back, hands under his head, staring up at the ceiling. He already knew what he wanted—of course he did—because the last twenty years of his life hadn't really deviated too much from the first twenty years of his life—he wanted to be with Rayna. He wanted to be with her, make a life with her, enjoy their children together, grow old together and care for each other every day for the rest of their lives. And really knowing that fact—really acknowledging it in a way that dug deeper than his usual cursory examination of his feelings—made him feel sad and remorseful. When Rayna had ended things between them, and even when they'd said it was *mutual*, it hadn't been mutual. He'd wanted to marry her, give her children and spend every day of his life loving her. But she couldn't commit to life in Montana, and then what had he done? He'd married a woman who could not commit to living in Montana!

"I did love her," Dean said aloud as he walked into the kitchen.

"I'm sorry, Mr. Dean. What did you say?" Miss Minnie asked him. She was peeling potatoes for dinner.

"I'm trying to figure out my lunch. I'll be far enough out today that I won't be coming back to the main to eat."

Miss Minnie frowned at him, dropped the potato and peeler, wiped her hands off on her blue-and-white checked apron and scooted him out of the way.

"I've got ham for sandwiches…"

Rayna was a vegetarian, so ham wouldn't do. But Miss Minnie would think he needed medical attention if he said he wanted sandwiches without meat.

"Any egg salad?"

Miss Minnie grinned at him, snapped her fingers and moved some items around in the fridge before she found what she was looking for. She popped the top off, looked inside and then said, "Still fresh."

"I can make them, Miss Minnie. You've got your work cut out."

"Scooch, scooch," she said, shooing him away from the counter. "You aren't the boss of me, Mr. Dean."

Dean smiled, sat down on a bar stool on the other side of the counter. Technically, he *was* her boss, but lord knew he would never say it to her—or anyone else for that matter!

"Four, five?" she asked him, laying out the wheat bread on the counter.

"Is there enough for six?"

Miss Minnie's face lit up. "Six today! Hungry boy!"

She loved it when the people in the house ate. She had been making him sandwiches for most of his life, and it was nice to have someone so close to his mother still looking out for the family.

By the time Miss Minnie was done, she had packed him sandwiches, two choices of beverages, napkins, bags of peanuts for a snack in a basket and then presented it to him.

"You're the best."

Minnie turned her head to the side and tapped her cheek with her finger.

Dean leaned down and gave her a peck. "I love you, Miss Minnie."

She blushed and chuckled with pleasure, then waved her hands for him to get out of her kitchen.

"You'll be back at six for supper," she called after him.

"Yes, ma'am. I will."

Paisley and Luna had been dropped off at school; he would be back in time for dinner without any suspicion of where he had been. Dean walked over to his tractor with purpose, certain that his decision to spend time with Rayna without nosey eyes on them was a worthwhile, harmless endeavor. He put the basket off to the side, cranked the engine so it could warm up in the glassed-in cab and then sent Rayna a text. He was grateful that she responded right away, and the fact that she'd said "the package is in transit" made him smile.

Dean waved to some of the ranch hands on his way to the creek that crossed both properties, Legend and Brand. He drove the tractor up a hill, taking it slow and steady over the icy terrain. At the top of a hill, he saw the woods and the creek, and then he saw Rayna sitting in a sturdy John Deere Gator, waiting for him.

Rayna jumped out when she saw him. She waved her

arms, and she looked so beautiful in her excitement and happiness to see him.

"Well, that's an upgrade," she called up to him about the tractor. It was a one-hundred-thousand-dollar John Deere and certainly an upgrade from the antiquated tractors they used to have at their disposal.

"Your ride or mine?" he asked her.

"Yours!" She smiled up at him. "I want to drive it."

Rayna drove the Gator a few feet into the woods and parked it out of sight. Then she walked quickly to the tractor.

Dean opened the door, reached out a hand, and she took it, climbed into the cab and sat down on the small seat next the driver's chair.

"On the way back, she'll be all yours."

Chapter Ten

"Where are you taking me?" Rayna asked him.

"Now, why would I ruin the surprise like that?"

This new John Deere tractor was a monster and easily navigated the terrain that was rocky, snowy and, at times, slick like glass. And it didn't hurt that Rayna was impressed by it; Dean thought that picking her up in this tractor was similar to picking up a date in a Maserati when he'd lived in the city.

"Time to close your eyes."

"What?!" Rayna exclaimed.

"Trust me."

"Fine," she said with a teasing tone. Then she did as he asked and covered her eyes.

Dean loved the feeling of having Rayna back by his side. The sensation of having her body this close to his lit up the pleasure centers of his brain like no other experience had in recent memory. He didn't want to get ahead of himself, but the way Rayna was sitting beside him, leaning into his body instead of away toward the glass of the cab made him believe that the resurgence of comfort and love they'd had in their youth was being reborn in both of them in real time.

When he reached their destination, Dean stopped the tractor and turned it off. In front of him there was a project he had worked on, little by little, since he had moved back to Montana with his girls. This place was so special to him that he hadn't shared it with anyone, and he had never thought to share it with Rayna.

"Okay," he said. "Open your eyes, Ray."

He kept his eyes trained on Rayna's face; he wanted to remember this moment for the rest of his life regardless of how long this reunion would last.

Rayna opened her eyes, and she stared at what he had created. At first she didn't even blink as it began to sink in where he had brought her and what he had done. Then, when Rayna did blink her eyes, a couple of tears dropped off of her lower lashes onto her reddened cheeks.

"Our tree house?" Rayna brought her hand up to her mouth as she met his singular gaze.

"Yes," he said with a satisfied smile, "with a few minor upgrades. Do you want to check it out?"

She nodded wordlessly. He had imagined her reaction should she ever see his painstaking restoration and upgrade of their childhood tree house, but nothing in his imagination compared to the reaction he was witnessing now.

Dean grabbed their lunch and met Rayna at the front of the tractor. Her eyes were bouncing from one detail to the next, and it felt as if she were trying to take it all in and process the changes. He had installed a winding staircase up the original structure that they had built together, one piece of scrap wood at a time. Most of the structure hadn't been salvageable, but he had repurposed the wood to build the staircase and to flooring inside. What Ray would find on the inside was a lovely one-room space outfitted with thick insulation on the floor, walls and roof as well as a solar floor-heating system that would warm up the space.

"What do you think?" he prodded her, impatient to hear her thoughts.

"I'm shocked." She walked over to the stairs that would lead them to the front door. "In the best of ways. Shocked."

That made him smile, and her reaction was all of the validation he needed. "You're pleased?"

"Pleased, surprised, shocked, excited, nostalgic, loved. Pick any and all synonyms, and it wouldn't fully capture what I'm feeling right now." Rayna walked over to the old tire swing hanging off one of the large branches. "You kept this."

"I did." He nodded. "I couldn't bring myself to change it."

They had scored this tire from her father's large work-shop. Her father had stored many things in his workshop—Rose had called it junk and her father called it his treasures. Either way, that tire was special in that it had belonged to her father.

"I'm glad you didn't," Rayna said, and before he knew what she was doing, she had climbed onto the top of the swing.

"Push me!"

"Ray." He put the food basket down "I left it for show, not use. I'd bet money that it's not in usable condition."

"Where is Daredevil Dean hiding? Is he still in there, or has he been totally and completely crushed by *Get Off My Lawn* Dean?"

She was pricking his ego, and he knew that; he just didn't quite know what he was going to do about it.

"It's sturdy, Dean!" Rayna held on to the rope and bounced up and down on the tire. "Come on! Push me!"

When she called out to him to be pushed, Rayna had a smile of pure joy on her face, and it made her so lovely to

him and it took him back to a time and place that was simple, innocent, with a whole life ahead of him. And he found
that he was quite incapable of resisting Rayna now in the
same way he had been incapable of resisting her back then.

"Okay," he finally said. "If you get hurt, that's on you!"

Dean gripped the bottom part of the tire, backed up as
far as he could and then let go. Rayna laughed happily, leaning back and let the tire spin her around. When she came
back to him, he pushed her again and again. Her winter cap
had fallen off, and her hair, a lovely shade of mahogany red
brown, swung out behind her.

"I feel dizzy!" She laughed through those words.

"Ready to stop?" he asked.

"Yes!" She closed her eyes and sat up straight on the
tire. "Too dizzy!"

After he grabbed the tire, chased it a couple of steps to
get the tire to stop swinging, he asked, "Are you okay?"

She was holding on to the rope, her eyes still closed
tightly, but the smile on her face hadn't changed. After
a minute, she opened her eyes, grinned at him and said,
"Your turn."

She rejected his offered hand, pulled her body up an
inch, moved her legs apart like an in-air split and then
hopped down to the ground.

"No." He shook his head. "Not a chance. This rope *will
not* hold me. We got lucky with you. Look at this." He
pointed to rot on the rope that made it brittle and frayed.

Instead of making a verbal counterargument, Rayna put
her hands on her hips, bent over a bit and then started to
flap her arms and cluck like a chicken.

"Are you calling me a chicken?"

"If the feathers fit."

"I cannot believe that you would stoop that low, Ray."

Dean grabbed the rope, tugged on it, knowing that it was a terrible idea in advance. Rayna was half of his weight. He didn't have a whole lot of hope for things to go as well for him as they had gone for Rayna, but she was flat-out calling him out for being a chicken, and that was an accusation that *could not* go unanswered.

She was still clucking when he tried to jump onto the tire—this was something that Ray had made look very easy. The third time was the charm for him, and he finally hoisted himself onto the tire. His weight made the tire sink significantly, and he was sure that he had heard the tree limb moan along with some snapping sounds from the rope above.

"Ready?" Rayna grabbed the bottom of the tire with both hands, said, "Set," and then she did her best to pull him backward a bit. "Go!"

"More?" she asked. "Or do you want to tap out?"

"Bring it!" Dean refused to have only one turn on the tire as his legacy. But this pride he was clinging to did not change his awareness of the structural weaknesses in both the old, weathered rope and the tree limb struggling under his weight.

Rayna pushed him again, laughing happily. Her fun was his fun, so he held on for dear life and prayed that everything would "hold" until this terrible swing ride ended for him. She gave him one really hard push. He swung forward and then swung back toward her, and then it happened—the rope snapped like an uncooked spaghetti noodle, and he dropped, landing on his backside in the snow. The force of her preparing to pull him back and then the tire dropping instead sent her off-balance, and she landed on her backside next to him.

"Are you okay?" he asked as he lay flat on his back, the

snow melting beneath him seeping into the material of his jeans while he took a physical inventory.

Ray was still laughing. "God, yes! Are you okay?"

Dean pushed himself into the seated position and looked at her. "Didn't I *tell* you it wasn't structurally sound?"

"Yes, grouchy." Rayna easily stood up with a catlike grace. She reached down to help him up, and he didn't feel one bit of shame accepting the hand.

"Why does everyone keep calling me grouchy?" he asked, trying to brush the snow off the back of his body.

"Because," she said, "you are!"

"I'm just a man with a lot of responsibilities."

"Those two things are not mutually exclusive, right?" she asked, her lovely eyes a vivid bright blue. "You can be a man with a lot of responsibilities *and* a grouch."

He frowned at her. His daughters had, at times, wanted him to be happier, but the way Rayna said it to him—in a way that perhaps only Rayna could—sunk in.

Was he really a killjoy? Was he incapable of truly having fun?

Dean walked over, picked up the basket and joined her at the bottom of the stairs.

She reached out and put her hand on his arm "Don't let this ruin our time together. I haven't felt this...*free* in years. I want to hold on to it, okay?"

The way she looked up at him with eyes so filled with delight, he couldn't stay in the bad mood that had already begun to creep into this moment with Ray.

"Okay," he said and meant it. Together, they walked up the spiral staircase he had built. At the top of the stairs, there was a door that he had stained by hand. He took out a key that was on the key ring with the tractor keys, and he unlocked the door. Then he opened the door, pushed it open and backed up so Rayna could enter the tree house first.

"Oh, Dean." She turned around in a circle, admiring all of his hard work with wide eyes.

His enjoyment came directly from her response—she loved it, and that filled his heart. Dean put the basket down on a small café table while Rayna continued to explore his craftsmanship.

"It's pretty warm in here," she said in amazement, unzipping her jacket.

"We've got thick insulation top to bottom," he said with pride. "And radiant heated floors."

Dean took off his coat and hung it up on hooks made of horseshoes near the front door. He took her jacket and did the same. Everything he had put into the space had been chosen with Rayna in mind—knowing that even if she didn't ever see it, it had made him happy to do it.

"This is amazing," Rayna said. "*You* are amazing. Your daughters must love it."

Caught off guard, Dean thought for a split second before he said, "They've never been here."

"Dean. Why not?"

He breathed in deeply, blew it out through his nose, looked down at his feet for a bit and then lifted his head up. "I just needed something that was mine."

Rayna crossed the space between them. "And mine."

"And yours."

"Why do you need so many places to hide, Dean?"

That question hit its mark and after a minute, he said, "I feel like a camel who can't handle one more straw. Being a single father, Dad, divorce, the responsibility of the ranch. It's a lot." He said. "When it all gets too much, I find a nice comfortable hiding spot and regroup."

Wordlessly, Rayna walked over to him and gave him a hug.

After a bit, he said, "I'm hungry. Are you?"

"I am." Rayna laughed. "My stomach has been anticipating whatever goodies Miss Minnie packed for us."

"But," Dean said, grateful that Rayna was willing to pivot from a very serious topic and move on to the more safe territory of *food*, "my hind parts are cold and wet. And I don't want to come across as this being a part of my plan..."

"Can you ditch the drawers?"

Dean nodded and was grateful that she agreed. He pulled off his boots in short order and then yanked off his pants. Granted, his underwear was also damp, but he could handle that. His cheeks were feeling hot because he hadn't imagined that he would be in his tighty-whities and his old socks with tired elastic and a hole in the big toe on the left one.

Rayna must have sensed his discomfort because she kicked off her boots and stripped off her jeans. She had looked him over, but he did his darn best not to do the same. But in the peripheral, he saw her shapely thighs and legs. He had known that she was dedicated to her yoga practice from social media and he had seen her in figure-hugging yoga clothing in his feed, but to see it in person was different. She had always been beautiful, and that hadn't changed one centimeter for him.

Dean held out her chair for her and then joined her at the table. They unpacked lunch and fed their hunger. She had noticed a definitive uptick in her hunger since moving to Montana—no doubt it was her position as "Chief Mucker in Charge" was burning up calories with lightning speed. Hideaway Ranch was operating on a skeleton crew to save money. After Thanksgiving and in final preparations for their first guests, ranch hands would be returning. Most importantly, Wayne's youngest brother, Waylon, would be arriving from a visit to Texas in two days, and she would be able to shift some of her duties onto his shoulders.

"Oh my lord," she said when she polished off her second egg salad sandwich. "The woman is a genius in the kitchen. I shouldn't be cooking for our guests—she should!"

"Them's fightin' words, little lady," Dean teased her.

After a couple of minutes of comfortable silence, she said to him, "This is a weird scene."

"Very weird."

"If anyone had told me that I would be sitting in this tree house with you in our skivvies, I would have insisted they get their head examined."

Dean wiped off his mouth, tossed the napkin into the basket, closed the top and then leaned back in his chair with a satisfied look on his face. A mountain of a man had replaced the boy she had known. He was really tall, with broad thick shoulders and a full beard. His hands were rough and strong. He was showing his age with the wrinkles around his eyes and worry lines between his eyebrows. She liked his hair worn long like this and found herself returning to his lips. She had happily kissed those lips hundreds of times—would it be the same to kiss him now?

Dean patted his belly with his hands. He was thicker around the middle than she had ever seen him. He was active, but he wasn't burning off all of those calories he was consuming. It would be hard to resist down-home, stick-to-your-ribs home-cooked meals made from scratch by Miss Minnie or Paisley. When she had joined the Legends for dinner, she had taken two huge serving-spoon helpings of mashed potatoes, glopped them onto her plate, then added butter and salt and pepper, and then she had hoovered them in a way she could only describe as "unladylike." If she ate with the Dean's family regularly, all of the yoga in the world wouldn't prevent her from packing on the pounds.

In a thermos, Dean had brought coffee for the end of the meal. He took a couple of mugs out of a cabinet nearby and poured them each a piping-hot black coffee, just like the both of them preferred it. They moved over to the love seat.

"Mmm," she said when she tasted the coffee. "Strong."

Dean nodded, blowing on the coffee in his mug. "No other way."

"Totally."

They enjoyed their coffee, and Rayna felt relaxed with Dean. It was a strange sensation because in twenty years of marriage with Ben, she couldn't remember ever feeling this way. With him, she'd always been on edge; with his family, she'd always been on edge. Now that pressure was gone, and what was left was an overwhelming feeling of regret and loss mixed with eager anticipation for what might unfold in her life next.

She looked down at her mug and wondered if she should give voice to the loud, persistent words in her head.

"What?" Dean asked her. She had noticed how he examined her face; she noticed how she felt when he looked at her with total acceptance and appreciation.

"I'm sorry," she said with an emotional waver in her voice.

"For what?" he asked her, his concerned gaze on her.

She tapped her chipped fingernail on the ceramic of her mug. "For ending things between us the way that I did."

Dean reached out and put his hand on her arm briefly. "Let that go, Ray. I already have. Years ago."

She nodded, brushing a tear off of her cheek. She didn't

respond because she was afraid that more words would unleash the floodgate and all of the emotions—anger, frustration, disappointment and shame—might surface in a way she wouldn't want them to. No control.

"Talk to me, Ray," Dean said in a voice filled with concern and kindness for her. "Tell me what's on your mind."

"When I left for college, all I could think about was getting away from here. Going to college, I guess, was my get-out-of-jail card."

She saw the pain in his moss-green eyes as much as he tried to hide it from her.

"I didn't want to be knee deep in mud and cow manure during the rainy season for the rest of my life. I didn't want to spend winters out in the middle of the night birthing calves because for some reason, the time when cows felt compelled to give birth were always on the coldest, darkest, wettest nights."

That brought a smile to his lips. It was true, and he couldn't deny it. The life on a cattle ranch was never easy. It was, at times, rewarding, but the life was hard and exhausting. It always had been, and it always would be. The question for any rancher or farmer was a fundamental one that needed to be answered—was this life in their blood? For her, it hadn't been.

"That didn't mean that I didn't…don't…" She stopped and regrouped in her mind. "I loved you, Dean. I promise you that I did."

"I know you did," he said. "You showed it to me in so many different ways."

"I made a decision, and I have paid dearly for it." She stared into her mug.

"I'm not following."

She put her mug down on the nearby end table, threaded

her hands together and rested them in her lap. In that moment, Rayna didn't even feel like she could look him in the eyes.

"I lost time with my parents. I lost time with *your* parents. I lost time with…you." Those words hurt to think, and they were even more painful to say. She felt the guilt she had lived with for so many years and now it felt like she was drowning in it. "But I can't go back."

Dean put his mug down, tugged her hands free of their clutch and held them in his. "Neither of us can go back, Ray. None of us can."

She nodded, swallowing back her tears.

"Hey," Dean said gently, still holding her hands in his. "If there was a switch on this wall right here, and if you pulled it and it would take us back to when were eighteen or nineteen, would you do it, knowing that you wouldn't have your boys and I wouldn't have my girls?"

She shook her head. "No. I wouldn't."

He shook his head too. "And neither would I."

"So you forgive me?"

"There's nothing to forgive, Ray," he said. "Was I hurt? Absolutely, I was. But I forgave you a long time ago. You need to forgive yourself because you didn't do anything wrong. You lived your life the best way you knew how to do."

That short conversation seemed like the period on the end of their clandestine tree house rendezvous. They both needed to get back to the real world, so they put on their wet jeans, cleaned up the space and then headed back down to the tractor. As good on his word, Dean let her drive the tractor back to where she had left her Gator. When they reached the Gator, Dean climbed down to the ground and walked her to the all-terrain vehicle.

Before she got into the Gator, Rayna paused. "I didn't know how I would feel having you back in my life. I was nervous about it, really."

"Me too," he acknowledged before he asked, "How about now?"

She gave him the truth that he deserved: "I've never felt more comfortable around anyone, other than my boys, than I feel with you."

"Bless it, Ray." Dean looked away and pinched the top of his nose with his fingers to stop tears from forming. When he turned back, he said, "I'm grateful to have you back in my life. I'm doing my best not to focus on the future because I don't want to miss the moments I have with you right now."

He looked directly into her eyes and held her there and then said, "I love you, Ray. I always have, and I always will."

It took her longer to say the words that she already knew were in her heart: "I love you, Dean. I always have, and I always will."

They hugged each other and promised to meet back at the tree house soon. Before Rayna let him go, she rose up on to the tips of her toes and kissed him on the cheek. "Thank you, Dean, for one of the best days of my life."

"I'm pulling the plug on the new build for now," Charlie said on video. Then she started to cough and sneeze at the same time. After she could manage to speak again, she said, "We've been fighting this build for over a month now, and we just can't get it done."

While on their trip to Helena, Charlie and Wayne had both gotten COVID, which had put the kibosh on the already painstakingly slow process to build another cabin for guests. Charlie's face was beet red, her eyes were watery and puffy and her voice was weak. "One minute I'm hot, then next I'm freezing. My skin hurts. Can you believe that? It actually hurts."

They were having their weekly meeting about the ranch with all three of them in attendance—Rayna was in the camper, Danica was in her real-estate office in LA and Charlie in her cabin that she shared with Wayne.

"It would've been nice to have, but it's okay to put that on the back burner," Danica said. "Skiing season starts right before Thanksgiving, the Big Sky resort is booked and running a cancel list, and from what I'm seeing, all of the Airbnb options are booked too."

"What does that mean for us?" Charlie coughed, blew her nose and then threw away the crumpled tissue.

"With the exception of the blocked weeks designated for our families, we're booked now through the end of April," Danica said with her million-dollar brilliant white smile. "This is redemption for our family on steroids!"

Charlie was not known for her silence but was quiet while she processed that information. Rayna asked the question for both of them: "As in, we're booked for five months? The entire skiing season?"

"Yes, that's it. We're officially in business. I hope we—i.e., you guys—are ready for it. The block of weeks for our families will give you some time to breathe, get some rest and then get the place ready for the next group." Danica tucked her ice-blond hair behind her ear, showing large sparkly diamond studs. Even though Rayna and Danica were identical twins, she didn't resemble Danica all that much. A person would really have to search their features to come to that conclusion. She was beautiful and glamorous in a way Ray would never be, and Ray loved that about her and she was happy for her. As early as she could remember, Danica had wanted to be a model and actress. Now she was a Realtor for the rich and famous, and she had built, along with her longstanding boyfriend, Grant, an empire.

Charlie dropped her head into her hands. Wayne walked by sporting a bathrobe over his jeans. "Hey."

"Feel better!" Danica and Ray shouted.

"Your lips to God's ears." Wayne, keeping on brand, disappeared as quickly as he had appeared.

"Charlie?" Rayna said. "What's wrong?"

"I thought you would be thrilled," Danica said.

Their sister lifted her head, and she had tears on her face. "I'm happy. I'm relieved. I'm overwhelmed with gratitude. I know our parents are looking down on us now, so proud that we came together and saved this ranch. We saved our family legacy."

Charlie had carried the burden of trying to save the family ranch. She had refused to sell off land bit by bit, and she'd clawed and scraped and fought until all was almost lost after their mother had died. Now she had the support from her sisters as well as Wayne and his brothers. Of course it was overwhelming for her. It would be for almost anyone.

"We love you, Charlie," they said in unison.

Charlie wiped the tears from her eyes, blew her nose again and then said in her hoarse, rough voice, "I love you so much."

Danica then asked, "Are you willing to stay on until end of April, Ray? Even if Aspen is back in Montana, she'll have a newborn at home."

"I can stay until April."

"Well, that was easy," Danica said, surprised. "I was expecting some sort of objection."

After a coughing jag, Charlie said, "She's been sneaking off with Dean Legend. Maybe *that* has something to do with it!"

Danica's face lit up. "Okay, now we're cooking! Pun totally intended."

"I have not been *sneaking* anywhere!" Rayna denied, but the truth was all over her face to be read by her sisters. "Besides, I'm too old to sneak."

"Well, I say good for you! I hope I still have some romantic trysts left in me."

"Danny! What about Grant?"

Danica frowned with a dismissive shrug. "He's not invited. I swear that man could suck the fun right out of a balloon."

Chapter Eleven

Even though Dean and Rayna had promised to plan a secret rendezvous at their tree house, everything had worked against them. Charlie and Wayne had caught COVID, and that put them out of commission, so all of the farm chores fell to Rayna. On his end, Paisley had caught the flu and his focus needed to be on getting her well in advance of her mother's arrival. He was still seeing a regular list of clients for hoof trimming and shoeing, but when one dropped off, he didn't replace them. Today he was heading over to Hideaway to trim and shod the horses; he was looking forward to seeing Rayna. Even though they hadn't seen each other in person, they were texting regularly now and video chatting at night after the girls had gone to bed. He had begun to rely on those talks, begun to rely on hearing Rayna's infectious laugh and admiring her pretty face. And he liked the fact that he felt *connected* with her again.

Dean pulled off the road onto the long drive leading to the heart of the Brand ranch. Right after he turned, he saw Rayna standing off on the left side of the road, looking around like she'd lost something, snapping pictures with her phone and making notes in a binder she carried. He slowed down, rolled down his window and waved her over.

When she saw him, her face so lit up with love, acceptance and joy that it touched his heart in a way that he hadn't known existed; he loved Ray in a way that he hadn't known existed. And when she looked at him like she was right now, he knew that his deep, abiding love was returned.

"Hey!" She reached him, her auburn hair tussled by the wind and her pretty face with a natural glow.

"Hey yourself." He held out his hand to capture hers. "What are you up to?"

"I'm planning out the Christmas decorations! I'm thinking that I'll put garlands on the two poles and the top pole above the gate, with a festive wreath, of course, and along the drive, I'll put lights on all of the trees, which are evenly spaced thanks to my mom's precise measuring when she originally planted these trees, and maybe I could even hang some wreaths on the trees or tie huge red-and-green bows on the trunks? So many options! My head is teeming with them! When I go to sleep, I fall asleep with twinkling Christmas lights in my head, and when I wake up, my first thought is *Christmas*!"

Dean just loved watching Rayna when she was excited about something, and she was certainly excited about decorating the ranch for Christmas. Her light, her energy and her zest for life were infectious.

"Can I give you a lift?" he asked.

"Sure!" Rayna nodded happily, trotted around to the passenger side and climbed in. "This way I can tell you the rest of my plans for the decorations!"

She asked him to drive more slowly so she could explain her vision. "So with these trees that line the drive, I'll use alternating red-and-green lights. I want the colors of Christmas to be ever present but in a *less is more* kind of way."

"You'll be using solar to get the energy way out here?"

"Yes," she said. "Wayne said he would be able to do it,

but honestly, he's really struggling getting over COVID. His brother Waylon is willing to help, but we're still running a skeleton crew until after Thanksgiving and there's more to do than one man can handle—heck, more than five men could handle! So I may just do it myself. Ben didn't help me decorate for the holidays, not even with the outside lights. Nope! That was all me. So I can do it here too."

"Well," Dean said, "if you need help, you'll let me know."

"Okay," she said. "I will."

Rayna pointed out all of the decoration details for the main house and the barn. "The guests want to pick out a tree, and then they'll decorate it. I've bought some *amazing* ornaments!"

Dean pulled in through the second gate, drove around the circular drive and then backed his rig until it was nearly touching the barn door.

"Well, this was my lucky day to find you needing a ride."

About to overflow with Christmas excitement, Rayna threw caution to the wind, leaned over, gave him a quick peck on his cheek. "This isn't the first time you've come to my rescue."

Darn it if he wasn't blushing like a teenage boy on his first date after Rayna had kissed him. "Well, it's been my pleasure."

She opened the door, but before she got out, she turned back to look at him. "Dean Legend, are you blushing?"

He looked at himself in the rearview mirror. "No. I'm a tough Montana cattleman, Ray. We don't blush. But on occasion, we do get windburn."

Rayna understood the joke, and she laughed along with him as she jumped out of the truck without thought. Her transformation had been swift from the time he'd first seen her when she'd been wearing so many layers of clothing that she could barely walk and couldn't bend her arms in any meaningful way. The woman who was "woman-handling" the barn door open had transformed: she was wearing a normal amount of winter clothing, she had boots that helped her stay steady on the icy patches and she now walked with renewed energy, shoulders back and head up with what he would characterize as self-confidence and self-pride.

They walked into the barn together. She helped him lug some of his tools into the barn, and then they closed the doors behind them to keep the warmth generated by the animals inside.

"Don't you just love the smell of manure in the morning?" he teased her.

"Okay. Don't judge me—I actually *do love* the smell of the barn in the morning."

"No judgment here." Dean smiled. "I've got the same affliction."

He started with Atlas with the heavy soup-plates for hooves. While he worked, they talked about everything and a whole lot of nothing—just keeping each other company. It was easy between them, and he really liked that.

"How's Paisley?" Rayna asked.

"She's feeling better, thank the Lord."

"I'm glad to hear it."

Dean nodded and then asked, "How about Wayne and Charlie? You said Wayne's still struggling—what about Charlie?"

"They're getting better every day, but I'm telling you, it really knocked them back. Wayne's brother, Waylon, came back after a quick trip and I was never happier to see someone. I've built up some stamina for barn work, but I'm still adjusting. And it never stops. That's the thing—this never stops. But it also motivates me: I have a reason greater than myself to get up in the morning. For the longest time, my sons motivated me. Now…" She looked around at all of the animals in the barn. "These lovely creatures serve as my motivation. Yes, I give to them, but they give tenfold back to me."

Dean looked up from his task and smiled at her. "Spoken like a true-grit cowgirl."

"You know what?" Rayna lifted her chin with what he read was a sense of pride. "I'll own that. True-grit cowgirl. Yes, I guess I am after all."

"Well I'm glad you've finally come to that conclusion." Dean moved around the horse. "By the way, Dad has asked that you join us for dinner tomorrow and Luna wanted to remind you that you promised to come watch her ride tomorrow."

"I thought we were going to insulate Paisley from…" She pointed to him and then to herself. "This. Especially when we don't even really know what *this* is."

He stood upright, turned around, looked her straight in the eye so both of them didn't mistake this moment when he said, "I think we both know what this is, Ray."

"Maybe we do," she said, chewing on the side of her nail. "But we agreed to take it real slow."

"I know. I get it. So slow that a snail could pass us by."

That returned a smile on to her face. "So slow a glacier could beat us in a head to head race!"

"Yes, we did say that. And we will. Okay." Dean patted Atlas on the rump, "But Dad wants to see you regularly, and what reason could I possibly give him that you won't come over? You lit up his life, Ray. I haven't seen him that animated and, God damn, *happy* in months!"

"I am always so happy to see him."

"And Luna thinks you're the coolest person ever."

That brought a pleased smile to her face. "So why shouldn't she get to spend time with you?" he asked her before he returned to his work.

"I don't know, Dean. I really don't know."

Dean moved onto another hoof. "What don't you know, Ray? We aren't going to French kiss in front of her. I'd like our first kiss in twenty years to be a private affair."

He looked up at her, and she was listening, not trying to interject. He finished Atlas and walked him back to his stall. Before he started on another horse, he walked over to where she was standing.

"Here's the deal, Ray—as you know, my ex-wife is engaged."

"How are the girls taking it?"

"Not well. Either of them, actually," Dean told her. "Cat was planning on Nico joining them on this ski trip and we agreed, finally, that this was not the best idea."

Rayna kept on biting the skin on the side of her nail. "So actually you made my point for me! Paisley is already facing so much in her young life. Why pile on?"

"Do you know one of the traits that I love the most about you, Ray? You're so thoughtful and kind to everyone and everything around you. I know that you're sincere in wanting to protect Paisley from more heartache."

"Yes," she said.

"You're back in my life now, and I have no intention of losing you again. Paisley's feelings get top billing from me, but she has to accept that Cat and I are not getting back together. I know that's what she wants, but it isn't grounded in reality." He stopped to make sure Rayna was focused on his words. "But I'm worried that you're using Paisley as a way to keep me a safe distance away from you, Ray."

"I don't think I'm deliberately keeping you at bay, Dean.

I just don't think it's fair for us to give your eldest girl yet another reason to be destabilized, insecure, hurt or replaced. Especially when we don't even know what we're doing."

Dean closed the distance between them. "I know exactly what we're doing, Ray. And I think you do too."

Rayna frowned, and she was quiet for a couple of seconds before she said slowly, "If I'm being honest with myself, yes, I love being with you and being around you. I feel like a giddy schoolgirl whenever I think of you, and I get really excited when I know we're going to see each other again. But this is not the time for us to be selfish—the last thing I want to do is cause your dad, your daughters, you, me…"

Dean took hold of her hand and led her to the nearby tack room. In the dark, he put his hands gently on either side of her lovely face and touched his lips to hers. It was a sweet kiss that for him held so much promise about tomorrow and the rest of their lives. They stood together in the barn where they had shared their very first kiss; and now, to share another first kiss, twenty years later, felt like a divine appointment. Dean believed in his gut that this was their path—to build another relationship that included her sons, his daughters and all of the rest of their extended families.

"You kissed me," Rayna said to him.

"Our second first kiss." Dean put his arms around her and drew her close to him, grateful that she didn't pull away.

He could feel her heart fluttering and her breathing deepen, and what Rayna decided to do next could solidify the path they were going to forge together—one path would take them in the direction of a holiday fling that ended when the snow melted; the other path led them to love and marriage. A real second chance for them—that was what he wanted more than anything else. The question was, did Rayna want it?

A long sigh escaped from her parted lips, and then she put her hands on his chest, raised up on the tips of her toes and kissed him. Slow and easy, with an invitation for more—and he didn't need to be invited twice. He wrapped her up in his arms and kissed her like the hungry man that he was. The feel of her body next to his, the feel of her soft lips kissing him back and the sweet smell of her skin sent him to the moon and back. When he broke the kiss, they stood together, both breathing with shallow breaths, holding on to each other as if neither of them wanted to let go.

"So, you'll come tomorrow?"

"Yes," she said, "I will."

And now with all of the formalities out of the way, Dean was mighty pleased that they were *both* smiling when he went in to seal their deal with a fourth kiss.

Later that day, Rayna's car and belongings were delivered. Waylon had arrived a few days ago and was on hand to help guide the semitruck through some slushy spots on the long drive. Waylon Westbrook looked like a younger, much taller version of Wayne—they had the same intense blue eyes, the same strong nose and chin, and while Wayne had more salt than pepper in his hair now, Waylon's hair was a deep brown that he now wore long enough to put in a ponytail. From what she could tell, Waylon was a hard worker who wasn't much of a talker—just like Wayne.

Waylon whistled as the driver began the process of offloading the top-of-the-line Jaguar F-Type R75. "She's a beauty. Mom has a similar one. It wouldn't be my first choice for Montana, but she's right pretty."

Ben had given her this car for what had turned out to

be their last Christmas together. At the time she hadn't approved of the purchase, but since it was a gift, she'd chosen to accept it in the spirit she'd believed it had been given. That car was one of the things that had needed to be paid off when their house had sold—one hundred and fifty thousand dollars.

"Does she want another one?" Rayna asked about the Jag.

That question made Waylon smile before he stopped the driver. "We've got to back her up more. This car will get stuck the minute the tires hit the ground, and the engine is so ramped up that it won't be able to get traction."

Thankfully, with Waylon's help, her Jag was off loaded into her father's enormous workshop, which had been labeled in the past year as the "Everything Barn" where it would be safe while she figured out what to do with it. No matter if she stayed in Montana or returned to Connecticut, this Jag didn't represent her any longer. When she'd played the role of Rayna Fortier, long-suffering wife of aloof Benjamin Fortier, perhaps it had been a good fit, but not now and not ever again.

Waylon helped the driver take boxes off of the truck. She offered to lend a hand, but Waylon respectfully asked her to let him take care of it for her—the ground was slippery, and the boxes were heavy. Once the boxes were stacked neatly in her father's office that had climate control, Waylon guided the driver out of the main area of the ranch and sent him on his way.

"Need anything else?" He stopped by the office where she had been standing looking at the boxes her friend had packed for her.

"No," she said distractedly. "I'm good."

"Okay." He gave her a thumbs-up. "I'm going to get started on some chores."

"Thank you," she said. "I started out strong, but I've kind of fizzled a bit…"

"You did great holding down the fort, Rayna. You're a rock star."

She called Zuri and left a message thanking her for all of the work she did to help her transition from Connecticut to Montana. Then she stood staring at the boxes for what seemed like a rather long time until she found a knife in her father's desk, and she cut the tape on one of the boxes. She opened the box slowly and then looked at the clothing neatly folded inside. Could she have changed so quickly in such a short time that these clothes seemed to belong to someone else? She dug through the box filled with de-signer-label suits, dresses and business casual until she hit a gold mine of yoga clothes. She pulled those out and then shut the box. She now had boxes of clothing that seemed foreign to her and then the car. Even if she did decide to keep it, where would she get it serviced? Now, hindsight being twenty-twenty, it wasn't the best idea she'd ever had to ship it here in the first place.

Dean sent her a text, and she read it quickly and then sent the reply Heading out now.

She pulled the heavy barn door shut, dropped her yoga clothes into the camper and then hopped into her father's old truck and headed to the Legend ranch. Recently the window in the truck had decided to stop rolling up, so she had put on a wool cap, a thick scarf and braved the cold air as she cautiously navigated the long drive to the main road. When she was driving this old rust bucket of a truck that had arthritic doors that groaned and creaked as it was opened or closed, a tendency to fishtail when it hit any water or ice, with the stuck speedometer, the driver's door that could only be opened from the outside and now, the window that wouldn't roll up—with all of that to speak against it, Rayna preferred it to the luxurious, sleek, with windows and a heater that worked, Jaguar.

Rayna felt her stomach flip-flop as she turned onto the drive that would take her to the Legend family home. The scene today was much different than her last visit—horse trailers were parked on the side of the drive, and girls who appeared to be around Luna's age were walking horses into the barn. There was a palpable energy in the air that managed to take her out of her head and focused her attention on what was unfolding before her in the moment.

"Rayna!" Luna was racing down the steps leading up to the main house. She'd been about to head left to the barn, but when she spotted Ray, Luna changed direction and ran over to where she was parking the truck.

Rayna felt her body fill up with unconditional love for Dean's younger child. The girl's lovely eyes were alight with joy at seeing her, and how could she deny that it felt incredible to be accepted by Luna in this way?

She managed to get the door open, stepped out and Luna threw herself into her arms and hugged her tightly. The girl was still light enough to spin her around in a circle while she laughed contagiously.

"I'm so glad you came!" Luna shouted when Rayna put her down.

"I promised I would." She held on to Luna's shoulder for a second until she didn't feel dizzy.

"Okay! I'll see you later!" Luna peeled away, went to go get her cowgirl hat that had flown off when she'd launched herself into Rayna's arms. Once the hat was back on her head, Luna waved at her and then ran full tilt to the barn.

Before heading to the barn, Rayna wanted to see Buck. He'd been asking for her every day, and she never wanted to do anything that might upset him. And it might have taken her a minute to process it, but keeping herself away for Paisley's sake had hurt Buck unintentionally. She did see Dean's point about balancing everyone's needs, not just his eldest daughter's needs. And having come over to his side of the topic, Rayna would be patient with Paisley and make sure she set boundaries with Dean that were sensitive to the emotional burden she was carrying. Just inside the door, she took off her jacket and hung it up before she headed to the library.

"Hi, Dad," Rayna said.

Buck's expression brightened. "Daughter! Where have you been? I thought you forgot all about this old man."

She waved at Greta, who sitting near the wall of windows where the sun was flooding into the room, watching the activity outside. She walked over to his bed, where he was propped up so he could watch the day unfolding outside. She hugged him tightly and said, "I'm sorry, Dad. I was the only one holding down the fort. Charlie and Wayne came down with COVID."

The nurse perked up when she heard that, and Rayna added, "I haven't been anywhere near them."

"Come, sit," Buck said, waving his hand at a nearby chair.

She pulled the chair closer, sat down and took his hand in hers.

"Dean said that you'll be staying for dinner?" he asked.

"Yes. Thank you."

"Good, good," he said and then repeated, "I've missed you."

"I'm sorry, Dad. Truly I am." She squeezed his hand. "I'll do better."

"Okay, dear one," Buck said after a coughing fit was over. Rayna felt Buck Legend had always been such a force in everyone's lives who encountered him, and it was very difficult to accept that he was now slipping away from them little by little. She did her best to keep those thoughts hidden but it was difficult, and hiding those feelings from Buck didn't make them hurt any less on the inside. It cut clean and deep like a hot knife through butter.

"I'd better get out there so I don't miss Luna."

"Yes, of course, go quick!" Buck said having difficulty catching his breath. "I love you, my daughter."

Rayna stood up, hugged him tightly. "I love you too, Dad."

Dean looked around the bustling activity in the equestrian barn he had built and saw his vision, his idea coming to life before him. The stalls were filled with well-groomed horses, the tack room was the epicenter of activities for the girls in Luna's 4-H club and the parents and trainers alike were complimentary and impressed by the design of the facility. He felt proud of his work and like he had done the exact right thing for Luna.

"How's it going, ladybug?" He found her in the tack room, talking loudly and happily while grabbing some snacks off of the table.

"This is the best day ever!" Luna lifted up her arms and spread them apart and grinned at him.

He gave her a quick hug. "I'm glad."

"Rayna's here."

"She is?"

"Yep. She is."

Figuring she was in the main house, Dean set out to find

her. On the way out of the barn, cutting the corner close, he bumped into her as she was also cutting the corner.

"Hey!" Rayna laughed.

"Hey yourself." Dean's heart filled up with happiness whenever he laid eyes on her. Every moment with Rayna was precious to him. "Good thing you still wear so much padding."

"Very funny."

He smiled at her and said, "Did you see Dad?"

"Yes." Rayna nodded and a cloud came into her eyes. "I have to do better. I would never hurt him intentionally."

"You wouldn't hurt *anyone* intentionally, Ray." As they walked together, side by side but not hand in hand, toward the barn, Dean asked her about the event he had planned. "What do you think?"

"You built it and they came, Dean," she said proudly. "The barn has come to life."

"I'll see you later," he said as he dropped her off at the tack room. "Feel free to help yourself to the food on the table, and there's also hot cocoa and coffee."

She watched him walk away. He had built all of this—he had planned all of this—for his daughter. Seeing Dean as a father had touched her more than anything else. His love for his children, so steady and true, had allowed her to see another layer of the man she now loved, and it made that love for him grow and strengthen. Dean Legend was exactly the man she had once dreamed him to be, even more of a man than she had imagined. And it certainly didn't hurt that she found his *Grizzly Adams meets modern cowboy* look a real turn-on.

Rayna mingled with the other attendees, filling a small plate with veggies drizzled with olive oil and eating them slowly while her mind considered what it would be like to make love with Dean again. When they'd both lost their virginity to each other, they had been naive kids who hadn't had the foggiest idea of how to do what they'd been attempting to do. Now? She was more in tune with her body, her wants and her needs, and she doubted she would be shy asking for those wants and needs to be fulfilled.

"Perhaps it's time for a hands-on mini anthropological study?" Rayna whispered aloud to herself while chewing thoughtfully on a carrot.

"My son wanted to be an archeologist," a woman with her own plate of veggies said.

"Is that right?" Rayna asked as seriously and curiously as she could.

"Yes. But my ex-husband wanted him to have a trade," the woman said. "He's a plumber now, has his own business and is a good provider for his kids. But I do think he would have been much happier as an archeologist."

Rayna ran into some women she had gone to school with, and seeing them with their own children felt heartwarming and strange all wrapped up in one. They didn't have a chance to catch up with the first horse showmanship class about to start, but she did exchange phone numbers with a promise to get together at another time. With her belly full of hot cocoa that had warmed her up from the inside out, she found a seat in the bleachers that were on either side of the large indoor arena. Right when the girls were leading their horses into the arena, Dean found her and took a seat next to her.

"It's been such a long time. What will they be doing?"

Dean said, "Leading their horses at the walk, leading

them at a jog or trot. They'll need to stop and back up, set them up for inspection and then pivot."

She nodded, her memory being jogged. "There's Luna! She looks so tiny next to Duke."

He chuckled. "She does, doesn't she? When she wanted to get the biggest horse in the herd, I almost said no. But then I thought, working with this gelding will build confidence like nothing ever could."

Without much thought, she put her hand on his hand and said, "I love watching you be a dad, Dean."

He smiled at that compliment, his eyes trained on Luna and her big quarter horse gelding. Before she could take her hand away quickly, Paisley appeared at the bottom of the bleachers. Rayna removed her hand and cursed inwardly.

"Come sit with us," Dean said to his daughter.

Paisley sent her a sullen look but climbed up the steps and sat next to her dad.

"Hi, Paisley," she said.

Paisley gave her a peace sign with her fingers but seemed determined not to speak one word to her. Instead of feeling frustrated or rejected, Rayna wanted to hug Paisley. She could see the pain and the hurt in the girl's eyes, and it hurt her to see it.

After a minute, Paisley said, "I'm going to shoot content on the other side. The angle is totally wrong here."

"Okay, sweet girl." Dean hugged her and gave her a quick kiss on her head. "I'll see you later."

"Bye, Paisley," Rayna said.

Dean's eldest didn't look back at her but did give her a quick, dismissive wave and then headed off. Both of them ignored this interaction and focused in on Luna, who was walking her gelding beautifully.

"It's okay." Dean was looking ahead, but in a voice only meant for her ears, he said, "I love you, Ray."

Without any hesitation, Rayna looked at him and said, "I love you, Dean."

Chapter Twelve

The 4H event was a huge success, and Dean felt relieved for that success. He was well aware of the feast-or-famine way of life on a cattle ranch, and he wanted to secure the future of the ranch and, more importantly, secure the future of his daughters. There was a palpable tension in the air when Paisley was around Rayna, but Dean believed that with time and patience, she would embrace Rayna. For now, he was happy with how things were unfolding. Rayna was embracing life in Montana, and she seemed to be embracing the spark that had been relit between them. While she had said that she wasn't sure what the future held for her or for them, he found it difficult to believe that she wouldn't *eventually* commit to him and be his wife. They were a long way off from a proposal, but he would be lying to himself if he couldn't admit that he had already begun to plan the "how" and "where" that he would propose marriage to her.

"This is what I like! All of us together!" Buck had just finished a second plate of food, and this was an unusual enough of an occurrence that Miss Minnie commented on it.

"I'm glad to see your appetite come back, Mr. Legend."

"I feel like I could eat the whole cow tonight." Buck talked through a couple of deep coughs.

"Save room for dessert, then," their cook said. "I've got something special in there, and you won't want to miss it."

They all helped clear the table while Buck teased everyone to hurry up so he could get to his dessert. Once the table had been cleared and coffee poured, Miss Minnie emerged carrying a pie piled high with fluffy, made-from-scratch whipped cream.

"Here she comes!" Miss Minnie said with a smile on her round, chubby face.

"What in the world do you have there, Minuet?"

Miss Minnie's name was Minuet, but Buck and Nettie had been the only two people—other than her mother, who had passed several years ago—who could use that first name. Miss Minnie never felt up to carrying the mantle of such a fancy name.

"Miss Nettie's chocolate cream pie with a Miss Minnie twist."

Miss Minnie cut the pie, and Paisley, always a willing sidekick for the cook, served the dessert, starting with Buck.

Dean noticed the sheer happiness on his father's face when he took his first bite of his wife's chocolate pie. He chewed with his eyes closed, and a frequent, nagging thought came to Dean's mind again: If Buck could hold on to this happiness in his life, would he reconsider accepting treatment for his cancer? He had his granddaughters and now Rayna. Was that enough? Was it too late?

"Cinnamon!" Paisley shouted. "You added cinnamon!"

Miss Minnie, hands held in front of her body, rocked back on her heels with a pleased smile on her face. "And what else?"

Paisley closed her eyes in the same manner as his father, chewed deliberately and then opened her eyes with a look of satisfaction on her face. "Nutmeg."

Miss Minnie pretended to pull on a chord to a bell. "Ding, ding, ding! That's my smart girl!"

The group finished their desserts. Luna was always done first; she asked to be excused, not for tablet time but to go to the barn to spend time with some of the horses that were now boarders. Then Paisley asked to be excused; she had been working on editing the video she'd shot today to upload on social media platforms.

"Did you hear me, son?"

His dad's question snapped him out of his own mind and brought him back to the present.

"No, Dad. I'm sorry. It's been a great day, but I'm plumb worn the heck out."

"No need to apologize. My daughter and I were just talking turkey over here."

Dean glanced over at Rayna, and she had the appearance of someone who was trapped in a corner and didn't quite know how to fight her way out.

"Dad thinks we should have a Legend-Brand revival Thanksgiving here," she explained to him.

"One the best damn ideas I've had in recent history," Buck said with some of the vigor of his younger, healthier years.

"Dad, Cat is coming on opening day of Big Sky..." Dean told him. "I think opening day is November twenty-second."

"Okay?" the elder Legend asked. "I don't see a problem."

"We invited her over to spend Thanksgiving with us."

Cat and he had agreed, mostly because her fiancé wasn't going to be on this trip, that they would spend Thanksgiving together at the ranch. The girls were excited about it, and now he wondered if his dad had completely forgotten.

"I remember." Buck's bushy, unruly white eyebrows drew together. "I'm not senile yet!"

"I didn't mean that." Dean backtracked quickly. "I just wanted to remind you that plans have been made."

"And? It will be a Legend-Brand *family* Thanksgiving. Cat is family." Buck looked over at Rayna. "You don't mind about that, do you? More the merrier! That was Rose and Nettie's way. We need to honor them. Remember them."

When Buck started to talk about Nettie, he couldn't hold back, and often didn't even attempt to hold back, his tears. Buck took his napkin and wiped off the tears from his face.

Dean looked at Rayna in his peripheral vision. At first she seemed to be shrinking in her chair. He thought if she could bolt without Buck taking notice, she would be half-way back to Connecticut by now. But the moment Rayna saw Buck's tears, her body language changed. Still, he wasn't convinced that this was a great idea mixing a bunch of oil and a barrel of wine.

"I think Rayna plans to spend Thanksgiving with her sons, Dad."

Dean hoped that this would satisfy Buck that it wasn't in the cards for this two-family blended, exes included, Thanksgiving meal. There were so many landmines attached to an event like this that Dean was certain he wouldn't survive the day without getting a foot blown off.

"Well, of course she is, son," Buck said. "They'll be here with us."

"Okay, Dad," Rayna said. "I will invite them. Does that invitation include Charlie and Wayne? Wayne's brother?"

"Yes! Invite them all!" Buck hit the table with his fist, and for a rare moment, the Legend patriarch was reinvigo-rated with the strength of the man who had ruled this ranch over decades. "Everyone is welcome!"

* * *

"What was that?" Rayna had walked with Dean out to the truck.

"A sneak attack by a very determined old man."

"I couldn't think of one reason that the Brands couldn't attend. Not one reason. Everything that came to mind seemed flimsy and lame."

"And he would've rejected those excuses anyway."

"Exactly. That's what I thought," Rayna agreed with a good dose of bitterness in her tone. "He's still a force to be reckoned with. I haven't seen him that feisty for over a year. But maybe he's right? Lump everyone together, and see what happens."

"I'll have to tell Cat."

"Will she be a *yay* or a *no way*?"

"I think she'll be a *yay*," Dean surprised her by saying. "She's pragmatic. If it helps the girls accept life as it really is, she'll support it."

They reached her truck, and his expression turned curious. "It appears that you have snow inside of your truck."

"Yeah, I know." She pulled the door handle up and then tugged on it hard until it finally gave way and made a cracking, creaking sound as it slowly opened. "The window won't roll up now."

"You should have mentioned it. I'd have fixed it for you," he said, starting to fiddle with the window. "At least if it's rolled up, it will keep the snow and rain out of the cab and it will make it a little warm inside."

She brushed the snow off of the driver's seat. "But if it can't roll down, I can't open the door."

"Because it won't open from the inside."

"Smarter than your average bear." She gave him a half smile, still processing being ambushed by Buck and now on the hook to spend Thanksgiving as one big blended family.

She was about to get in the truck so she could be on her way. She needed time alone to think through what was now on the horizon. She could see all sorts of flashing warning lights signaling to the driver that dangerous roads are ahead. Thanksgiving with Dean's ex? What could possibly go wrong?

"Hey, wait, Ray." Dean reached out to capture her hand in his. "Are you mad at me?"

She turned toward him but slipped her hand out of his. "I don't know. No. Scratch that! Yes. Maybe I am."

"May I ask, what was the nature of my crime?"

Rayna sighed heavily, watching the cold air forming swirls of white in front of her. It was cold, she was tired and she wanted to go home.

"Can we talk about this tomorrow?" she asked him. "I just need to sleep on it."

"Yes. Of course." He nodded, stood by while she got into the truck and cranked the engine. While the truck sputtered and idled to get the thirty-year-old engine warmed up, Dean said to her, "It's okay, Ray."

"You keep saying that, Dean. But is it really okay? I'm not so sure about that right now," Rayna said, feeling more frustration building as she began to mull it over. She was freshly divorced, embarking on a relationship with her childhood sweetheart, and the *L*-word had been said and put on repeat. She had a car she didn't want and didn't need, and clothing that she hated! Not five hours ago she was contemplating disrobing Dean down to his birthday suit and taking all sorts of advantage of him, and now, all of a sudden, she was having Thanksgiving with Dean's ex-wife and mother of his children.

"Be careful, Ray. Please text me when you get home."

She heard Dean say "I love you," but she didn't say it

back. A mile down the road, she felt like a real jackass. It wasn't Dean's fault that Buck wanted to have a revival of their shared holidays. The minute she got home, she would text hi and make it right.

"Because I do love him," she said as the frigid air began to hurt the exposed parts of her face and her fingers were aching from gripping the wheel to keep it on the road. "That is my truth. For the second time in my life, I have fallen in love with James Dean Legend."

"I am so sorry about last night," Rayna told Dean on the phone. "Normally you're the grumpy one."

Dean laughed. "Is this an apology or an attack?"

His laugh broke the tension, and she knew that he had accepted her apology in his own way.

"I called my boys today, and they're actually excited to have shared Thanksgiving. They've heard about it their whole lives, and they've obviously seen my photo albums."

"Photo albums! Can you believe that's what we use to do with our pictures?"

"I know, but there's some upsides. I've lost plenty of pictures when I've switched to a new phone and my pictures floated away on whatever cloud they were supposed to be in."

"Well, I'm looking forward to meeting your boys. Do they know…?"

"About us?" she asked. "No. But I think Ryder suspects."

"And when they do find out? What kind of reaction are you expecting?"

"I don't even know. I suppose we'll just have to find out together." Then she said, "Charlie, Wayne and Waylon are a yes, if you want to tell your dad."

"Okay. Game on."

After a small pause, Rayna asked "And did you let Cat know of these rather seismic shifts?"

"I did."

"And?"

"She believes that if you're there then her fiancé should be there as well."

"We aren't engaged, granted, and I'm not trying to insert myself into your relationship with your ex or your coparenting, but I kind of see her point."

Dean sighed a frustrated sigh and said, "I'll think about it."

"Okay."

Then he changed the topic: "Now, Ray, don't get your hackles up, but I don't think it's at all a good idea for you to be driving your father's ancient…"

"Antique…"

"Antique truck at night. You need a vehicle. A safe vehicle."

"We're back on each other's wavelength. I was just about to say that to you! Can you come over later today? I have something I want to show you."

"What about keeping this thing between us secret?"

"Charlie already knows, so that means Wayne and probably Waylon know—not that they care."

They hung up with an agreement for him to come over around noon. The girls were in school, and he could spend a block of uninterrupted time with her.

"I'll look forward to seeing you then," Dean said.

"Me too."

Dean arrived at Hideaway on time. She greeted him with a big hug and a quick kiss, knowing that on her ranch they had more leeway to express their feelings. Rayna led him over to her father's workshop and as the door opened, his eyes locked onto her Jag. He couldn't seem to take his eyes off of the car and, right on time, he whistled low and long.

"Why does every man who sees this car whistle?"

"Because this a sexy car! Is she yours?" Dean started to circle the car like he was a tiger circling a gazelle.

"For now." Rayna stuffed her hands into her coat pockets. "I'd like to sell it, but I doubt there will be a line out the door of people looking to buy a Jag for the same amount they can spend on a house here."

She could see how enamored Dean was with the car, and she couldn't blame him. This car was an incredible marriage of power and design, and it needed to find itself a new home.

"Man." Dean came back to stand next to her. "What did she set you back?"

"Paid it off when we sold our house—it was one hundred fifty thousand and some pocket change. The Christmas gift I never wanted or asked for. Ben loves to show off his wealth."

"So not great memories."

"No. Not at all," she said. "If I had been thinking at all clearly, I would have had it sold instead of shipped it here."

"You've had a lot to deal with, Ray. Give yourself a break."

She crossed her arms in front of her body; just looking at this car and the boxes upon boxes filled with things that she no longer wanted made her feel anxious and exhausted. It sometimes felt to her like if she took one step forward into her life, these tangible artifacts from her failed marriage kept dragging her backward.

"Are you sure about selling?"

"Yes," she said emphatically. "I want it gone."

"Well, I do know a guy who owns a luxury rental-car business out of Bozeman. I think he'd love to have this in his stable."

"Will you call him? Set something up?"

"Of course I will." He put his arm around her shoulders, and she leaned into him. "Actually he's Scott Johnson's nephew, Red."

"Danica's prom date Scott?"

"The one and the same. He'll give us a fair deal," Dean said.

"Thank you," she said, pinching the inside of her eyes to stop tears from forming.

Dean looked down at her, and when he saw that she was struggling emotionally he turned her body toward his, wrapped her up in his strong, burly arms and hugged her tightly. She hadn't expected to cry; she hadn't expected to feel *anything* beyond being glad to get the car off her hands.

"Ray, this is tough stuff, but I don't know anyone as tough on the inside as you."

She nodded and wiped the tears from her cheeks. "I just want it to be gone. I don't want to look at it anymore."

"We'll get it sold and get you into something that makes sense."

"A cowgirl truck?" She asked after a loud, unladylike sniff.

Dean laughed, hugged her again and then gave her a sweet butterfly kiss. "Damn straight."

They parted ways with a promise to meet at the tree house the next day; they both seemed to be craving alone time with each other.

Dean climbed into his truck, rolled down the window and reached for her hand. "Tomorrow at noon?"

She laughed, squeezed his hand before she let him go. "High noon."

* * *

"How are you feeling, Charlie?" Danica asked during their video meeting.

"Better. I'm still weak, though. I've never been sick like this before. Wayne's been really knocked back on his heels," Charlie said, bringing a glass of water with her to the butcher-block counter.

"Well, I hope you keep feeling better. Drink plenty of fluids and get lots of rest," Danica said.

Charlie held up her glass of water for her sister to see. "I've got the fluids part down, but plenty of rest, not so much."

"What's keeping you up?" Danica asked.

"The same thing that's keeping me up," Rayna speculated. "The bookings!"

Danica rubbed her forehead—she suffered from migraines on and off, and it seemed like every time they spoke, she had a headache. "But why? This is the answer to our prayers, isn't it? Save the ranch by turning it into a destination spot for companies, families and winter-sports enthusiasts! We had projected being profitable in three years—if we keep this pace, we're going to meet that goal ahead of schedule.

"You believed in this so much, Charlie, and I didn't think it had even a remote chance," she said. "I stand corrected. I'm a believer. The rental-house market in Big Sky is on fire—I'd really like to tap into that! It's just all gravy all the time. So will someone explain to me why this is causing you stress?"

"Would saying 'everything' be too vague?" Charlie said with a cough.

"Yes, it would." Danica picked up a pen. "Let's talk this out."

"We will need more horses so they can be rotated out and have time off."

"Okay. Sugar Creek is right there in Bozeman. They're family, so bonus, and they have great horses. Check! Figure out the number of horses and a budget. Next?"

They hashed out all of the concerns to include a laundry service, housekeeping service, hiring more ranch hands with twelve-month contracts to keep them around during the summer season. But Danica didn't seem too concerned overall; she seemed to have embraced the Big Sky market and the possibilities for making money with the ranch and other ventures beyond the ranch.

"Didn't you mention something about goat yoga, Ray?" Danica asked her.

"Well, yeah. But I'm not sure if I'm ready for that right now. The space available in the town center didn't feel keen to have goats in the space."

"Crazy people!" Charlie smiled but then began to cough again.

"No. Find a different way! The goat yoga idea is going to hook all sorts of people to come out to the ranch. It's a niche market that will draw in the people. I promise you it will. Once they see the place and what we have to offer, they may book us next year instead of the resort!"

"I will think about it. I promise," Rayna said. "But after I get the place ready for a classic Christmas. I have a solid plan, and my orders are starting to arrive. I'm going to pull out all of the stops for this family—chestnuts roasting on an open fire, decorating Christmas cookies for Santa, singing Christmas carols, helping them pick out their own tree, and I can't even begin to tell you how amazing the ornaments I've selected are…"

"I got the bill," Danica said off-handedly. "I hope they're worth the expense."

"They're beyond worth it. *Charles Dickens Christmas* meets *Thomas Kinkade*. It will be perfection."

"It does sound wonderful, Ray. All of those details are essential," Danica said and then she snapped her fingers. "We need a photographer! When did you say you were going to start the outside installation?"

"The day after Thanksgiving. I'll have about two weeks before the guests arrive."

"That's a tight timeline," Danica said.

"We know." Charlie blew her nose again. "Sink or swim."

After the discussion about the decorations and hiring a photographer, Danica said, "Meeting adjourned?"

"No. Just a minute more," Rayna said. "I do want to mention something."

"The floor is yours." Danica looked up from her pad.

"So, I had my Jaguar delivered here and I intend to sell it," she told them. "Dean has a lead on a luxury car-rental business in Bozeman. If I'm lucky, he'll take it off my hands.

"If he does, I'll use the proceeds to buy myself a gently used truck," she continued. "I'd like to invest in the ranch with the rest."

"Are you sure you want to do that?" Charlie asked, surprised.

"Yes, I am. Danny gave us the seed money, you've kept this farm afloat for years and I want to contribute too. I have faith in us. If I didn't, I wouldn't do it. Hideaway is my history too, and maybe, just maybe, it's my future as well."

Chapter Thirteen

Rayna watched her Jaguar, secured on a flatbed truck, disappear around the corner. She had a very healthy check in her back pocket, and in an unexpected twist, Ben had given her the gift of a nest egg.

"So, it's done." Charlie walked over to where she was still standing even though the Jag had already disappeared from sight.

"Yes." Rayna felt frozen in that spot. Her legs felt rubbery and too weak to hold up her weight. "It's done."

The three of them had drifted apart in their twenties and thirties. Now in their early forties, fighting to keep the ranch had changed all of that for them. They were always texting or calling when one of the three was experiencing hardships or happiness, and it had been a blessing for all of them. Even though Rose was gone, they were fulfilling her dying wish—for her girls to support each other and love each other even when they disagreed.

Today Rayna knew that this moment, while of her choosing, was symbolic of the end of her marriage. Yes, the divorce papers had been signed, but somehow selling the Jag made it symbolically final to her.

"It's okay, Ray. It's okay, and you're okay."

Rayna gratefully accepted her sister's hug. "Thank you."

"Of course. I love you. Danny loves you."

After they broke the hug, Rayna fished the check out of her back pocket and handed the folded check to Charlie. Her sister didn't unfold the check, and she immediately gave it back.

"I want to help."

"You are helping. I spoke with Aspen this morning, and she just can't come back for the foreseeable future. When she brings the baby home to Montana, she wants to focus on her blog so she can work from home. We suspected that, but now we know. The ranch needs you, Ray. We need you to cook, run the main house and start that goat yoga class before Danny blows a gasket over it. Things are ramping up, and I have to tell you, when I'm super stressed and I remind myself that you're here with me, it helps me calm down."

"Maybe you need to attend one of my goat yoga classes to manage your stress."

Charlie read on her face that she wasn't convinced. "Look, Ray, Danny and I already discussed this, and we *will not* accept this money from you under any circumstances. Not now and not until you know what you really want to do. That money will give you options, and if it's all tied up in the ranch, your only option will be to make your life here long term. Are you ready to commit to Big Sky?"

When Rayna looked out into the distance, Charlie said, "That pause means *No, I'm not ready to commit.*"

"If I do decide to make a go of it here, after I get my yoga business up and running, I do want to invest in this ranch. Is that a deal?"

Charlie shook her hand. "Trust me, if that's the case, I will happily accept your money!"

Before they parted ways, her sister said, "You need a vehicle. I mean, I appreciate your bravery, but Dad's truck is questionable as a road-worthy method of transportation."

"I know. It was kind of fun roughing it and figuring out how to survive ice mixed with slick oil spots without power steering or four-wheel drive." Ray laughed. "Dean's going to take me to the Chevy dealer in Bozeman once my check clears."

"That relationship seems to be moving right along. Exactly how far have things *gone* with Mr. Legend?" Charlie raised her eyebrows suggestively.

"Well," Rayna said, "I will admit to this and *only* this—Mr. James Dean Legend does look mighty fine in tighty-whities."

Charlie winced and put her hands over her eyes. "Darn it, Ray! I'll never be able to get that image out of my head now!"

"You asked, I answered."

"I know I did. And I know it's my own fault." She shook her head with her eyes closed. "But God bless! I can't seem to *unsee* it! The harder I try, the worse it gets."

"That's karma, Charlie. Plain and simple. Karma."

Dean picked her up and took her to the Chevy dealership where she used a sizeable down payment and a small loan to rebuild her credit, which had been damaged after the divorce. She had gone to the dealership with the goal of buying a certified used vehicle like a Chevy Blazer—not too big, not too expensive, with four-wheel drive. However, what she drove off the lot in was far from her original plan. It was gently used, it did have low mileage and it was certified; and that was where the convergence of her previous plan to her eventual purchase ended. She proudly drove a monster 2500 HD biodiesel truck with the High Country package—black interior, black exterior, chrome accents. And when she pulled up to the barn in her new truck, she felt proud of herself and *more* herself than she had in years.

Charlie and Wayne, who was feeling better, greeted her like she was a warrior returning from a battle. Waylon gave his stamp of approval, and in his own way, so did Bowie— he gave it a really good sniff and then promptly lifted his leg and peed on the front left tire.

"Really Bowie?" she asked him. "Was that *really* necessary?"

Dean had nearly a full stable, and it had kept him busy as all get-out. He had to fill his coffers with hay, feed and bedding. He had some of these items already stored for Luna's two 4-H horses as well as for the horses that had been Nettie's pride and joy—in their mid-twenties, they were loved and cared for as family pets. There was another herd of well-bred, stock Quarter horses—the horses that did the bulk of the cattle work on the ranch. They had shelter on the north barn but were hardy enough to brave the Montana winters.

As his regular veterinarian was sick with the flu, Rayna had suggested Dr. Tonia Vislosky to conduct basic health exams on the horses.

"You must be Dean." Dr. Vislosky jumped down from her truck.

"Nice to meet you." He shook her hand. "I've heard great things."

"The Brands are good folks," she said with a small smile while she took a blue plastic animal carrier out of her back seat and then held it out for him to take.

He looked at her and she looked at him, and then he looked inside of the carrier.

"Kittens?" he asked, hearing the distinctive high-pitched mews of young kittens.

Dr. V. nodded and continued to offer the carrier to him.

"I don't believe I ordered these," he said.

She looked at him strangely. "These are Rayna's kittens. She said to put them in your care until she could get things on her end set up."

"Rayna's kittens," he repeated.

"They're so good, you won't even know that they're here!" the vet said. "I'll just get my things while you get them settled."

Dean lifted up the carrier to look at the very young, very adorable tuxedo cats. One sassy kitten stared back at him with his or her giant green eyes, and then it came forward, bumped its head against the inside of the carrier and then stuck his tiny paw through, as much as he could, one of the air holes.

"No. Don't even try it. It won't work on me," Dean said, taking the kittens to his office where it was warm. "As soon as I call Rayna, all three of you are advancing to Hideaway Ranch—do not pass *Go* and do not collect two hundred dollars."

Dr. V. met him in the aisleway, and he fell in beside her. He had long legs and Dr. V. was petite, but she managed to keep pace with him.

"This happened overnight," she commented.

"It did," Dean said, pleased. "I held one event, and just like that, I'm in business."

"Places as nice as this are few and far between."

"We're having some major growing pains, but it's getting there."

Once Dr. V. got started, she was focused and thorough. None of the horses took advantage of her small stature. Dr.

V. was fair, kind but firm, and all of the horses responded well to her.

When she was done, she said, "I'll send electronic copies of the invoices to each owner individually to the emails provided. The owners will also receive Coggins electronically, so ask them to be on the lookout for that. Overall, you've got a nice bunch of healthy horses."

"Thank you, Dr. V." He shook her hand. "It's been a pleasure."

"Likewise," she said. "I hope to do more business with you in the future."

"You can count on that."

"Hi, Dean!" Rayna answered the phone cheerfully. She was happy to hear from him as always, but she was also very happy with how well all of her plants were faring in the insulated but sunny greenhouse.

"How are you? Having a good day?"

Rayna was about to respond in the affirmative, but when she stepped back, she tripped over the hose she had failed to coil and landed rather unceremoniously on her backside.

"Ow!" she grumbled. "Stupid hose!"

"Are you all right?"

"Yes." Rayna stood up. "My hind parts and my ego just got bruised. How are you?"

"Hmm," Dean said, "how should I put this?"

"Put what?"

"I have kittens."

"What?" she asked, attempting to kick off the garden hose that was now wrapped around her foot.

"I. Have. *Kittens!*"

"Why didn't you lead with that?!"

"Why did you have Dr. V. drop off kittens?"

She looked at her phone and saw that Dr. V. had texted her, but she hadn't heard it.

"Mystery solved!" she said.

"Maybe on your end."

"Dean, I love you. Don't worry your pretty little head over it. I'll be there in a sec."

Rayna hung up and walked quickly, but not overly so, in order to evade detection that something wasn't right by her investigative sister. She climbed into her truck, which she now lovingly called the Beast, cranked its bad-boy engine, gave it a minute to warm up and then drove slowly, casually onto the gravel drive until she was well out of sight. Then she stepped on the gas and went full-throttle to the main road. The Beast didn't need her to take frozen-over potholes timidly; she drove right over them like they were little baby ice cubes being crushed by the extra thick, knobby-as-all-get-out tires.

Rayna got to the end of the drive, turned right and headed toward Legend Ranch. She had been waiting for these sweet fur babies to come home, and she almost had everything situated on her end. For now, she had everything a kitten would need in the back. Dean would eventually get on board—she had noticed that her second-time-around boyfriend was just taking life too seriously. She just hoped, with time, she would be able to help Dean enjoy his life in the same way he had helped her embrace a new, sometimes intimidating, life path.

"Did you fly here?" Dean asked when he opened the driver's door and held out his hand to help her down.

She accepted the help but quickly pulled her hand away; they were still, and would continue to be, cautious on his turf so as to be mindful of Paisley's feelings and to explore their feelings without feeling any pressure one way or the other.

"The Beast!"

Her unwavering happiness over her truck and now the arrival of the kittens seemed to put Dean in a better mood.

"Are you hiding kittens because Charlie specifically told you—and anyone in a ten-mile radius, it was so loud—that anything that eats, makes manure or racks up vet bills is not to be brought on the property?"

Rayna rolled her eyes. "She was just all bent out of shape about the donkeys I bought over the summer. That's all. Plus, that ranch is just as much mine as it is hers, and I'm giving these poor homeless kittens a home."

"If all that is true, then why, might I ask, do I have *your* kittens?"

"Stop looking so disapprovingly at me! I need to get things set up on my end, that's all."

"Just let me know when you break the news to Charlie because I'd like to set up a lawn chair, get a cooler of beers and enjoy the fireworks coming from the general direction of Hideaway Ranch."

"Don't worry. Just help me."

She opened the back door of her truck and slid out a new kitty box that held supplies for the kittens—food, toys, bowls for food and water, and comfy warm beds that all of the kittens could share.

She handed that load to Dean. He took it automatically, then realized what she had just handed to him and tried to hand it back to her while he said, "They aren't moving in, Ray."

Rayna grabbed a bag of kitty litter, held it in her arms and bumped the door shut with her hip. "Well. Not forever. Just for right now."

"Didn't you think that you might need to ask me if I could keep the kittens before having Dr. V. drop them off here?"

"Well, yes, of course I did," she said easily. "But I realized if I asked you, you would say no."

"Hit that nail right on the head."

"So I thought it would be best if I just did the petty crime and apologized for it later." She smiled up at him. "You're right, I was wrong. Please accept my apology and take me to my kittens!"

"Barn cats sleep in the barn. Hence the term *barn* cats," Dean said. "You have a barn."

"They're too young to be in a cold barn right now," she retorted. "When they get old enough, they'll have a job keeping mice out of the barn."

When they reached his office, Dean was grumbling something about the kittens being all sorts of trouble, but what trouble could three tiny little kittens cause? Dean opened the door for her, and when he followed her into his office, they found Luna sitting cross-legged on the ground, her face awash with excitement as the three kittens crawled on her, chased each other, stalked pieces of cedar bedding carried in by the boots of the riders and tore around the place, bumping into each other and jumping straight up in the air, Halloween cat bristles on full display.

"I love them, Dad!" Luna exclaimed.

"No."

"Can I keep them?" she asked, ignoring the no.

"No."

"But why not?" Luna had a whiney squeak in her voice.

Rayna sat down on the ground beside her, letting the kittens get used to her. She picked up one kitten, put the little girl against her cheek, feeling the softness of the kitten's fur before she kissed it and let it go back to exploring the space.

"See what you did? Trouble. Nothing but!" Dean asked her before he said to Luna, "They belong to Rayna."

Luna's expression crumbled, her lip pooched out and her shoulders dropped in disappointment.

"But you can come over to my place any time you want to see them," Rayna tried to smooth it over.

"Really?"

"Of course, ladybug." Rayna hugged her. "Any time you want, you just ask your dad and we'll work it out."

Luna leaned her body into Ray's and put her hand on her thigh, and that closeness with Dean's youngest made her feel so darn welcomed and good.

"What are their names?" Luna asked.

"Well," she said, "those two look like twins, so I was going to name them Big Tux and Little Tux."

Luna nodded her approval. "What about him?"

"I don't know. What do you think?"

"Well, he has that white spot at the tip of his tail and it kind of looks like one of those wands that magician's use? So maybe Magic?"

"That's the most perfect name for him." Rayna hugged Luna again. "Magic it is."

Chapter Fourteen

"I've reviewed your plans for the guests—the food, the decorations, outdoor and indoor. Everything looks impeccably planned, Ray. Makes me wish I had you on the payroll to plan all of my open houses!"

"Thank you, Danny. It's actually been a joy. I had no idea how much I needed to be *needed*. Before we go, I do want to run something by you. I was reviewing the client intake form for our first family, the Baron family, and it's puzzling to me."

"In what way?" Charlie asked.

"They state that they want to experience a classic white Christmas with a real tree…"

"Not a problem there," Charlie said. "We can source that right here on our property."

"They want to help with the decorations in general…" Rayna added. "So, decorating the tree and maybe hanging stockings, that sort of thing."

Her sisters nodded.

"I looked him up and his bio on the university website states that he is proud of his Israeli roots, is fluent in Hebrew and Yiddish. Perhaps they are a mixed-religion family?"

"Well," Charlie chimed in, "maybe we can purchase some Chanukah decorations just in case? Chanukah col-

ors are blue and silver—if they would like, we could decorate the fur trees with blue-and-white lights while doing
the full-blown red-and-green Christmas extravaganza on
the inside."

"Perfect idea," Danica said, and Rayna agreed.

"I don't know if this was by design, but Chanukah be-
gins on December twenty-fifth at sundown," Rayna told
her sisters.

"I just got goose bumps!" Charlie exclaimed. "I think
this family is going to be the most incredible first guests—I
feel it in every fiber of my being. We'll never forget them."

"And," Rayna added, "if we get this inaugural booking
right, the Barons will never forget *us*."

They were just about to adjourn the meeting when her
phone rang. It was Dean, and he sounded odd but she
couldn't pinpoint the exact emotion.

"Can you come over?"

"Right now?"

"Yes," Dean said. "If you can."

"Let me wrap up with my sisters, and then I'll be right
over."

"Consider yourself finished!" Charlie said. "If he needs
you enough to call, go!"

Dean heard her sister and said, "We're in the barn."

"Thank you!" Rayna jumped up, rushed to the door,
grabbed her coat and hat and then took the steps quickly but
carefully. She jogged over to her truck, got in and cranked
the engine. The Beast always needed a minute to warm up,
and those seconds that made up that single minute seemed
like an eternity to her.

A text came through the triplet sisters' group chat: If you
need help, let us know.

She didn't respond, and they wouldn't expect her to. She

shifted into Drive and floored it. She had figured out in a very short time how to handle the Beast, and she got to the main road in record time, barely stopped when the coast was obviously clear, and then she turned and headed to the Legend ranch. Her mind was racing with thoughts about what could possibly make Dean place a call like that to her.

"Quit speculating, Ray, and just *get* there. You can handle anything that comes your way."

Dean heard Rayna arrive, and he left his office to meet her. As always, things just seemed better when Rayna was nearby. She had a calming effect on him, and he had quickly grown to rely on it.

Rayna pushed aside their agreement to be discreet, and she walked into his arms and they hugged each other tightly.

"What's wrong, Dean?" she asked, her worried eyes on his face.

"I need help with Luna."

"Okay." Rayna nodded her head. "Whatever I can do to help, I will do it."

He walked in long strides to his office with Rayna keeping pace with him. Almost every time they went several days without seeing each other, Rayna had seemed to evolve just a bit more. Little by little, day by day, Rayna was transforming into the cowgirl she had always been, and it gave him hope that she could make a life she loved right here in Big Sky with him.

Dean opened the door to the office, where Luna was sitting on the floor with Magic curled up on her lap while Big Tux and Little Tux slept in the cozy bed, their limbs intertwined. She had tears streaming down both of her cheeks and down to her chin. Her eyes were starting to puff up, and she sniffed loudly every couple of seconds to clear it so she could breathe better. It broke his heart in the true sense of that phrase. He could handle anything—losing his mother, his divorce, watching his father die slowly of cancer because he refused treatment—but what killed him and made him feel like a horrible single dad was when either of his girls cried.

"Ladybug!" Rayna went straight over to Luna and sat down beside her. "What's wrong?"

Luna had to take several quick breaths in before she said, "Dad says that Magic is your cat, but I know he's mine. I love him, and he loves me!"

Dean's youngest used the sleeve of her sweatshirt to wipe the tears from her face, but new tears only followed those tears.

"Do you have tissues?" Rayna asked him.

He went over to his desk, got the box that he had used to dry his daughter's tears before he'd called her.

Rayna took some tissues out of the box, wiped Luna's face and then put her hand gently on the back of the girl's head to keep it steady, put the tissues over her nose and said, "Blow."

It took several rounds of nose blowing for Luna to settle down and, at least temporarily, stop crying.

"I can see that he loves you very much," Rayna said.

Dean could see it too; Magic was curled up in Luna's lap, purring steadily and loudly, and his emerald-green eyes were at half-mast as if he had just found his new favorite thing in the world: being next to Luna.

"He does! And I love him! Why can't I keep him? You have two already!"

"Luna…" Dean always supported his daughters' right to speak their minds, but when they spoke their minds and it sounded disrespectful, that crossed the line.

"It's okay, Dean." Rayna looked up at him. "She's made a valid point. I do have two."

He took a step back, leaned against his table, arms crossed in front of his chest. Rayna was already making more progress with Luna than he had managed to do—it made him wonder if his girls were losing out by being with him when they could be living with the parent who would understand them more than he ever could. This wasn't the first time he'd contemplated that, and this moment seemed to be powerful evidence that he couldn't give his daughters everything that they needed.

"I want him, Rayna," Luna repeated. "Dad says I can't have him!"

That was the end of the short reprieve from crying for her.

"Lovebug," Rayna said, "your dad has his reasons, and we need to respect them. You can come over to see Magic anytime. I promise."

"I don't want him to be at your house. I want him to be in mine. He'll be sad if he's not with me!"

Rayna wiped Luna's tears and looked over her shoulder at him. "Magic can't stay in the barn?"

"No," Dean said. "The last time we tried, the dogs scared the barn cats half to death. They always ended up in the rafters or stuck up a tree, and Mom decided that as much as she loved her cats, when Bandit and Radar died, we wouldn't replace them."

"He could live in the house with me," Luna tried to bargain.

While he formulated his response, Paisley opened the door, and the moment she saw Luna on the floor crying, she immediately went to her side.

"What's wrong,?"

"Dad won't let me keep Magic."

"But you knew that," Paisley said. "Dad already told us that."

Luna took several shallow, rapid breaths in and then got out in a wavering, stuffy voice, "Magic is mine. He's mine!"

Paisley stood up, walked over to the desk, got the tissues and then returned to her little sister. She knelt down in front of her sister and wiped her face off. "Luna. Cowgirls don't cry, remember?"

She nodded, but he knew her well enough to know that she wasn't the least bit convinced—she was dedicated to her cause, and he had to respect that, just as he respected how both Ray and Paisley were working to help Luna.

"It's a big responsibility," Rayna said.

"I take care of them every day. I feed them, I play with them, I make sure they have water *and* I scoop the kitty boxes. If I did it with three why can't I do it with only one?"

Dean had always been grateful that God had given him two brilliant daughters, but at times, he wished they weren't as logical as they were. He often found himself unable to argue his position and win when they cornered his king and yelled *Checkmate!*

"Thank you, Luna, for taking such good care of the kittens."

"Okay," Dean said after Rayna caught his gaze. "I know when I'm outnumbered. If it's okay with Rayna, Magic can live in the main house."

"Is it okay with you?" Luna asked her.

"It is," Rayna said. "I do think that he's chosen you as his person, and we need to honor that choice."

A broad smile mixed with surprise brought the light and joy back to his daughter's face. Luna carefully picked up Magic, handed him over to Rayna, then stood up and ran over to him, throwing herself into his arms.

"Thank you, Dad."

She cried a fresh batch of tears—happy ones now, ones she dried off on his flannel shirt. He held her tightly, kissed her head, and when he looked over his daughter's head to catch Rayna's eye, his love for her, already so deep, expanded. He needed Rayna like he needed air; and now he was convinced that not only did *he* need her, so did his daughters.

Paisley was petting Magic's head, and Rayna asked her, "Do you want to hold him?"

Paisley nodded and accepted the kitten into her arms. She stood up and walked over to where Dean was still holding Luna.

"I guess we can put him in the laundry room for now," Paisley suggested. "Just until we get everything set up for him."

"That's a good idea," Dean said.

"I'm going to take Big Tux and Little Tux home today. You can take the food, the bowls and the kitty box for him. I have extras of everything at home," Rayna said as she stood up with a sheepish expression on her face. "I think our job here is done."

Dean met his true love's eye and winked at her. "Good work, cowgirl."

And as a total surprise, he meant it. It was good work—in a roundabout way, he'd learned that Luna had deep emotions hidden inside and somehow Magic had brought them to the surface. To that point, Magic was helping her emotionally and would continue to help moving forward. Luna broke away from him, threw herself into Rayna's arms and squeezed her tight. In a very natural manner, Rayna kissed his daughter on the top of her head.

He saw the expression on Paisley's face, and her reaction to the scene unfolding was one of unhappiness. She tugged on her sister's sleeve. "Come on, Luna. We need to get him settled in the house."

The girls picked up all of the supplies and took Magic up to the main house. Rayna gathered up her remaining kittens and put them into the carrier.

"Sorry about that." She tucked her hands into the back pockets of her jeans. "Totally not my intention."

"Crime doesn't pay," he said, teasing her, then added, "Come here."

The barn was quiet at the moment—a lull in activity—so Rayna came right into his arms.

Dean wrapped her up in his arms. "I know you didn't intend for this to happen, but it *did* happen and that unintended consequence taught me something about my baby girl. She needs Magic just as much as he needs her."

"So my major muck-up actually helped?"

"Yes." Dean used his finger to gently lift her head up. "It did."

They kissed, her soft lips against his, her body pressed against his, and the reaction was sudden and urgent.

He kissed her lips one more time and then asked, "Meet me at the hill?"

This was their code for *Let's have a secret rendezvous at the tree house.* As of late, neither of them had the time to indulge in that alone time, but he felt that being alone with Rayna, kissing her, loving her, talking to her had become less of a luxury and more of an aching need.

She combed her slim fingers through his beard, and he could read in her eyes that she was ready to take that next step with him. "Yes. What time?"

"Four?"

She nodded and then kissed him again with her cool hands on his face, her body leaned into his. "Don't be late."

"Not a chance of that."

He picked up the carrier and walked her out to her truck. "I believe these belong to you?"

"You're never going to let me live this down, will you?"

He smiled at her, knowing that his love for her was on full display as he looked at her. "Not a chance, Ray. No chance at all."

With the kittens safely stowed away in the camper, and after having spent time with them so they could adapt to their new home, Rayna prepared to meet Dean at the top of the hill. She didn't have to guess at what might transpire between them. She was well aware that they were going to make love. He wanted it, and she wanted it just the same. They had become friends again, and now as when they'd barely been adults, they would become lovers.

She drove the Gator up to the hill and didn't much care who saw her on the Brand side of the fence; on Dean's side, and until Paisley could adjust to the reality of her parents moving on, they still needed to downplay their feelings.

"There she is." Dean was waiting for her and greeted her where she parked. "Do you want to drive us in?"

She nodded, and he joined her. "I'm happy to see you."

"I'm happy to see you." She leaned over and met him halfway for a quick kiss. "I've really missed you."

"I've missed you."

"It's been tough—you taking on boarders and getting ready for Thanksgiving, and me swamped getting ready for our guests."

"It's been busy, that's for sure. I've had to give up trimming for now. I don't even have time to trim the horses on-site. Did you get ahold of Katie?"

They hit a bump, and she laughed as the Gator caught some air. "I did. She's super cool."

"Good. I won't admit this to anyone else. She's actually a much better farrier than me."

"So we've been getting second-rate service, Mr. Legend?"

"Only second rate in that department." He put his hand on her thigh. "Every other service I would like to provide for you is top notch."

They reached the tree house, quickly took the stairs, and once inside, Dean flipped on the stored power and the small space began to heat up quickly. They both stripped off their outerwear, and then Dean pulled her into his arms and kissed her face, her neck, breathed in the scent of her hair.

"You're so beautiful, Ray. God, I love you so much."

Rayna held on to him, feeling secure and happy in his arms. He was a mountain of a man with a thick beard and a hairy chest. He was masculine—a protector, a provider, and she felt love for him that was deep, unconditional, and that extended to his daughters. The only way to know that this kind of love existed was to *feel* it firsthand.

"I love you, Dean."

He touched his forehead to hers. "I needed this, Ray. I needed you. I just want to be able to hold your hand wherever we are. I want to kiss your sweet lips every single time I see you."

Dean kissed her, long, slow, seductively, and that kiss sent sparks of desire lighting up her entire body, head to toe.

"You feel so good, Ray. I love to touch you." He kissed her neck.

Rayna reached up and ran her fingers through his beard. "I want you, Dean."

"Are you sure?" he asked. "I mean *really* sure?"

She nodded, stepped back and pulled her sweater over her head and dropped it on the floor.

"Bless it, Ray." Dean's eyes drank her in. "You're too damn pretty for me. I've got a five biscuits for breakfast dad bod over here."

Rayna walked right over to him, moved his hand out of her way and started to unbutton his shirt. "You are handsome, James Dean Legend! If you have a 'dad bod,' then I love it!"

Once she got him out of his shirt, she ran her fingers through his chest hair, which was much thicker and more abundant than when he'd been a young man. "Sexy man."

"If you like it, then I'm good with it. You're the only woman I want to impress."

Dean sat down and yanked off his boots. "I had a vasectomy."

Rayna kicked off her boots. "I had my tubes tied."

He stood up and unzipped his pants. "So two goalies are on deck."

Clothes off, they stood looking at each other, stripped down to their underwear, with twenty years behind them.

"You're the most beautiful woman I've ever seen."

"Thank you, Dean. Somehow you always know the exact right thing to say to make me feel better."

"I know you."

"You do," she agreed, walking over to where he stood, rooted in one spot like an oak tree.

She wrapped her arms around him, resting her head on his chest, listening to his rapid heartbeat. "I want you to know all of me, Dean."

He said, "Hold that thought! Don't move, and don't get out of the mood."

"Okay," she said with an amused smile.

Dean left her for a moment to throw the love seat cushions onto the ground so he could pull out a single bed.

He laughed at her expression. "I promise no one has ever been here. This was a 'just in case' purchase."

"Just in case I showed back up into your life at some point and we rekindled our romance and then came here to make love?"

"Build it, and she will come." He grabbed a blanket out of a nearby chest.

"And here I am." She laughed because his long-shot plan had actually worked.

"And here you are." He kissed her again, and she loved the way he felt, so burly and strong, and she loved his scent, so woodsy and masculine. In his arms, those sparks of anticipation of desire and anticipation were still lighting up her body, giving her that feeling that had eluded her for too many years.

"It's been years since I've…" she started to say.

"Me too," he said. "I just want to ask one more time—are you sure you want this? Are you sure you want me?"

"Stop talking, cowboy." She grabbed his hand and led him to the bed. "I've got a very long honey-do list for you, so you best get started."

They made love two times. The first was intense, fiery and urgent. The second time was slow, languid, and it had given them a chance to have long kisses and let their lips and hands roam as they would. Rayna loved the way Dean's body felt skin-to-skin with hers, his lips on her body and her lips on his. After their second helping, they lay together, their bodies intertwined like vines on a tree.

"Was it always like this?" he asked her.

"No." She laughed. "We were so young. We didn't even really know *how* to do it, much less how to make it 'bells, whistles and fireworks' for either of us."

"Yeah." He laughed. "I think I struggled to see how our puzzle pieces were supposed to fit together, and my only education was from my buds—and they didn't know what the heck they were talking about either. All I knew was that I was supposed to last all night and then somehow take you to heaven and back on a wave of orgasms."

"I had no idea of the kind of pressure you were putting on yourself!"

"Did you get all of those elusive bells, whistles and fireworks today?"

She smiled. "I went to heaven and back on a wave of orgasms with Fourth of July fireworks lighting up the sky as I descended back to Earth."

He chuckled, pulled her closer and kissed her head. "Well, that's a relief."

"Quite a relief for me too!"

"Naughty girl," he said, his voice sleepy as he started to doze off while he kept her close to him. "I just love you so much, Ray. Every day I love you more than the day before."

"I love you," Rayna said, the rhythmic sound of Dean's steady heartbeat lulling her asleep. "You're the perfect man for me."

Chapter Fifteen

The week leading up to Thanksgiving felt like a blur. All of the decorations had been delivered one truck at a time. Every box felt like its own Christmas present, and she loved opening each one to see her holiday goodies that she had selected. There were lovely, delicate balls that were hand blown and incredibly delicate.

"Where are you off to?" Wayne intercepted her on her way to her truck. "I thought we were setting up the solar panels today."

"Wayne! I'm so sorry. I forgot to tell you that I have to go next door."

He seemed relieved to be off the hook, and she said, "You really need to get more rest and stay out of the cold, Wayne."

"That's not my temperament."

"I know. But we need you in full health when the Barons arrive."

"I'll do my best," Wayne said before he headed back in the direction of the house he now shared with Charlie.

"Hi, Dean," she answered an incoming call.

"It's not Dad—it's me, Luna. Are you coming over? My turn is coming up."

"I'm on my way now."

She heard Luna say to Dean, "She's on her way, Dad."

Luna was practicing again for a 4-H competition, and she *persistently* wanted Rayna to be there to watch. In Montana, she seemed to always be running late; it made her Type A personality crazy, but it didn't change anything. There was so much to do, and everything seemed to take longer.

She pulled onto the drive that would take her to the barn and found a spot big enough for her truck, parked, hopped down and rushed to the bleachers. She saw Dean sitting in their previous spot. She waved to him and then climbed the stairs to sit next to him.

"Has she gone?"

Dean pointed to the arena. "Right now."

"Oh, thank goodness."

"She was persistent, oh, buddy," Dean said. "When my Luna gets an idea in her head, God bless, she will not stop until she gets it. And she wanted you here today."

"And she got me." Rayna smiled and tucked her hands into her coat pockets.

Luna took her horse through the horsemanship paces and faltered a bit on the back-up portion but all in all had a clean showing. When she was finished, Dean and Rayna stood up, clapped, and when Luna saw her in the stands, her face lit up and she smiled a huge smile that made Rayna feel so special. She still had a lot of work to do with Paisley, but Luna was one of her greatest fans and she returned that feeling.

"She's a really good one, Dean. I love her."

"She is that. And she loves you."

They watched the rest of the girls perform, and then they went to find Luna, who was brushing her horse in the stall. She rushed over to Rayna when she saw her and launched herself into her arms. "Did you see me for the whole time?"

"I did. And you were phenomenal."

"Thank you," Luna said, hugged her dad and then got back to her horse.

"How's Magic?"

"He's taken over the entire house. He spends a lot of time helping Miss Minnie in the kitchen, and he hangs out with Grandpa even though he says he's allergic. But every day when I get home from school…" Luna shrugged. "He's on the bed with Grandpa."

"I'm glad he's doing so well." Rayna smiled.

"I didn't hear a bomb go off at Hideaway Ranch. So, I'm thinking that…"

"No, I haven't told Charlie. I don't want to pester her with minor details."

He smiled at her. "Two minor *kitten* details. My suggestion? Rip that band aid right off."

"You doubt the wisdom of my plan?" she asked playfully.

"Absolutely I do."

Dean introduced her to the other parents as they walked by. In a short amount of time, the word had gotten out that Legend Ranch was the place to board a horse, and at the pace he was going, he could have a full stable by spring. He was experiencing some growing pains for sure; he was doing most of the barn maintenance until he could hire a full-time person to take over. The girls helped him at feeding time before and after school, though. And he'd managed to secure the hay, grain and bedding he needed, and he was in the process of figuring out where to build a compost pile away from the main house and the barn.

Dean reached out and brushed the top of Rayna's hand with his, and that was her signal that he missed their physical touch. After they'd consummated their relationship at the tree house, they'd had yet to find another time to slip away. They spoke every night after the girls had gone to bed, and this helped them connect at least once every day. Someday they would have more time together; for now, they both had too much important business on their plates to blithely put their budding romance ahead of everything else.

"I've really got to get back," she said reluctantly. "I'm still inventorying my decorations and checking and re-checking my ingredient list. And I still need to get ready for Thanksgiving."

Her mother, Rose, had always baked the pies when they had their joint Brand-Legend holiday dinners. Rayna felt grateful that she had taken the time to learn from Rose how to make all of her pies—classic apple with plump raisins, deep-dish pumpkin pie, crunchy cherry pie and decadent chocolate-pecan pie.

"Are you making your mom's greatest hits?" Dean asked.

"All four." She nodded. It was a tradition that Rose would bake the Thanksgiving pies and Miss Nettie would bake the pies for Christmas.

He pat his belly. "I'm ready for a slice of each."

Without thinking about it, she happily leaned into him, put her head on his shoulder and said, "I'll make sure you get the biggest slices."

"I'm going to hold you to that!"

As she was heading out of the barn, Luna spotted her, yelled her name while she ran full tilt in her direction.

"Yes, ladybug?"

Luna's cheeks were flushed, and she was out of breath. "I forgot to tell you! One of the parents got hurt and can't ride in the Christmas parade."

"I'm so sorry to hear that," Rayna said, not sure why Luna had tracked her down so urgently to tell her this.

"So, I told Mrs. Post that you would do it."

"I'm sorry. What did you do?" Dean looked at his youngest with curiosity. "Volunteer Rayna to ride in the Christmas parade?"

"Uh-huh." Luna's head bobbed up and down.

"Ladybug, I can't ride in a parade," Rayna said kindly to her. "Mrs. Post will have to find someone who can ride."

"You can ride," Luna countered. "Dad says you used to race him bareback."

"I did," Rayna said slowly. "But that was a long, long, *long* time ago."

"I'll speak with Mrs. Post," Dean reassured her. "I think you had a great idea, Luna, but in the future just run any of your big ideas by me first. Okay?"

"Okay." Luna frowned, her brow furrowing as she fist-bumped her dad. "But I want Rayna to be with me. I need her."

Dean looked at Rayna. "I'm sorry. This came out of left field."

"It's okay," she said. "It's nice to be loved."

Luna wrapped her arms around her body. "I love you, Ray."

The way she was holding on to her, the love that she felt from Luna in word and in deed made her feel incredibly special. Luna had already won her heart. In fact, even though it was rougher waters with Paisley, she loved Dean's girls.

"Please, Ray!" Luna was still holding on to her.

Rayna ran her hand across the girl's silky hair and asked, "Why do you think you need me, Luna?"

"Everybody has somebody in the parade," she said with genuine pain in her voice. "I don't have anybody."

"Are you sure you want to do this?" Dean asked Rayna. "I know you *can* do it."

Rayna was standing on the bottom step of a very tall

mounting block less than an hour after Luna had volunteered her for the parade. She was wearing a safety vest and a riding helmet, and her facial expression could only be read as fear mixed with resignation.

"Why do you keep asking me that?" she snapped at him. "Don't you think I know my own mind? I did manage to survive over twenty years without you asking me that question!"

It was rare that Rayna was snappy, and all it meant was that she felt insecure and stressed—two feelings that should stop them from moving forward.

Rayna closed her eyes, took a deep breath in and then let it out slowly. Then she opened her eyes, seemed to give herself an internal pep talk, and he could see that she was resolved to getting back in the saddle.

"Why can't I say no to that sweet little face of hers?" she asked Dean, still standing on the bottom step of the mounting block. Her would-be steed, Apollo, a geriatric Quarter-Clydesdale cross, had fallen asleep while Rayna made up her mind.

"I ask myself that same question all of the time."

Rayna set her jaw, nodded her head in response to some internal dialogue, put her hand on Apollo's large round rump, reached out for Dean's hand, which he gave to her. She squeezed his hand hard while she moved up to the second step. Apollo's head dropped lower, completely unbothered by Rayna's nerves or the length of time it was taking for her to attempt a mount.

"You've got this Ray."

"Quit talking to me!"

Dean zipped his lip and did his best to support her *quietly* while she contemplated moving up to the top step.

"Don't let go!" she said.

"I won't."

"Don't let go!" she said again, stepping up to the final step.

"You did it Ray!"

"It's too high. Why is it so high?" Rayna wobbled on the top step. "Were horses always this tall?"

He waited for her to calm her nerves again before he said, "Only one more step, Ray. When you're ready, just swing your leg over his back and sit down."

"Quit rushing me!" she barked at him, and he could see her hands shaking when she reached over to get a hold of the saddle horn.

Dean moved over to stand next to Apollo's head. He put the reins over the sleeping horse's head and rested them on the horse's neck so she could easily reach them.

"Don't let go, Dean. If you let go, I swear…" Rayna slowly swung her right leg over the top of the saddle, balancing her body weight on the saddle horn.

"I've got him, Ray. You're doing great."

She was stuck straddling the saddle with her left foot still on the top step of the mounting block.

"Just sit down gently and, slow and steady, bring your left foot over."

Rayna followed the direction and sat down in the saddle. There was a flash of self-satisfaction on her face, and she picked up the reins with one hand while still holding on to the saddle horn.

"Good job, Ray," Dean said. "I'm proud of you."

Now that she was in the saddle, she actually smiled at him. "I'm proud of myself."

He showed her where to attach the safety vest hook that, if pulled on, would inflate, saving her from major injury should she fall. "Do you want him to walk forward?"

"Okay," Rayna agreed. "But don't let go. Don't leave me!"

He caught her eye and said, "I will never leave you, Ray."

Together they walked slowly around the indoor arena—the only speed that they could walk was *slow* because that was the only speed Apollo had.

"Ray!" Luna waved at her from the bleachers. "Good job!"

Rayna smiled at her and waved, then she realized her hand wasn't on the saddle horn anymore, so she grabbed for it.

"How does it feel?" he asked her.

"Scary," she said honestly. "I have no idea how I used to ride horse bareback with only a lead rope and halter, fully galloping and jumping over anything in my way."

"We were young," Dean said with a smile.

After two times walking around the arena, Rayna said, "I think I can do it on my own now."

He stopped walking and looked at her. "Are you sure you…"

When he realized he was just about to ask the question that ticked her off, he shook it off and said as he backed away from Apollo, "If you need me, I'll be right here."

Dean watched Rayna ride for the first time since she'd been in high school. She probably didn't realize it, but she still had a great riding seat and was intuitively doing what she had been trained to do when she'd been a young girl helping her father round up cattle. When she was ready to get off, she rode over to the mounting block, had a momentary freak-out when Apollo shifted his weight while she was straddled with one foot on the block and her right leg over the saddle.

"It's okay, Ray," he said in a voice that he deliberately tried to sound like he was being bossy. "He's not going anywhere."

Ray nodded, holding on tightly to the saddle horn while she slowly and cautiously swung her right leg over the saddle until she had both feet on the third step. A smile of pure happiness lit up her face as she raised her arms over her head. "I did it!"

She took a step backward and downward.

"Wait!" Dean said. "You forgot to…"

He didn't finish that sentence because the saddle strap lanyard hooked to one of the stirrup straps was pulled when she stepped back, and it activated the canister of CO_2 and inflated the vest in one fell swoop. The sudden inflation of the vest caught Rayna completely off guard, she wobbled to the right, reaching for Apollo, and then she lost her balance and fell off the mounting block.

"I've got you!" Dean caught her in his arms and gently set her down on the ground.

Once Rayna's feet were safely on the ground, she looked at the vest that was now inflated.

"Are you okay?" he asked.

She nodded, running her hands over the inflated vest. "This thing really works."

"Yes, it does."

She looked up at him. "I would have to practice *a lot* before the parade."

"I'll help you get ready."

"Will I ride Apollo?"

"If you want."

She walked around to Apollo's front side and wrapped her arms around his neck. "Thank you for taking such good care of me."

She patted the sturdy horse on the neck, kissed him on the softest part of his nose and then said to Dean, "If I can ride Apollo, I'll do it. I'll ride with Luna in the parade."

* * *

"Mom!" Ryder Fortier opened the front door of the main cabin. "Everyone's ready to go."

"Come in here and help me with these pies, please!"

Ryder came inside to help her. Her boys had arrived the day before and jumped right into the whirlwind that was her life as she prepared for Thanksgiving *and* the Baron family.

"You look handsome." Rayna looked up at her tall, slender son.

Ryder wore his long hair slicked back off his face and secured at the back of his head with a black hair band. His round John Lennon spectacles combined with his slim-fit forest-green suit hemmed at the ankle, black pointy-toed shoes and festive socks decorated with turkeys made him look like a throw-back hipster from the nineteen sixties.

He hugged her, kissed the top of her head and then picked up the stack of pies housed in individual plastic containers. "You look real nice, Mom."

"Thank you," she said, looking down at her chosen garment.

They had always dressed up for Brand-Legend holiday get-togethers; it had given everyone an opportunity to wash off the mud, dirt and manure, strip off the jeans and boots and get a little fancy. Even with her hectic schedule, she had taken the time to get her roots colored and she had put on makeup with a very light hand. When she looked in the mirror, she liked the image that was looking back at her.

"Okay." She slipped into a new cashmere long coat for dressier occasions. "Go, go! We're late!"

"You stole my line!" Ryder laughed, and that laughter did her heart good. She had been busy enough at the ranch to not pine for her boys every second of every day, but that didn't mean she didn't miss them like a constant ache in her body.

She held on to his arm as they descended the stairs to where the others were waiting on her. Charlie, Wayne and Waylon were in one truck, and Rowdy was in the Beast.

"Mom's gone country on us, Ryder!" Rowdy teased from the back seat.

While Ryder seemed more slender from his regular yoga practice, Rowdy had bulked up from his daily weight training with the junior varsity team. For his "dressy" clothes, Rowdy was wearing a dark-wash jean with a button-down shirt and boots that were scuffed at the toes and mostly clean.

Ryder handed the pies to his brother before he climbed into the front seat. Rayna got behind the wheel, waved to Charlie that she was ready to go. They had always traveled as a pack when they headed over to the Legend ranch, and it felt nostalgic in the best way that she was able to continue this tradition with her own boys. That was an unexpected blessing.

She cranked the Beast, revved the engine and shifted into Drive. She followed Charlie out of the inner sanctum and onto the long drive leading to the state road.

"I have to admit, Mom, I would never pin you driving a monster truck."

She smiled, liking the fact that she had surprised her sons. "I feel more like myself in the Beast than I have in any other vehicle I've owned."

Ryder looked back at his brother before he said, "You've changed."

She heard the note of concern in her son's voice. "Does that upset you?"

"Naw," Rowdy said, and she knew he meant it. He took

things in stride in a way Ryder had never been able to do. "Why should it? It's your life."

"What about you, Ryder?"

His wheels were spinning for a second before he said, "You've changed everything. How you dress, what you drive, your hair color, where you live! It's a lot to process."

"I can understand that, Rye, but..." She shrugged. "I have changed a lot, but it's been organic, not planned or deliberate. It just *is*."

"I think it's good," Rowdy said. "You seem happier to me."

Ryder looked out the window, and she could sense his internal conflict—of course he wanted her to be happy, but she knew from their weekly conversations that he was struggling more than Rowdy about the divorce. And this was the first holiday after the divorce; she would be lying to herself if she thought that, even with all of the good things that were unexpectedly happening in her life, this Thanksgiving was not a hurdle they all had to jump. And Christmas was the next hurdle. Rowdy and Ryder were spending Christmas with their grandparents and their father, and it would be their first Christmas as a fractured family.

Rayna parked her truck next to Charlie's, and bearing pies and her mother's incredible ambrosia, they walked as a family toward the front porch steps. Dean had told her that family didn't knock, so she didn't. They all filed into a line behind her as she walked through the door. The minute she walked into the house, her senses were delighted with the smells of the holiday—buttered biscuits fresh out of the oven, sweet-potato casserole, gravy and stuffing, all homemade from scratch.

The minute Dean saw them, he walked with long strides to greet them. He shook each of her sons' hands, and then did the same for Waylon and Wayne. He hugged Charlie, but even though Rayna knew that Dean wanted to greet her as his love, Paisley's eyes were on them. Instead, he helped her out of her coat and then quietly he said, "You look beautiful, Ray."

She spun around, looked up at him. "You trimmed your beard."

"I figured I could spruce myself up a bit," he said. "Do you like it?"

She wanted to touch it in the worst way, but she used her powers of self-control. "Long beard, short beard, no beard...you always look good to me."

The minute the two families began to mingle, the kitchen and dining room were filled with booming voices and so much laughter. Her sons gravitated to Dean, and when she happened to glance their way, they were engrossed in conversation. She made her way through the group, delivering the pies to Miss Minnie and asking if she needed help in the kitchen. After Miss Minnie shooed her out of the kitchen, she found Buck, who was holding court with Charlie, Wayne and Waylon.

"Daughter!" Buck reached out his arms for a hug. "Happy Thanksgiving!"

She hugged him and kissed his cheek. "This is all because of you, Dad."

Luna found her and glued herself to her for a good long while until she noticed the door opening. When she saw her mother at the door, she yelled "Mom!" and ran as fast as she could to her side.

Catrin had arrived alone and Rayna knew from Dean that Nico had decided that a big family get-together wasn't the best way to get to know the girls, so he had stayed back in Monaco. Before entering, Catrin had taken off her shoes, and Rayna had an acquaintance who had grown-up in Cambodia and she knew that this was Cambodian tradition. Dean's ex-wife set her shoes down just outside of the door before she absorbed her youngest daughter into her embrace. When Paisley heard Luna yell, she raced toward the door and joined in.

Catrin kissed both of her girls, told them that she loved them in Khmer. With one daughter holding on to each of her hands, she walked toward the kitchen flanked by her girls. Rayna wasn't one to be starstruck, but she kind of was with Catrin. The clothing designer had a petite frame, standing no more than five feet. She had a beautiful round face, soft brown eyes and full lips. Her straight black hair was bluntly cut just above her shoulders with bangs just above her perfectly shaped eyebrows. She wore a jumpsuit with palazzo pants, a wide belt highlighting her small waist, and she wore a strand of brilliant diamonds around her slender neck.

Rayna felt her heart pumping so fast that now she felt jittery—she just didn't know how Catrin would react to her when she knew that Dean had always held back a piece of his heart that he had reserved for her only.

Dean walked over to greet his ex-wife, and Rayna couldn't stop herself from watching the interaction and picking it apart in her mind. The greeting was cordial but cold: they shook hands and then they walked together so Catrin could spend time with Buck.

"Catrin!" he said. "I'm so glad you came."

"Happy Thanksgiving, Buck." She kissed him on the cheek. "Thank you for inviting me."

"Have you met my daughter, Rayna?" Buck asked Catrin, pointing at her.

"No," Catrin said quietly and offered her hand, "I have not had the pleasure."

"It's so nice to meet you. I'm a huge fan of your work." Rayna shook the slender, small hand of Dean's ex-wife; up close, Rayna believed that Catrin was one of the most stunningly beautiful women she had ever met.

"I must have made that dress just for you." The designer said, appearing to check over the details of her dress, her shoes, her make-up and hair. And, for some unknown reason, Catrin's examination of her made her feel both nervous and hopeful that the designer would approve of her choices. "Quite striking."

"I've never worn anything more beautiful than this. What inspired you to make it?"

"It was a nod to the traditional Cambodian Sampot Hol. I bought this fabric during my last trip to Cambodia," Catrin said of the cobalt-blue silk with floral patterns at the bottom of the long, narrow skirt of the dress.

"I feel honored to own it," Rayna said sincerely. "I wasn't sure if I should wear it for this occasion."

That brought a genuine smile to Catrin's face. "Of course you should have. It is the perfect complement to your lovely eyes."

When Miss Minnie called them all to the table, Rayna could not fully wrap her head around the fact that everyone was getting along. Meetings that could have spiraled into an awkward, painful dinner that felt like it was never going to end hadn't turned out that way at all. Her boys had taken a liking to Dean, and she had taken a liking to Catrin. Dean positioned himself across the table from her, and at one point he gave her a fleeting wink and a smile, and that smile set her heart to fluttering. Perhaps it seemed too soon for a romance to flourish between them from the outside looking in, but for her and for Dean, it seemed as natural as breathing air.

Chapter Sixteen

The week after Thanksgiving had been a mad dash to get the ranch ready for the Baron family. Wayne had finally fully recovered from his bout with COVID, and it was just in time to get the firepit—which was slated for toasting marshmallows, hosting holiday singalongs and roasting chestnuts—spruced up. Ryder and Rowdy pitched in with the decorating effort. They had helped her every year back in Connecticut, so they already knew what she wanted and knew that sloppy work was never acceptable.

"I'm sad to see you go," Rayna said to her boys. "Be safe driving. Crazy people on the roads this time of year."

"We will." Rowdy engulfed her in a giant hug.

"I love you, Mom." Ryder hugged her tightly. "I just want you to be happy."

"Okay," she said, holding on for just a minute longer before letting him go.

Rowdy started their rental car and rolled down the window.

"Hey, Mom," he said, "we both like Dean. He's a good guy."

She hadn't expected to hear that at all, so she didn't know exactly what to say. She had never needed to discuss her dating life with her sons, but they had known about her high school sweetheart—they had seen pictures and heard stories.

Ryder leaned forward so she could see him when he said, "We just thought you'd like to know."

Rayna waved as she watched them drive away. Would it always be this difficult to say goodbye to them as they went off on their own life adventure in the world?

"Sad to see them go." Charlie walked up behind her with Bowie in tow.

"It is," Rayna said, grateful for the distraction of finishing the outdoor decorations.

"The house looks amazing, Ray." Charlie turned her attention to the main house after Rowdy and Ryder's car was out of the line of sight.

"The boys knew exactly what to do down to the last detail," Rayna said. "They took a major weight off my shoulders."

Her sister took in the garland wrapped around the porch banister, the large wreath with white lights hung on the front roof gable and the large red bows that adorned every other porch spindle.

"What's left on your to-do list?"

"Just the main-road gate, the trees lining the drive and the barn. I am going to decorate the chicken coop…"

"Of course." Charlie smiled.

"Waylon is already started on the barn—he's a hard worker."

"Westbrooks."

"Did you say that Dean was coming over tomorrow to help with the lights up front?"

She nodded. "Having a boyfriend comes in handy."

"We've gone to labels now?" Charlie teased. "Hideaway Ranch can give you a great rate on an all-inclusive wedding package."

Rayna laughed. "Let's not get too ahead of ourselves. I'm not even sure I'm staying in Montana after snow season."

"Yes, you are," Charlie said. "I saw how you look at Dean and how Dean looks at you."

Rayna couldn't deny that there was a strong chance she would build a life in Montana—leaving Dean now seemed improbable if not impossible. But they were dedicated to moving slowly and letting his children have time to adjust in a way her grown boys didn't need. And even though Luna was her biggest fan, Rayna knew that there were deep waters in that little girl's heart and she felt everything so intensely. Dean and she both wanted to help Luna navigate unfamiliar waters as easily as she could.

"How are Big Tux and Little Tux doing?" Charlie asked her.

Rayna's brow lowered and then she asked, "You know about the kittens."

Charlie laughed heartily. "Ray! Everyone knows about the kittens! People as far away as Bozeman know about the kittens!"

"Who blabbed?"

"I'm not naming names. Suffice it to say that I know, and I'm not upset at all," Charlie said easily. "Why did you think I'd care one way or another?"

"The donkeys."

"Well, I was wrong about them," Charlie said. "This is your ranch as much as it is mine, and if you wanted to add donkeys to the fun of the ranch, I should have accepted it."

"We were on a very tight budget."

"Yes, we were, but two miniature donkeys weren't going to break the bank one way or the other. I was a lone wolf here for many years, and I guess I needed to adjust to sharing it even with my sisters. But if you wanted them to be barn cats, you should have had them sleep in the heated tack room. Now that they are used to sleeping with you in a comfy bed? They will hunt you down and cry at your door until you let then in."

"That's what Dean said."

Charlie shrugged and gave her a look that said, *And he's right.*

That night, Rayna was propped up in her bed, Big Tux upside down next to her with his pink toes curled, so content that he looked like he was smiling. Little Tux was on her lap, curled into a tiny ball, purring with happiness while she scrolled through more Christmas ornaments on her favorite websites. It had become kind of an addiction, and she was finding it difficult to just say *I have enough* and stop herself from obsessively searching.

"Enough, Rayna!" She turned off her tablet and put it on the small nightstand by the bed. Little Tux opened her eyes, looked at her to let her know that her outburst had interrupted her good rest.

"I'm sorry, little one." Rayna pet her soft fur and scratched her chops to make amends. "I'll try to do better."

Those kittens weren't the only ones that had grown to enjoy bedtime; Rayna couldn't imagine how to fall asleep without her silky soft, loving, purring kittens.

Her boys sent her a text and let her know that their plane had landed and they were safely in Oregon. She texted that she loved them both before she closed her eyes, so tired from her workload and feeling now as if she were never going to finish. Some of the bloom was off her rose. She hoped that once it was done and she had checked everything off her list, and the ranch was decorated in a way that screamed *classic White Christmas*, she would feel a resurgence of excitement. It would be wonderful to see all of her hard work enjoyed by the Barons.

Her phone rang, and it caught her off guard because she must have dozed off. She searched around herself, looking in the folds of the comforter and finally found it under Big Tux. She tried to slide it out from under him without disturbing him too much. Big Tux rolled over onto his side, toes curling; he opened his eyes and meowed at her in a way that definitely sounded like a complaint.

"Sorry," she said to her handsome boy. "Hi, Dean."

"What did you do wrong?"

"What?"

"What did you do wrong? You said that you were sorry."

"Oh! No. Not you—Big Tux."

"Well, I wouldn't mind an apology about Magic the Cat, who has taken over every inch of my house."

"You're welcome," she said with a smile. "How are you?"

"Tired. But good," he said before he yawned loudly. "The girls are with their mom, so it's quiet. Too quiet."

"I know." She petted Big Tux and made him purr loudly. "The boys left today."

"Man. What great boys you have, Rayna! I wish they lived closer."

"Me too!"

They chatted for a bit about the Christmas parade and what was left that needed doing in the decoration department. Then Dean said, "I did have a talk with Cat about us."

"Well, that curveball just hit me in the face."

"Sorry," he said. "That was actually the reason for my call. Not that I think I need a reason…"

"You don't."

"So, we had a productive talk—she really liked you and in her own way approved of you being in her daughters' lives."

"Wow," she said slowly and then repeated it. *"Wow."*

"And we both sat down with the girls and explained the changes that were happening in their lives."

She listened and gave him plenty of time to work through what he wanted to relay to her.

"Luna seems to be more resilient, but Cat and I agree that we can't assume that she's okay. Paisley, on the other hand, doesn't hide anything. She doesn't keep a whole lot hidden..."

"No."

"And in one way, that's easier, and then on the other hand, she can give us a run for our money," Dean said. "But the most important thing that Cat said to Paisley was about you."

Rayna leaned into the conversation, her brain hoping for good news while her body tensed up on her.

"Cat told her that it was important for her to give you a chance and that she's okay with any relationship that I have with you—friendship or otherwise."

"Wow." She said it again.

"And to be fair, I let the girls know that I was happy for their mother's engagement and that, while we still needed to meet him and such, I trusted Cat's judgment."

Rayna couldn't say anything in return because it was all so unexpected. She had thought that things would move slowly and orderly, but that wasn't the case.

"Are you still there, Ray?"

She cleared her throat. "Yes. I'm still here."

"Did I just freak you out?"

"Yes and no."

"Just because we had this talk, doesn't mean we need to rush anything. I'm happy with how things are between us. Do I want more one day? Yes, of course, and I don't think that comes as any big surprise."

"No."

"So, what's on your mind, Ray? Talk to me."

"Um... I'm thinking that I love you."

"And I love you."

"And I love your girls and your dad," she said. "And I think Cat is absolutely fangirl worthy. I mean, Dean, she's gorgeous, intelligent, a good mother, an incredible artist and she's an international phenomenon."

"Are you trying to talk me in to remarrying her?"

Rayna laughed. "No. I'm not. But I do wonder..."

"Why we couldn't make it work?"

"Yes! I mean, honestly, I haven't ever wanted to be in a relationship with a woman, but in Cat's case, I think I'd give it a try!"

He laughed along with her. "I may not be able to handle you leaving me for my ex-wife, Ray."

"You know what I mean..."

"We ended our marriage because we had both stopped loving each other in that way. I wasn't going to jet all over the world as her purse holder, and she had no desire to spend her life on a cattle ranch. The special place I have always had in my heart for you was not the main reason we ended things. We found ourselves at a crossroad and I took one path and she chose another."

How did Dean always seem to slice through the minutia and hit that hidden place in her mind that worried about that very thing?

All she could say was "I love you, Dean. This relationship I have with you, this friendship that we share... I'm grateful for it."

"I love you, Ray," he said. "I want you in my life always. You are my best friend."

"You are mine."

"So let's just stay on the ride and see where it takes us."

"Agreed," Rayna said. "And by the way, my boys gave you their stamp of approval."

"That's damn good news, Ray."

"I'm tired. I'll see you tomorrow, bright and early for decoration installation."

"Good night, my love. Don't forget to dream about me."

The day before the Baron family was set to arrive, Rayna finally felt as if all of her Christmas plans had come to fruition. At night, the main cabin looked like a scene right out of a Christmas story, and during the day the garland, the bows and the wreaths gave the house a Christmas flare that was both nostalgic and festive.

"How does that look?" Dean was on the top rung of a tall ladder

"Cock-eyed."

"What's the usable translation? Do I move it right, left?"

"I think just a hair to the left," Rayna said, watching Dean put the last gold star on the top of the very last tree in the line of trees that followed the drive to the main hub of the ranch.

"How's that?"

"It's…" she said and actually felt an emotional response. "Perfect. Just perfect."

Dean gave a hallelujah salute to heaven above before he climbed down the ladder, and she hugged him and thanked him. He put his arm around her and kissed her. They finished as dusk arrived, and around them, as if planned by grand design, all of the lights on all of the trees on either side of the driveway lit up and cast hues of green and red and gold onto the snow on the ground.

"Dean." She spun around slowly, mesmerized by the

magic of the moment. "It looks like it was taken right out of a fairytale."

"It has always amazed me the way you design this in your mind and find a way to transfer it from your mind, to paper and then into...this."

She hooked her arm into his. "I couldn't have done it without you."

"I didn't do much, but if what I could do made a difference, then I'm pleased."

"Walk with me?" she asked.

"Absolutely my love."

Together they walked along the drive, the reflection of the twinkling lights dancing all around them. Never in her years of creating a plan for the Christmas decorations in her home in Connecticut, each year a different design, had she felt this sense of accomplishment and pride. Yes, she had delighted children and their parents in their neighborhood, and that had been rewarding. But nothing ever compared to this. Every string of lights, every tree topped, every wreath was chosen specifically to give the Barons the experience they wanted.

"It's starting to snow!" Rayna laughed, stepping away from Dean to stretch out her arms, tilt back her head and open her mouth to catch a snowflake on her tongue.

"I just love you, Ray," Dean said, watching her with so much love in his eyes for her.

She stopped twirling, walked over to him, wrapped her arms around him and kissed him.

"I love you, James Dean," she said, enjoying the feel of his arm on her shoulders and the warmth of being in his arms as they walked back toward the main house.

"This is going to be amazing," she said. "The Barons are going to love us!"

Dean stopped to pick up the ladder to take it back to Butch's workshop.

"I tell you what, Ray. They'd be crazy not to."

"They're here!" Charlie shouted. "They're here!"

"How do I look?" Rayna asked her sister. "Too much… not enough?"

"You look great," her sister said. "You're serving modern cowgirl vibes."

"Thank you," she said. "Same."

Wayne and Waylon were standing in the kitchen of the main house with them. Neither of them had said more than five words between them in the last thirty minutes.

"How do I look, Waylon?" Wayne asked.

Waylon appeared to be studying his older brother. "I think you're serving modern caveman."

"That's what I was going for!" he said.

Rayna and Charlie turned back to look at the brothers who were so obviously teasing them.

"How do I look?" Waylon posed to the left and then struck a pose on his right side.

"Sensitive cowboy."

"Will the two of you knock it off?" Charlie said. "This is serious."

"Are we going to stand in here chewing the fat, or are we going to greet our guests?" Wayne walked over to the door and took his hat off the hat rack, dusted it off with his hand and then put it on his head. "I'm going to greet these folks. Anyone else care to join me?"

Charlie and Rayna faced each other and said in unison, "We have guests!"

They hugged each other happily and then grabbed their winter gear and followed the two Westbrook brothers out the door, down the steps and marched forward into the new life for their family and their ranch.

Dr. and Mrs. Leonard Baron and their daughter, Hadassah, who went by the nickname Dasi, arrived with a couple of large suitcases that were taken inside of the home by Waylon and Wayne. Rayna had made two eggnogs, one virgin and one spiked, passed down to Rose from her mother and grandmother. Wayne lit a fire in the cozy living room and then asked the Barons to let him know if there was anything he could do to make their visit an authentic one.

"I'd like to get myself a hat like yours," Leonard said.

Dr. Baron was a man of medium height, thick black hair cut short, with some silver at the temples, and his eyes were a deep sable brown. He was heavyset and had the look of a professor with his wire-rim glasses that slipped down his nose frequently. He wore a midnight-blue yalmaka adorned with an outline of silver Stars of David. Any doubt that Rayna had about the family being tied to Judaism dissolved.

"We can get that done for you," Wayne said. "Just let me know when, and I'll take you into Bozeman. You'll also need some cowboy boots."

"The sooner the better. I want to get the works—boots, jeans, a plaid shirt like you've got on there, maybe a silver buckle with a bucking horse and, of course, a cowboy hat."

"The whole cowboy experience," Wayne said.

"Yes! That's exactly right," Leonard said. "And my daughter has asked to have an authentic experience as well."

"Not a problem. After we get you lookin' like ranch hands, we'll have to get you both on a horse and teach you how to drive a tractor."

Leonard stood up, crossed the short distance to Wayne,

offered him his hand and said, "Thank you. That's exactly what I want. The whole experience."

Wayne shook his hand and said, "We can get you to Bozeman as early as tomorrow."

"It's a deal," Leonard said. "Let's get it done."

"Will Mrs. Baron be joining us?"

Jenny Baron was making herself at home in the kitchen, unpacking some groceries and well on her way through a third helping of eggnog. While she worked, she hummed along to the looping Christmas carols that she had turned on for ambiance.

"Mrs. Baron will *not* be joining—thank you for the offer." Jenny smiled.

Rayna liked all three of the Baron family members, but she felt an immediate comfort and connection with Jenny, and she believed that the two of them would complement each other in the kitchen. The other woman wore her wavy dark brown hair in loose layers just past her shoulders. Her hair had a life of its own, bobbing and bouncing and dancing as she moved about. She had lovely hazel-green eyes, dark lashes and pronounced eyebrows. Her face was clean, without any makeup, and she wore simple, comfortable clothes that weren't fussy. Her energy was happy, upbeat, and joyous. She smiled and laughed easily, and Rayna believed it would be very difficult to be in a bad mood with Jenny Baron around.

After Wayne left, Leonard returned to a large rocking chair in the living room, looking content with his surroundings.

"Will your daughter be joining us for carols around the campfire?" she asked Jenny.

"I believe she will," Jenny said of her twenty-five-year-old daughter. "Dasi takes some time to adjust to a new surrounding. She does have autism—high functioning. New places, new people are hard for her. But she's excited to be here, and she's excited to immerse herself in this experience. We feel grateful that you opened your beautiful home to us. We see how much time you have put into making this Christmas wish come true."

"We feel grateful to have you and your family with us, Jenny. I hope we all make holiday memories that will stand the test of time."

On the Barons' first night with them, everything was going according to Rayna's plans. They enjoyed the eggnog—her spiked version being the favorite—and when it was empty, she just added a good deal of rum to the non-spiked version. After Jenny acquainted herself with the kitchen layout, she and Rayna worked together to prepare a light meal. Rayna came to an early realization that cooking was Jenny's delight, so she would be doing the most cooking for her family. In a way, she was relieved because this freed her up to create other experiences for Dasi and practice for the Christmas parade that was looming on the horizon.

At dusk, and after everyone had eaten dinner, everyone gathered at the firepit that Wayne had built using stone pavers and wood benches that he had made from wood sourced on the ranch. The upgrade from a campfire, which did have its charm, was now a perfect place for guests and hosts to gather. Rayna handed out sturdy mugs of hot chocolate while Waylon carved marshmallow sticks for toasting. When the younger Westbrook brother finished handing out sticks, he took a harmonica out of his jacket pocket while Wayne tuned his guitar. All of the Westbrook men were musical, playing multiple instruments between them. They used to tour Texas as the Westbrook Brothers, but Wayne in particular didn't want a life of gigs. He felt like he'd been born to be a rancher, and he fully intended to die a rancher, boots still on.

The Baron family sat huddled together on one long bench, and though clearly they were feeling the cold, none of them seemed deterred. Dasi was toasting a marshmallow for her mom while Wayne began to play his guitar. When Rayna looked around at the twinkly lights everywhere the eye touched they had transformed the ranch into a Christmas wonder. It had turned out so beautifully that it was emotional for her. She had applied skills that she had considered to be "unmarketable" and used her ability to plan a Christmas installation and execute it flawlessly. It was the best Christmas gift she had given to herself and to her family.

"Waylon and I thought you'd like to hear some old campfire songs," Wayne said, tapping out a tempo on the lower part of his guitar. Waylon, his eyes closed, nodded to his brother when he was ready. "Sing along if you know it, and if you don't know it, clap or stomp along with us. This is Roy Rogers's 'Home on the Range.'"

As the music started and Rayna saw the contented, excited faces of the Baron family, she caught Charlie's eye across the campfire and *felt* her sister let out a breath that she had been holding in for nearly a decade. She had fought, clawing and scratching and screaming at the universe, to save this five-generation ranch. Her plan to keep the ranch for generations of Brands to come had been to open the ranch for families like the Barons looking for that wild west experience or corporate retreats or overflow from Big Sky Resort winter-sports enthusiasts. And this night was that plan coming to fruition.

They sang around the campfire for nearly two hours before the Barons started to yawn and notice the cold as the fire died down.

"Thank you for a wonderful first night," Leonard said to all of them.

"Yes, thank you again." Jenny's laugh sounded like little bells ringing, and it was charming. "I'm afraid you will get tired of us thanking you!"

Rayna and Charlie walked with the family back toward the main cabin while Wayne and Waylon cleaned up the firepit. They reached the three large trees that made a triangle on the side of the main house.

"If you wouldn't mind stopping right here for a moment," Rayna said.

The family stopped and listened to her as she spoke. "I did see on the university website that you were born in Israel."

"Yes, that's true."

"So, I wanted to do something to honor that heritage, and I hope you will accept this gesture in the same spirit with which it was done." Rayna walked over to the trees and turned on the lights that she had decorated them with.

The Barons stared at the white-and-blue lights for longer than she would have liked without any feedback. She was beginning to think that she had made a *major* mistake. Until Leonard, Jenny and Dasi walked together to the space inside of the natural triangle the trees had created, hugged each other, and she could hear the raw emotion in Leonard's voice when he said, "He's here with us. He is here!"

Chapter Seventeen

Waylon Westbrook had been following his big brother, Wayne, around the western part of the country for most of his adult life. But cattle and ranch work wasn't where he saw himself in the future. He had quietly earned his bachelor of science and master of science degrees online in astronomy, and he wanted to earn his doctor of philosophy. But to get the most out of that course of study, he needed to be in-person on campus. And when he saw himself ten, twenty years down the road, he imagined he would be working as an aeronautical engineer or an astrophysicist or even as a planetarium director. His brothers Wyatt and Wade needed to be back in Texas and he needed to help Wayne hold down the fort. But after that? He had to follow his dream to earn a PhD.

After everyone went off to bed was his favorite part of the day. It was quiet, and with the holiday lights turned off on the main house and barn and the moon just a sliver, the expansive Montana night sky delivered a payload of stars! Waylon got his telescope out of the roomy tent, which was his choice of living space. He used the refurbished bunkhouse to shower and such, but the tent gave him the unencumbered, minimalist life that made the most sense to him.

Waylon set up his telescope near the firepit and turned

his attention to the stars. "Ah, there you are, my queen. What a beauty you are."

"You can see Cassiopeia?" A question came out of the dark, and it made him jump.

"Yes. I can," Waylon said, realizing that the voice came from Dasi Baron. Now that he was looking at, and focusing on, the bench on the far side of the firepit, he could see her as a shadowing figure.

"Can I?"

"Sure," Waylon said politely, but his time with his love, the universe, was an affair that he was used to having alone.

Dasi walked over to him, and he moved back as she quietly took her turn with the stars. "Polaris is so brilliant! I've never seen it like this before."

Waylon moved back to his spot. He adjusted the telescope to search the sky for Cepheus and its distinctive house shape.

"Cepheus," he said to her. "Do you want to look?"

Dasi looked into the lens of the telescope and then she said, "Cepheus constellation, named after a king of Aethiopia in Greek mythology. The major stars in the Cepheus constellation approved by the Astrological Union, also known by the acronym IAU, are Aldermin, Alfirk, Errai and Kurhah."

Waylon felt like a steamroller had flattened him, and that made him take a closer look at his unexpected company.

"You know astronomy," he said.

"Yes," she said.

"Do you study it?"

"No. Not really."

Waylon felt like now Dasi was a puzzle he needed to solve. "It took me years of study to know what you know."

"Oh," she said in a slightly halting manner that was only

noticeable if he focused his attention on it. "Well, I have autism, so I tend to be socially awkward, but I also have a photographic memory, so I can always find something to discuss with people."

"It's pretty amazing, Dasi."

She nodded, and then after a pause, she asked, "Do you live here?"

"Temporarily," he said while scanning the stars. "I have a tent."

"You don't smell like someone who lives in a tent," she said seriously.

That comment made Waylon take another short break from his stargazing to look at Dasi. Her features were mainly in shadow, and now he was curious to see her face, look into her eyes and match the brilliant mind with the woman.

"Well, that's encouraging."

Dasi said, "Okay. Bye."

"Bye, Dasi," he said, watching her walk back to the main cabin. "If you want to look at the stars again, let me know."

Rayna was at the Legend ranch for a dress rehearsal for the Christmas Day parade at the town center. She was surprised how easy she felt in the saddle now that she had a safety vest and a horse whose fast speed was "sleep."

"How did your first day go?" Dean asked, holding Apollo while she dismounted.

"Amazing. Perfect," she said. "They loved the house, they loved the decorations. They're such lovely people, and they're so appreciative of what we did to give them that Montana Christmas."

"Congratulations, Ray," Dean said. "Triple threat Brand sisters. Unstoppable when you work together."

Paisley was nearby helping Luna adjust her Christmas

costume, and when she was satisfied with Luna's outfit, she came over to Ray.

"Do you want me to help you with your costume?"

Rayna blinked several times before she jumped on that offer. "I would love for you to help me. Thank you."

"I think the pants are a good fit on you. The shirt is too large—it makes you look bulky and heavier than you are." Paisley looked her over thoughtfully. "I could pin it in the back so it's more form flattering, and we could add a festive belt to hide the pin."

"Okay."

"As for the sash," she said about the sash each rider would wear with Big Sky's 4-H club, "I can put a tack in it with my sewing machine, and no one would be the wiser."

Paisley lifted up the sash to the position she wanted, then said, "See? Much better, and you can see the name of the troop and it would be better for pictures."

"You have your mother's gift," she said to Dean's oldest. "I appreciate you using that talent to help me."

Paisley pinned the sash where she wanted it and then asked her to take it off carefully. "My mom likes you."

"I like her. Very much."

The girl made rare eye contact with Rayna. "Mom says that I should find a reason to like you."

Rayna laughed. "Have you managed to find one?"

"Um…" Paisley said. "I guess. You're really nice to Luna. I do like that about you."

When she walked away with Rayna's sash in tow, Dean walked over to her, hugged her tightly without a care of who was watching.

"What *was* that?" she asked him, hugging him back just as tightly.

"Dare I say *progress*?"

* * *

Rayna returned to the ranch in time to see Leonard and his daughter arrive back from their shopping trip to Bozeman. Leonard got out of the truck in his new duds—he hadn't even put his old clothes back on. He must've had the salesman clip the tags and wore the dark-wash jeans, button-down plaid shirt, new black boots, belt with a huge silver buckle and, last but not least, a black Stetson. For the cold, he had purchased a heavy sheepskin jacket lined on the inside with sturdy, water-repellent canvas on the outside.

Jenny came out from the house, her hands over her mouth and her eyes drinking in her husband transformed from a college professor to a Montana cowboy,

"What do you think, little lady?" Leonard asked, posing for her and using his best attempt at a John Wayne voice.

"I think you are the most handsome cowboy I've ever seen in my life!" Jenny took the stairs quickly down to greet her husband.

"Well, thank you, darlin'." Leonard kissed his wife before he lifted up his cowboy hat and showed her his yalmaka. "Still me, just in different duds."

"Well, thank goodness for that! I don't want to lose my husband of so many years." Jenny let out her joyous laugh.

"And what about you, Dasi, dear?" Jenny asked her daughter, who was standing a bit apart, holding a large shopping bag. She was in her regular clothes, but she was wearing a gray hat that had a twisted accent around the brim.

"Look at you, Dasi." Jenny put her hands affectionately on her daughter's face and kissed her lovingly on the cheek. "A cowgirl in the making."

"This hat is called the Drifter 4X. It has a pinched front crown." Dasi pointed to the top of the hat. "It's made of buffalo felt—that's the 4X part. It has a satin liner and a genuine leather sweatband."

"Do you like it now that you have it out of the store, my gift from God?"

"Yes," Dasi said seriously. "I do. It comes with a nice hatbox, it was handcrafted in the USA and it cost one hundred and sixty dollars. Montana doesn't have a state tax."

Dasi followed her mother into the house to show her all of the items that her father had bought for her. When she reemerged from the house, she was wearing her brand-new cowgirl clothing.

"Let me get a real good look at you," Leonard said. "Well, you look pretty as a picture, Dasi."

"Thank you, Dad." Dasi ducked her head down and smiled a small, pleased smile.

Rayna saw Waylon come around the corner driving one of the older model tractors he'd found in her father's Everything Barn, which he had tinkered with long enough that he'd actually managed to get it running. Waylon liked the older model rather than the state-of-the-art John Deere they had recently purchased. Behind the tractor he was hauling a trailer big enough to hold a giant Christmas tree.

"Are you all ready to find your Christmas tree?" Rayna asked loudly.

"Go get your mom, Dasi! It's Christmas-tree time!"

The Baron family bundled up and chose to rough it sitting on the wooden floor of the trailer—Rayna could have easily taken them in the Gator, but they refused the comfort. She did follow behind them in the Gator just in case they wanted to hitch a ride home with her. On the way out to the spruce trees, Charlie jogged over to her so she could be there to help get the tree down safely.

Waylon stopped the tractor in the spot where spruce trees were plentiful.

"Take a look around and pick out the one you want," Rayna said.

"Any tree?" Jenny asked.

"Most any," Rayna told them. "We've got headroom in the house for a seven footer."

The Barons took their time, weaving through the spruce trees, knocking off the snow from the branches to get a better look at the trunk. While they focused on the trees, Rayna noticed how closely Waylon was watching Dasi while doing his best to camouflage it. This ranch seemed to inspire love and romance: Wayne and Charlie had found love together and were now engaged, she had reconnected with Dean and their love has blossomed, and Waylon's older brother, Wyatt, had married her friend Aspen, and now they were expecting a baby girl.

"Do you see what I'm seeing?" Charlie whispered.

"Love blooming at Hideaway Ranch?" she whispered back. "We may have to put that in the advertisements."

"This is the one!" Leonard called out to them.

Rayna, Waylon and Charlie joined them, and it looked like a solid choice. Waylon went back to the trailer and returned with rope, a chainsaw, gloves and a tarp. Charlie got a rope, lassoed it near the top part of the tree while Rayna held the tree steady and Waylon got down on the ground to begin cutting the trunk at the base. The Barons were watching from a safe distance on the opposite of the direction the tree should fall given the correct cut.

"Can I give that a whirl?" Leonard yelled the question over the loud sound of the chain saw working its way through the trunk.

Jenny put her hand on his arm. "I don't think that's a good idea."

"You can help cut down your tree," Rayna said and signaled Waylon to stop cutting.

"Don't worry, my love." Leonard patted her hand. "This is meaningful to me. I promise to be careful, and I know Waylon will keep me safe."

Leonard put on noise-dampening headphones, an extra pair of gloves and carefully and cautiously followed the instructions. He lay down on the tarp so he could reach under the branches and then started to saw. Waylon called out directions to Rayna and Charlie when the cut hit the halfway mark. It was slow, steady progress until the saw jumped and then stopped. Jenny had her arm around Dasi, and she covered her eyes for a second when the saw kicked back.

"What did I do wrong?" Leonard asked.

"Nothing! It happens. Just adjust the angle downward."

With Jenny nervously watching from the sideline, her husband cut through the tree trunk, and Rayna and Charlie eased it down onto a second tarp that would help them move it. Leonard had to work to get up from his side position. Standing upright, he held his arms up triumphantly. Jenny and Dasi rushed over to him and hugged him and then helped him brush the snow off his clothes, and Dasi handed him his cowboy hat.

The Barons looked at the spruce they had selected for their Christmas tree.

"Now how do we get it home?" Jenny asked.

"I'm going to cut off some of the lower branches," Waylon told her. "We'll put a chain around it and hook it to that Gator over there, and then we're going to pull it right up onto the trailer."

While Waylon and Charlie worked to get the tree prepared for the move, Rayna stood by to offer her help. It made her feel incredibly rewarded to watch the Barons as another Christmas wish came true. Motherhood and making a happy home for her family had given her that feeling of reward—even when things hadn't been good in her marriage, being Rowdy and Ryder's mother had fulfilled her. Now, seeing her hard work pay off for such a wonderful, loving, appreciative family gave her a renewed sense of purpose. And, it made her realize that Montana was the place where she would build her future.

The tree was loaded onto the trailer, and Leonard decided to ride with the tree while Jenny and Dasi took her up on her offer to take them back to the house in her Gator.

Jenny was bursting with pride over her husband cutting down their Christmas tree. "I've never seen Leonard use power tools before!" She lowered her voice when she said, "It's kind of sexy."

"Eww, Mom. No!" Dasi shook her head as if she were trying to pry those words loose from her ears. "Just no."

Waylon and Charlie did the heavy lifting to get the tree in the house, put in the stand with a bucket designed to hold the tree upright while keeping it watered. Before they put the tree upright, he showed Jenny how to drill a hole in the bottom of the trunk to make it easier for the tree to absorb water.

Jenny stood up and admired her work. "Now *I'm* using power tools!"

When the tree was in place, Rayna started to bring up the decorations she had purchased. The Barons had wanted to decorate the tree, and she had brought them the mother lode of ornaments.

"What have you done, Rayna!?" Jenny looked at the

lights, shiny balls and beautiful detailed Santa Clauses and reindeers and small gift boxes with pretty little bows.

"I wanted to make sure you could make the tree your own."

Without words, Jenny hugged her tightly, and when she stepped away, Rayna saw unshed tears in her eyes.

"So?" She pepped herself back up when she asked, "Where should we start on this glorious Christmas tree, Baron family?"

Rayna sensed how personal this tree was to the Barons, and she left the main house to give them their privacy. Before she left, she turned on the Christmas music and put on a pot of coffee.

She found Charlie in the barn, mucking stalls. When her sister saw her, she leaned her pitchfork on the stall gate, walked over to her and hugged her. They hugged each other for a long time, each feeling a tidal wave of emotions.

"We did it, Rayna," Charlie said. "We did it."

"We did," she agreed. "We're going to be okay, Charlie. This ranch is going to be okay. We aren't going to lose it."

Charlie dried her tears, and then they called Danica on video chat. "I've been on pins and needles! How was the Christmas-tree hunt?"

"Pins and needles?" Rayna teased, "Was that a pun?"

"Maybe!" Danica laughed. "Tell me everything!"

That night, it was a clear sky and the temperature had dropped with a chance of snow the next day. Waylon had spent the day with Dasi, and once he really focused his attention on her, he had discovered that she was, by far, the most beautiful woman he had ever seen in his life, bar none. She had thick black ringlets that she wore long nearly to the small of her back. Her eyebrows were nearly black and framed her golden-hazel eyes and thick, long lashes. Her skin was creamy, and she had two freckles on her left cheek, pretty unadorned ears and a small cleft in her chin. He had found it very difficult to focus on the tree and not focus on her. Once during that time, she'd walked by him, hadn't meet his gaze but had said hello. That was the only word that she had exchanged with him, and it made him believe that while he was fascinated and enamored by her, she was not interested in him. And it didn't feel good to be friend-zoned.

After another jubilant time at the firepit and after roasting chestnuts over the open flame and eating their fill topped off with Rayna's chocolate-peppermint hot cocoa, everyone said good-night and headed off to their beds. Waylon cleaned up, and then he grabbed his telescope. He had hoped that maybe Dasi would ask for another night stargazing with him, but when it didn't happen it was difficult to understand why it was bothering him so much. He'd always been the shy Westbrook brother—he was taller, lankier and awkward, whereas his other brothers knew how to talk naturally with the opposite sex. That had never been his gift and, in reality, he was looking for something deeper—a once-in-a-lifetime connection—that missing puzzle piece. And he was willing to wait for it, alone.

"The stars are so bright tonight. Even brighter than last night."

Dasi's voice coming out from the darkness startled him *again*.

"Where are you?" he asked her.

"I'm enjoying these trees," she said.

"Well, can you come out of the trees?"

Dasi emerged from the three spruce trees that were decorated with the blue-and-white lights to honor their Jewish heritage.

"Have you come for the stars?"

"Not really. But I do like to do that," she said. "I'd like to talk…is that okay?"

Waylon stopped breathing for a split second and then quickly said, "Okay."

He left his telescope and joined her on one of the benches by the firepit. He stoked some of the embers, bringing the fire back to help keep her warm.

"I was worried that you didn't want to talk to me again," he said.

"Why?"

"Because you didn't talk to me all day."

"I said hi."

He smiled. "Yes, you did."

She glanced over at him with a small smile on her face; the flames of the small fire cast orange and red and gold hues on her face, and it enchanted him.

"I have autism," she said. "Does that bother you?"

"No," he said quickly. "Absolutely not."

That garnered another small smile. "That's good."

"What do you do, Dasi?"

"I'm studying to be a cantor," she said, moving her thick ringlets over her shoulder, "Do you know what that is?"

"I do. I've always been interested in theology. Judaism is one of the major religions I studied as an undergrad," he said. "If I'm remembering correctly, the cantor is a member of the clergy…"

"Yes."

"And you will lead the congregation in song and prayer."

"Yes!" Her smile broadened. "And I will organize the music for the temple."

"Is that a master's degree?"

She nodded. Then she said, "You are very tall."

He laughed again, "I am. It's true."

"How tall are you?"

"Bare feet? Six foot and a couple of inches."

"Can you stand up in your tent?"

"Not all the way."

For a long while, they stopped talking and listened to the crackling of the dying fire.

"If you love to sing, how come you don't sing with us around the fire?" Waylon asked.

"Oh, well," she started, stopped, tried to restart and then finally she said, "I don't know. Shy, maybe."

"I'd like to hear you sing."

She glanced at him quickly again. "Well, then, okay, I'll sing for you tomorrow."

"I'd like that."

There was a question that he wanted to ask Dasi, but he kept hesitating and hesitating until finally he mustered the nerve to ask, "I know you're Jewish."

"Yes, I am."

"And you practice Judaism."

She nodded.

"Do you have to marry someone who's Jewish?"

"Um…" Dasi tilted her head a bit, stretched out her legs in front of her. "We practice Reform Judaism, so it's not a rule. But because I will be a cantor—and even then it would be allowed—I want to marry someone who shares my faith."

Something in his heart snapped, and he took in a deep breath as if someone had hit him in the gut. "Does this man need to be born Jewish, or can he, for instance, convert?"

"I think for me, yes." And then she stood up. "I'm cold now."

Waylon walked her to the porch steps and then when she reached the porch he asked, "Are you going on the trail ride with us tomorrow?"

"Yes," she said. "I like all of the animals very much."

"Good night, Dasi."

She gave a small wave of her hand. "Good night, Waylon Westbrook."

When Waylon climbed into his sleeping bag in his modest tent, he couldn't get Dasi out of his mind. To him, she felt like a dream that he had always kept very close to his heart, hoping that one day this dream of his true love would become a reality.

Dasi did clearly have a neurodiverse, autistic brain, but that was what made her so uniquely *Dasi*. She was a positive light in an often-dark world; she was sweet and kind and she loved the stars. He hadn't ever fallen in love—there were women on one ranch or another, but he'd always passed on the wrong and waited for the right. This was love; what he felt instinctively for Dasi was genuine and real, and it *was* love. If Dasi would ever reciprocate those feelings, the rest of his life would be made.

Chapter Eighteen

The week leading up to Christmas had settled into a routine for all of them. Dasi loved to collect eggs from the chicken coop, and Jenny loved to pick herbs and vegetables from the greenhouse. For Leonard, learning how to groom, lead and ride a horse was his top priority, and he had joined Wayne on several two-hour trail rides. The comfort and peace the Barons were feeling—enough to kick off their shoes and settle in as if they were at a home away from home—made Rayna feel unspeakably proud of herself and her sisters. This first booking, so far, seemed to be a home run and, though she doubted this would be the way for all of their guests, the Barons felt like family. There was a part of all of them that saw the end of this adventure together coming to a close, and it gave Rayna mixed emotions—on one hand, Christmas Eve and Christmas Day were the culmination of so much hard work, but it also meant that this lovely experience with the Barons was coming to a close.

So, instead of dwelling on what she couldn't change, Rayna focused on her two favorite Christmas moments: Christmas Eve and then, of course, Christmas Day. Christmas Eve had always been a night of wonder and excitement for her. All of the decorating and cooking and shopping for the perfect gifts led her to activities that would "kick off" Christmas. She loved to go caroling in the surrounding neighborhoods, bake cookies, and then everyone got to find the presents hidden in the stockings hanging on the fireplace. And for the Barons, she wanted Christmas Eve to be a magical evening for them. For caroling, Rayna wrangled everyone, including Charlie, Wayne, Dean and Waylon, to join her in caroling for the Barons. *But* what Leonard and Jenny didn't know was that Dasi had been learning the Christmas caroling playlist, and with her vocal talent and photographic memory, she would be leading the caroling this evening.

"Christmas carolers!" they all shouted to get Leonard and Jenny to come out to the porch.

"What is this?" Leonard emerged in his new winter coat, and Jenny soon followed.

"We're going to sing for you," Dasi said, standing in the lead position up front. Rayna, Dean and Charlie sounded more like croaking frogs with a sore throat, but Wayne, Waylon and Dasi would, hopefully, turn their sour notes sweet.

"Dasi!" Jenny stood close to her husband for warmth and being close during a shared experience. "Have you been practicing behind our backs?"

"No," Dasi said, seriously. "I've been practicing in the barn mostly, sometimes in the chicken coop. Chickens respond well to Christmas carols. I conducted a small research study and learned that each chicken had their own preference in carols."

"What would you like us to sing?" Rayna asked from the back row.

"How about 'We Wish You a Merry Christmas'?" Jenny suggested.

With their daughter leading the way, Leonard and Jenny heard six songs that night. And when everyone was too cold to do one more carol, they all went inside to drink hot buttered rum and decorate Christmas cookies.

"You did an amazing job on this tree," Rayna said, admiring the way the Barons had used the ornaments to create their very own special Christmas tree. Under the tree, there were three boxes wrapped in classic Christmas wrapping paper with wreaths and snowflakes and trees.

"I get so much pleasure looking at it," Jenny said. "I had no idea what would greet us here." She touched Ray's arm, "And we were greeted by angels. You and your sister and Wayne and Waylon…our Christmas angels."

Rayna hugged Jenny and thanked her for such kind words. "You feel like family to us, Jenny. It has been our blessing to have your family as our very first guests."

Charlie turned up the Christmas music, filled everyone up with rum, and then the cookie decorating was under way. The more rum they drank the more they wanted to drink, and the cookie decorating suffered as an unfortunate side effect of cookie decorating while tipsy.

"In the morning, we are not going to be proud of our work here today," Jenny said with a tipsy giggle.

"No," Rayna said, looking at the cookies that were smudged or decorated with animals that weren't currently represented in the animal kingdom.

"What is this supposed to be?" She pointed to a cookie in the middle of the pack.

Jenny squinted and studied the cookie, "Moose?"

"I don't know," Rayna said. "And I'm not sure I care."

That got the two of them giggling together until Dean walked over and put his arm around her. "I have to head back. Will you be able to come over tomorrow after the parade? I'd like you there, and I know Dad would love to see you."

"Hold that thought!" She opened the pantry and took out two stockings she had decorated and filled for Paisley and Luna.

"I made these for your girls," she said after she'd followed him out to the porch.

"Thank you," he said. "You are so thoughtful, Ray. A heart of gold."

"I was happy to do it," she said. "But I think it would be best to let your girls have your undivided attention for Christmas day, Dean. I'll see them in the morning, and then they'll have you for the rest of the day. Everything is changing so quickly for them—they need times that seem like old times."

Dean put his hands on her face and kissed her sweetly. "I love you, Ray. For so many reasons. But the way you look out for my girls touches me in a way that I could never fully explain."

They ended the night with a kiss, and he promised to call her to make sure she was ready to ride Apollo in the parade. When she opened the door, she literally ran into Charlie, who was walking a little wobbly, holding on to Wayne's arm.

"Taking this cowgirl to bed," he said.

"Good night." She hugged her sister.

Waylon also passed her, and when she shut the door behind her, she realized that she had better get the stockings handed out because Leonard was dozing in his favorite rocking chair. The stockings hanging on the fireplace mantel were for show; the real ones were hidden in a nearby closet.

"It's my family tradition to open stockings on Christmas Eve," she said and then handed one stocking to each Baron.

"Rayna! You've done too much!" Jenny said.

"It's just trinkets and bobbles—locally sourced honey, locally manufactured soaps, stuff like that."

Dasi and Leonard thanked her and then disappeared to the back of the house.

"And so there were two," Jenny said.

"Moms are always the first to rise..." Rayna nodded.

"And the last to go to bed."

They both tapped their glasses and began to clean up the mess left behind. After they made short work of cleaning the kitchen, they sat together in the kitchen, both too wound up to go to bed.

"You've never asked me about the reason why a Jewish family wanted Christmas."

"I didn't think it was my place, Jenny."

"No. I suppose it's not," she agreed. "But you are curious."

"I was before you came, but most of my focus has been providing that classic Christmas, and I didn't focus on the why."

"If I may," Jenny said, her head down, a solemn aura surrounding her in the place of her standard "can do" optimism, "I would like to share the why with you now."

Rayna reached over, putting her hand over the other woman's, and looked at her sincerely. "Of course, Jenny. Of course you can."

Jenny looked down for a long while with her lips quivering, her shoulders tensed and her hands twisted together. When she did finally lift her head, tears were streaming down her cheeks. Rayna rushed for the box of tissues she had not too far in the past used herself. She took the tissues and dabbed the tears from Jenny's cheeks.

"You don't have to tell me if you're not ready."

Jenny reached out for her hand and held on to it. "We lost our son."

Those four words felt like real pain in her body. "I'm so sorry, Jenny."

"Thank you," she said. "Abraham. Abe. He was our oldest, and he was so creative and challenging and brilliant and loving. He wanted to forge his own path, buck the norm, think outside of every box he could find."

Jenny wiped more tears off of her cheeks. "I was raised Episcopalian. But I converted to Judaism when I married Leo. It was my choice because I found myself drawn to the principles of the Reform movement. But Abe wanted to be a cowboy, and he wanted to have Christmas. And, Leo—oh, how he fought with Abe about this. Leo said Jewish boys from Brooklyn could not be cowboys—not *shouldn't*—he said *couldn't*.

"And that's when Abe brought to my husband a documentary at the New York Jewish Film Festival about the Jews of the Wild West—cowboys who also happened to be Jewish!" she said. "But this didn't move his father. No, it did not. And it certainly did not go well when Abe began to push the idea of celebrating both Christmas and Chanukah."

Jenny pulled out her phone, scrolled through her pictures and then showed one to Ray. "There! This is my son. Look how handsome he is."

She looked at Abe's picture. "This Christmas business was just Abe's way of pushing Leo's buttons. He was like that Andy Kaufman—always finding ways to tweak somebody's nose, to make them think, get them riled up. But coming out west—learning how to work with horses and cattle—this was a real dream for Abe. He had always wanted this even as a little boy."

Jenny breathed in and let it out on a sigh, "Abe got sick his first year of college. Meningitis. And then we lost him."

Rayna didn't know what to say, so she reached out and squeezed the other woman's hand to offer some support, however small.

"So now we all live with regret of what we didn't say, what we didn't do, what we did say that we shouldn't have…"

Now, for Rayna, Christmas in Montana made perfect sense. It was a way to honor their son, Abe.

"When I was cleaning out his dorm room, gathering his things to take home, I found those three boxes in his closet. I kept them, of course, but I didn't know what to do with them." She nodded toward the boxes beneath the Christmas tree.

"So, I saw your advertisement, and I thought to myself, it's been a year now and my husband still suffers so much, and maybe this would help him heal. If he could become a cowboy and if he could have this wonderful white Christmas, perhaps he would forgive himself—perhaps he would heal. And so, here we are.

"And now you know why this Jewish family has traveled west, like many of our ancestors," Jenny said.

As she told the story of her son, slowly Jenny moved through that grief and her steady nature returned. "Now," she said, "you must go to sleep. You have a very big day tomorrow. And after your parade and your Christmas, you must come over for the first night of Hanukah. I'll teach you how to make my great-grandmother's challah-bread recipe."

Rayna stood up to give Jenny a goodbye hug, when she saw snowflakes swirling in circular patterns outside of the kitchen window. "Jenny! Look! It's snowing!"

"A white Christmas." She went to the kitchen window to look outside. "Mazel tov!"

The clock on the wall began to chime, and goose bumps raced up Rayna's arms and made her shiver. "It's midnight, Jenny. Merry Christmas."

"Oh, you dear, sweet soul. Merry Christmas!"

Rayna had a packed schedule on Christmas Day, starting with the parade. Riding next to Luna, waving to the surprisingly large group of spectators and feeling comfortable and confident on Apollo's back gave her a chance to really enjoy the parade and celebrate Christmas. It felt as if she had yelled "Merry Christmas!" hundreds of times; by the end of the ride, her voice was hoarse, but she didn't care. Dean and Paisley were at the end of the parade, and the smile on Dean's face, the look in his eyes—so much love and pride—that was the best Christmas present that she could have imagined. Her newfound love with James Dean Legend, and the relationships she was building with his daughters, was the gift.

"You did amazing, Ray!" he said after he gave a hero's welcome to Luna.

Rayna dismounted with his assistance, and once her feet were on the ground, she spun around and hugged him tightly. It was instinctual, natural, and even with Paisley watching, she couldn't let this moment go without celebrating it with the man she had loved when she'd been a teenager and now, again, when she was older and much wiser.

"Thank you, Dean," Rayna said, "for talking me into this! I had so much fun!"

"Merry Christmas, Ray."

"Merry Christmas!"

Both girls thanked her for their stockings, and Paisley, while still standoffish and not totally certain that she was thrilled with the idea of Ray being a permanent part of their family, had fixed her costume to fit like a glove, and the sash had been perfectly placed for pictures.

"I just posted this picture of you." Paisley showed her.

Rayna had to do a double take when she saw herself riding Apollo. In a way, it didn't look like her—at least not the *her* she remembered. She looked happy, completely, whole-heartedly, holding-nothing-back happy.

"It's a good picture," Paisley said. "I shot video too."

"Thank you, Paisley. You're very talented," Rayna said, and she almost asked for a hug but held back. It had to unfold naturally, and she could see Paisley doing her best to accept her.

Rayna gave one last hug to Apollo, giving him another apple and molasses treat that she had made at home as an experiment. They loaded the horses onto the trailer and then headed back home. At the end of the driveway to Hideaway Ranch, she had Dean stop so she could jump out and walk up the main house.

"I'd rather drive you all the way," he said.

"Nope! I'm going to enjoy the walk through my trees of light and enjoy them. After the first of the year, they'll be taken down, and I won't see them again until the end of November! Merry Christmas!" she said.

And in glorious harmony, Dean, Paisley and Luna all said in unison, "Merry Christmas, Rayna!"

She shut the door and waved before she walked at a brisk pace through the aisle of sparkling trees. Even in the daylight, the trees were simply magical. A decorating triumph!

Dean and she had agreed for her to come over for a private Christmas moment after she'd celebrated the first evening of Chanukah with the Barons. Her sisters and the Westbrooks had all decided to not exchange gifts; the success of their first booking was the only gift that they needed.

Rayna took the steps up to the porch easily and knocked on the door. Jenny opened the door and hugged her tightly. "Merry Christmas."

"Thank you, Jenny," she said. "Merry Christmas and Happy Chanukah."

She gave Leonard and Dasi holiday hugs, and Dasi's naturally pretty face was glowing and she was smiling brightly, holding a small scroll in her hands. A moment later, there was a knock on the door, and it was Waylon. Dasi ran over, grabbed her coat and opened the door. Waylon gave everyone a Christmas and Chanukah greeting before he offered Dasi his arm and they walked down the steps together.

Jenny said, "He bought her a star."

"Well, that's romantic!" she exclaimed, "And you approve?"

"Yes. Absolutely, we do. What a solid, intelligent, kind, patient young man. I mean, who knew Dasi would find love with a cowboy whose address was a tent? But you see, with Waylon, just as with Dasi, there is much more than meets the eye."

"True," Ray said. "Waylon *is* offbeat, but he comes from good stock."

"He has his master of science degree in astronomy *and* he has a plan to earn his doctorate. And," Jenny said, "Dasi has had difficulty dating—most men find the autism too difficult to handle. But Waylon, yes, he accepts her, but more importantly, he *appreciates* who she is."

Then Jenny waved her over to the table where the three Christmas boxes had been opened. "See, Rayna. See what my boy has done. Christmas on the outside, but Chanukah on the inside."

For his father, Abe had given Chanukah-themed socks and planted a tree in Israel in the family name. For Dasi, a beautiful Star of David necklace and Chanukah pajamas. "And, for me, my boy gave me this special challah board to serve the bread and a rolling pin with cut outs with a star and a dreidel. When you roll this over dough, it leaves these imprints."

Rayna felt so many different emotions that it was hard to make sense of them all—the magnitude of this moment for the Barons and the honor they were paying to their son, Abe, could not be described by mere words.

"Thank you for sharing this with me, Jenny. I will never forget it."

"And we will never forget you," she said. "Now, come! Let me show you how to make challah."

Rayna stopped by to see Charlie and Wayne and wish them Merry Christmas, then she spent a good hour touching base with close friends and her sons. As the sun set, she was back at the main house for the lighting of the first candle on the menorah. Leonard first lit the "helper candle," and while he was lighting the first candle, he spoke a prayer in Hebrew and then translated it into English for Rayna. And after, they ate the challah that she had baked earlier that day with Jenny.

"Thank you so much," she told Leonard, Jenny and Dasi. "This was a meaningful experience for me."

They hugged, saying goodbye, and as if on cue, Dean texted her to meet at his house in one hour. The entire day, time had seemed to be breaking speed records it had gone by so fast, but those sixty minutes until seeing her love on this magical night? Apollo speed.

After one exact hour, she turned the Beast toward the

Legend ranch. Dean was waiting for her, as always, at the bottom of the steps. Then he was by her side, opening the door to her truck and enfolding her in his strong arms. The moment was one of words, it was a moment of *feeling*.

After a lovely Christmas kiss, Dean took her hand, and they walked together to the barn, through the aisleway of sleeping horses and into his office. Once inside, he unlocked the secret observatory and led her up the stairs.

"Dean!" she exclaimed. "I've never seen something so beautiful!"

"That's my line," he said, standing close, his eyes only on her.

She smiled brightly at him, closed the distance and hugged him tightly. He kissed her gently, sensually, and she kissed him back with all the promise of a lifetime of love. He took her hand and led her over to the couch, and they sat together, holding hands and looking at the clear night sky above.

"The girls bought you a gift," Dean said, holding out a small box to her.

"Did you ask them to?"

"No," he said. "It was actually Paisley's idea."

She felt tears of happiness building as she opened the wrapped gift. Inside of the box was a beautifully blown glass cat curled up to sleep.

"Now I have three cats again. It's beautiful. I will cherish it."

"I cherish you."

She reached out for his hand. "And I cherish you too, Dean. I can't imagine my life without you."

He kissed her hand as she continued, "I do have something for you."

Ray pulled a large, ornately carved pocket watch and handed it to him.

"Is this your father's watch?"

She nodded. "My sisters and I want you to have it. You meant so much to my dad."

"I remember him pulling this out of his pocket to check the time," Dean said with a catch in his voice when he said, "Thank you."

"Merry Christmas, Dean."

He put the watch in his pocket and pulled a small box out, saying, "And, I do have something for you."

"Of course you do!" She laughed and clapped her hands together. "We both broke our one Christmas rule!"

He offered her the box, and she opened it and looked inside. "Dean...is this your mother's engagement ring?"

He took the three-carat mine-cut diamond that had never left Nettie's hand when she'd been alive. "Dad wanted you to have this, and so do I."

Rayna couldn't hold her tears back, and she wondered at the magic of this day.

Dean faced her, holding her right hand in his. "I need to tell you how much I love you, how much you mean to me. You have changed my life, Ray, and there isn't anyone else I can see in my future other than you."

She put her left hand over his. "I feel the same way."

He slid the ring onto her right hand. "I know you aren't ready, Rayna. But when the time is right for you, for our families, I want you to put this ring on your left hand, and I will know that you are ready to be my wife."

Rayna looked at the ring on her finger. "I do want to be your wife, Dean. In time."

"And I'll wait for you for a lifetime, Ray." He kissed her sweetly.

"Merry Christmas, Dean." She leaned her body into his so they could hold each other as the Christmas night came to a close.

"Merry Christmas, Ray."

* * * * *